DEAD MEN'S SANDALS

Previous Titles by David Wishart

The Marcus Corvinus series

OVID
GERMANICUS
THE LYDIAN BAKER
SEJANUS
OLD BONES
LAST RITES
WHITE MURDER
A VOTE FOR MURDER
PARTHIAN SHOT
FOOD FOR THE FISHES
IN AT THE DEATH
ILLEGALLY DEAD
BODIES POLITIC
NO CAUSE FOR CONCERN
SOLID CITIZENS
FINISHED BUSINESS
TRADE SECRETS
FOREIGN BODIES
FAMILY COMMITMENTS
GOING BACK

Other Roman books

I, VIRGIL
NERO
THE HORSE COIN

The Angus books

JAEGER'S HOWE HEXAGON

DEAD MEN'S SANDALS

David Wishart

Copyright © David Wishart 2020

www.david-wishart.co.uk

All rights reserved. No part of this publication may be reproduced, stored, or transmitted in any form, or by any means, electronic, mechanical or photocopying, recording or otherwise, without the prior permission of the copyright owner.

DRAMATIS PERSONAE

(Only the names of characters who appear or are referred to in more than one part of the book are given. The story takes place September/October AD44)

Corvinus's family and household

Alexis: the gardener, and the sharpest of Corvinus's slaves
Bathyllus: the major-domo
Meton: the chef
Perilla, Rufia: Corvinus's wife
Phryne: Perilla's maid

The Marcius family and connections

Atia: Titus Marcius Senior's widow
Brinnius, Titus: Marcus Cluvius's chief muscle
Capra: Marcia's elderly maid
Carpus ('Carver'): a Marcius employee and friend of Satrius
Cluvius, Marcus: Quintus Cluvius's son
Cluvius, Quintus: Titus Marcius Senior's erstwhile deputy
Frontius, Gaius: one of Fulgentia's tenants
Fulgentia: a landlady
Gellia: Aulus Marcius's wife
Marcia: daughter of Titus Marcius and Septimia
Marcius, Aulus: Titus Marcius Senior's younger son
Marcius, Titus Junior: Titus Marcius Senior's elder son
Marcius, Titus Senior: the murdered man
Septimia: Titus Marcius Junior's wife

Other characters

Eutacticus, Sempronius: a Roman organised crime boss
Felicia: a whelk-seller

Fulgentia: a landlady
Montanus, Gaius Julius: commander of the local auxiliary cohort
Pettius, Lucius: head of the rival firm
Pettius, Sextus: Lucius Pettius's son, and Marcia's fiancé
Satrius, Titus: Eutacticus's chief muscle
Sentia: Perilla's friend, and Montanus's wife

1.

As months go, September in Rome is one of my favourites. The heat's beginning to ease, and the weather's dry enough to make walking a pleasure. Okay, sure, the closer you are to the river, particularly in the low-lying areas, the niffier it is – old Father Tiber is still stripped down to his metaphorical summer smalls, and barring mid-stream he's mostly mud and worse – but a city boy like me is pretty much used to that. Up here on the Caelian where there's usually a breeze blowing you hardly notice.

So there I was, fresh off the boat from our Carthage trip, relaxing over a late al fresco breakfast and waiting for Perilla to surface, with nothing more taxing ahead of me but a stroll downtown for a shave-and-haircut followed by a half-jug and a leisurely chat with the punters at Renatius's wineshop. At which point our major-domo Bathyllus soft-shoed out through the peristyle and buggered the whole thing up.

'A visitor, sir,' he said.

Just that, and the little bald-head would've used exactly the same tone to report a king-size rat in the privy. Not a good sign. Still, Bathyllus has standards that would leave your average society matron nowhere, so I wasn't prejudging here.

'Yeah? And who would that be, now?' I dipped the last of my crusts into the bowl of olive oil...

...just as the guy himself appeared from between the pillars. I stared. The visitor, it seemed, was Titus Satrius.

Fuck. Double fuck. Me, I'd've preferred the rat.

'Morning, Corvinus.' He was grinning as he came over. 'Sorry to disturb your breakfast.'

'Then don't.'

The grin widened. 'Yeah, well, maybe I'm not sorry at that. One of life's little pleasures. The boss wants a word with you.'

'Is that so?' I said. Oh, shit. The boss in question being Sempronius Eutacticus, such was not good news. Eutacticus was to your run-of-the-mill crook what a crocodile is to a pond-newt; the two might be related in the technical sense, sure, but that's where any similarity ended, particularly with regard to dental development and general sunniness of disposition. Our paths had crossed several times over the years, and on my side it had never been a pleasure unalloyed. The trouble was that on the last occasion I'd ended up owing the bastard a favour. Hence, presumably, Satrius's visit.

Double, as I say, fuck. In spades.

'That is so.' He reached over for a stuffed olive, flicked it into the air, caught it in his mouth and chewed. 'Now for preference. Maybe earlier, if you can manage it.'

'He say what it was about?'

'Sure.'

I waited. Nothing. 'And?'

'Doesn't mean I have to tell you, does it?' Bastard. 'I've got a litter waiting outside.'

Well, that was to the good anyway. Normally I hate using those things, but Eutacticus's bijou little mansion was up on the Pincian, a fair hike away, and the less time I had to spend in Satrius's jolly company the better I'd like it.

So I told Bathyllus to tell Perilla where I'd gone – she'd worry, sure, but it was always best, when visiting Eutacticus, to apprise a third party of your whereabouts in case of accidents, viz. being fed to the bugger's pet eels – and set off. Hardly rejoicing, mind, but there wasn't much I could do about it.

The litter lads pulled up outside Eutacticus's gates. We de-chaired under the watchful eye of the gate-troll and carried on up the drive past topiaried hedges studded with serious bronzes and enough marble gods, goddesses and nymphs to equip a pantheon. Greek originals or specially commissioned, probably, the lot of them: in Sempronius Eutacticus's case, crime didn't only pay, it came with a six-figure annual bonus and an expense account you could've run a small province on.

The lad himself was sitting in a rose-trellised arbour communing with nature, the remains of a substantial breakfast on the table in front of him. Yeah, well, if you've a hard day of running an organised crime empire ahead of you you need a hearty breakfast to set you up for it. A bread roll, a few olives and a handful of grapes doesn't really cut it.

'Ah, Corvinus.' He was beaming. Bad sign; bad, *bad* sign. 'Glad you could make it. Sit down, boy. Pour yourself some wine.' I did, and glanced round at Satrius. I'd expected that, duty done, body duly delivered, he'd slope off to wherever tame gorillas go when they have some quality free time, but he'd taken up position against the arbour gatepost and was leaning against it, arms crossed and with a general air of being a fixture. 'Wife well, is she? Bright and healthy and so on?'

'Yeah. Yeah, Perilla's okay.' I tasted the wine. Caecuban. Not the imperial variety, mind, but it came damn close.

'That's good. You had a good summer?'

Oh, shit; small talk. With Eutacticus you never, ever got small talk. Forget bad; in terms of signs we were into fully-fledged omen territory here.

'It was interesting, yeah,' I said. 'We were away most of the time. Abroad. Carthage. We've just got back, in fact.'

'Excellent! So you won't have unpacked yet?'

'Ah...no, as it happens. Not altogether. We're planning to go down to Castrimoenium in a few days to see our adopted daughter and her family. They're—'

'*Were* planning.'

I blinked. 'Come again?'

'You heard.' The smile broadened even more, revealing an incisor. '*Were* planning. Past tense. You owe me and I'm calling in the favour. Plans change. You're going to Brundisium.'

'*What?*'

'A little job I want you to do for me.'

'Hang on for just one little second, pal!' I said. 'You can't just–!' I skidded to a halt; the smile had disappeared like morning dew at the first kiss of sunrise. Fuck. 'Brundisium. Right. Got it. And this would be in connection with what, exactly?'

'You remember my...we'll call him a colleague down there? Sent me that necklace your major-domo's crooked brother got his thieving hands on a while back?'

'Uh...yeah. Not personally, mind, I never met the guy, but–'

'Name of Marcius. Titus Marcius. His granddaughter's due to get married in a couple of months.'

'Is that so?' I said cautiously. 'And?'

'Seems he bought her a ring as a present. Not for her as such, for her to give to her fiancé on the day of the wedding. Only it's gone missing.'

'And you want me to find it, right? Or find whoever, presumably, was responsible for liberating it?'

'Partly, yes.'

I set down the wine cup. 'Come on, Eutacticus! The business you're in – your pal's in – you don't need me for something like that. Any run-of-the-mill, common-or-garden thief would chew his own arm off before he risked pinching something he knew you'd a connection with. Witness Bathyllus's brother. And if he was stupid enough to try you'd–' I stopped again as the qualification registered. 'Ah..."partly"?'

'The day after it went missing Marcius was found face down in Brundisium harbour with his head bashed in.'

Yeah, well, I reckoned that would just about do it where calling in the favour was concerned. Bugger. I reached for the wine cup and took a decent swig; if we were going to be saddled with an unexpected trip to Brundisium then I might as well make the most of things. 'Fair enough,' I said. 'You want to fill in some of the background details?'

He frowned. 'Listen, boy, when I buy a dog, I don't do my own barking, right?' Ouch. 'Sleuthing's your department and I've got a busy morning ahead. Everything's arranged, they know you're coming; you just get on down there, sniff around, do what you're good at. Find the bastard responsible and we'll call it quits.'

.Gods! 'Indulge me, okay?' I said. 'Just the basics. It's necessary. Believe me.'

The frown deepened. 'All right. Five minutes. What do you want to know?'

Grudging as hell. Still...'Who "they" are, for a start. We talking family here? Uh, what's your word, "colleagues"? Give me a few names.'

'Very well.' He shifted irritably in his chair. 'Like I said, the guy was Titus Marcius. We've had dealings with each other on and off over the years, and he was straight as they come.'

'"Straight"? That'd be "straight" as in "honest", yes?'

That got me a long, baleful look. 'Don't try to be funny, boy. You know what I mean. I'd a lot of time for Marcius, which explains why I'm giving you the job of finding the bastard who killed him. Family...he had two sons plus the granddaughter, Marcia.'

'The one who's getting hitched and who's suddenly short one wedding ring?'

'Correct.'

'So what's the connection?' I said. Eutacticus hesitated. 'Come on, pal! Coincidences happen, sure, but they're not all that common and you don't go for them straight off. You tell me someone half-inched this ring and the next day Granddad's found murdered. Okay, then we'll take it as a working hypothesis that the two events are connected until apprised otherwise. That fine by you?'

The baleful look went up another notch. 'I also told you not to get smart with me, Corvinus,' he said. 'Just don't push it, right?' I waited. 'The man Marcia's betrothed to is the son of a...let's just call him a long-term business rival, okay?'

'Is that so, now? This guy got a name?'

'Pettius. Lucius Pettius. His son's Sextus.'

'Uh-huh. So if they're, uh, business rivals then why the wedding?'

'The usual reason. It was part of a business agreement.'

'Yeah, well, I might've gone for that if you'd described them as colleagues, pal. In your own sense of the word, that is. "Rivals", now, that's something else, isn't it? Or am I wrong?'

Eutacticus grunted. 'Okay. Maybe "rivals" is pitching it a bit strong. Oh, sure, the two of them were in the same business, more or less, and in a small place like Brundisium there're only so many slices to the cake, so there was bound to be a bit of friction. Still, they got along together, most of the time.'

'Really?'

He frowned. 'I said: don't get smart. One thing you have to remember in this line, boy: if you don't want no trouble with the rest of the field you don't go looking for it. You keep to your patch, they keep to theirs and everything's bright and sunny in the garden. That's a lesson you learn pretty quick if you want to live to old age. You get me?'

I shrugged. 'You're the expert. Fair enough. Call them what you like.'

'The important phrase, though, is "long-term"; we're talking twenty-odd years here, so the two of them weren't getting any younger, right? Both well into their sixties. That age, you get tired, you're not as sharp as you were. Besides, the world's changing, there're pushy youngsters on their way up, out to make their fortunes any way they can. And where Brundisium's concerned there's the southern Italian gangs knocking at the back door. Oh, sure, ten, fifteen years ago these guys were just hicks from the sticks, small-timers with small ideas, but they're learning fast, and they're getting pushy. Seriously pushy. In another ten years' time, maybe less, they'll be real trouble, and not just down south, either.'

'You're breaking my heart, pal.'

'Oh, I've no worries on that score myself, Corvinus. Believe me. I've Rome stitched up tighter than a gnat's arse. Marcius and Pettius, now, they were different, old school operators, both of them, small-time but happy to keep it that way for the sake of peace and quiet. They were doing okay on their own for the time being, sure, but they could see how the wind was blowing. An alliance, pooling their resources, not pissing in each other's ponds, that made sense.'

'So what happens now that Marcius is dead?'

Eutacticus shrugged. 'Maybe nothing. No reason why it should. Like I said, it was a willing agreement on both sides, and Marcius has his sons to follow him. Plus his deputy's no fool. He'll take care of things until the dust settles.'

'Deputy?'

'He's the one you'll be seeing most of. Guy by the name of Cluvius. Quintus Cluvius. Him and Marcius, they've been together from the beginning.'

'You have any thoughts yourself? About who the perp might be?'

'I told you, Corvinus. That's your job. Me, I don't do theorising.'

I sighed. 'Okay. We'll leave it there for the present. Tell me more about this ring.'

Was it my imagination, or did his eyes flicker just for an instant?

'What's to tell?' he said. 'All you need to know is that it's gone missing, it's worth more than your fucking annual income, and the other half of your job is getting it back. Now you've had all the time you're getting out of me. Anything else you want you can find out for yourself when you and Satrius get down there.'

What?

'Uh...wait a minute, sunshine,' I said. 'Maybe I misheard. You said *Satrius?*'

'Sure. I'm sending him with you. Any objections?'

He'd reverted to basking crocodile mode. I backed water frantically. 'Ah...no. None at all,' I said. 'Absolutely not. Perish the thought.' I glanced sideways. Satrius was still leaning against the gatepost, only now he was grinning like a drain with the cover off. Bastard. 'You, uh, have reasons for doing that?'

'He's my rep and your authorisation. These guys aren't your normal poncey law-abiding pillars of the establishment; they don't play nice. You go poking your nose into their affairs and they'll cut it off for you without a second thought, for any reason or none at all, just on principle. Unless you're protected, that is. Which you will be, because with Satrius keeping an eye on things they know that if they so much as fart out of turn I'll find out, and I will not then be a happy bunny. Think of him as a guide and mentor.'

Guide and mentor, eh? Some images are just too bizarre for the human mind to entertain while keeping its sanity. 'Fair enough. So you, uh, want me to leave right away, do you?' I said. 'Us, rather? Me and Laughing Boy here?'

'No hurry, Corvinus. The day after tomorrow will do.'

'Very generous, pal. Thank you.'

That got me a long, hard stare, but then he grunted, shrugged, and stood up. 'Like I said, everything's arranged the other end; Satrius can fill you in on that score. Take your wife with you, take anyone you please. Take the fucking family cat if you like.' He patted me on the shoulder. 'Come on, boy! Smile! Think of it as an extra holiday, all expenses paid. Let me know when you've worked things out and I'll handle the rest. Now bugger off and enjoy.'

He got up, mopped his lips with his napkin, and ambled back towards the house, leaving me with Laughing Boy himself.

Gods!

2.

Perilla wasn't exactly over the moon about it, either. Understandably.

'Marcus, we're only just back,' she said when I told her. 'And the setup down there seems very dubious, to say the least.'

'Really? My, you don't say.' I threw myself down on the couch, reached for the wine cup that Bathyllus was in the process of setting down on the table beside it, and sank the contents. 'You care to go over to the Pincian yourself and ask Eutacticus to make other arrangements?'

'Of course not. Even so. Besides, Clarus and Marilla are expecting us.'

'You don't have to come if you don't want to, lady. You could go on ahead to Castrimoenium and I can catch you up later.' That just got me a look. Bathyllus refilled the cup. 'Fine. So stop beefing, okay?'

'How are we getting down there? Ship or road?'

'Road. Satrius is bringing round a sleeping coach an hour before dawn the day after tomorrow. Alexis can tag along behind in the luggage cart with Bathyllus and Meton.' Alexis being, technically, the gardener, but also, and more relevantly, the smartest of our bought help; in view of Satrius's shortcomings in that direction I might need an extra someone with brains on the team.

Bathyllus, on the point of exiting with his tray, froze.

'We're taking Meton, sir?' he said. '*Again?*'

So might Thyestes have looked when he pulled his sons' remains out of the stew pot.

'Yeah, I thought we might, Bathyllus.' I gave him my best smile. 'The accommodation's arranged, sure, thanks to Eutacticus, at least I hope it is, but we may as well have a decent chef along. You got any viable objections?'

'None whatsoever, sir.' If his teeth had been gritted any further you could've used them for a corn mill. Our major-domo and our chef do not get on. To put it mildly. Cat and dog doesn't even come close.

'Good. Just checking.'

Bathyllus sniffed and buttled off.

'We're not staying with the family, are we?' Perilla said.

'Uh-uh. According to Satrius we'll have the use of a house in town. Seemingly it belongs to a guy who had to go abroad suddenly for the sake of his health.'

'Hmm.'

'Don't knock it. It means we're independent. And it may even be true. Brundisium isn't the most salubrious of places.'

'Quite.'

'Come on, Perilla! We're stuck with the case. We may as well make the most of things.'

'Did Satrius tell you anything else?' She shifted on her couch. 'In the way of background, I mean?'

'Not a lot, beyond what I knew already. Only that what's-his-name, Marcius, was killed half a month ago and it was his daughter who discovered that the ring was missing. That's begging the question as to whether the two crimes are connected, of course. There, your guess is as good as mine.'

'You asked him about the ring?'

'Of course I did. He was just as cagey on the subject as his boss had been.' I frowned and reached for the wine cup again. 'Which was screwy in itself. I mean, Eutacticus told me the thing was worth a bomb, yes, and anyway given someone has taken the risk of half-inching it that much would go without saying. But that's not the end of it. Not even part-way there.'

'You think it was originally stolen property?'

'Yeah, well, knowing what kind of people we're dealing with I'd say that was a fair bet, wouldn't you? And if it was as valuable as all that I can see why he might be loath to supply too many details. Like who it belonged to before his pal got his hands on it and how the switch was made.' I took another swallow of wine. 'Even so, it's still weird. Oh, sure, when we had our conversation last time round over the missing necklace, the one that Bathyllus's brother and his partner pinched, Eutacticus was at pains to say he'd bought it legally. Or as legally as that bastard is capable of, anyway. This was different; the circumstances weren't the same, the ring wasn't his, and he knows I know the sort of business he and his pals are in, so he wouldn't be admitting to anything I couldn't've guessed, anyway. But still for some reason he was playing coy. And Eutacticus just doesn't do coy. Like I say, weird.' I shrugged. 'Ah, hell, it's a mystery. No point in theorising; leave it.'

'He told you nothing else? Satrius?'

'Uh-uh. Close as a clam. Mind you, that could've been out of sheer bloody-mindedness, because that's how the bastard's built. Anyway, we'll have plenty of time to soak him for information on the journey.'

'Ah, yes. Ten days plus in a coach with a hired thug for company. That I am really, really looking forward to.'

'Come on, lady! He won't necessarily be in the coach itself. And in any case we're hardly out in the sticks; we'll be on the Appian Road the whole way down. If there's no particular hurry we could even stop off for a few days, at Capua and Tarentum, say, maybe a couple of other places. Make it a holiday like Eutacticus said, do a bit of sightseeing.'

'And stay where? Marcus, I am *not* putting myself under any obligation for an overnight stay to one of Sempronius Eutacticus's associates, let alone putting up anywhere that Titus Satrius recommends. If we are going we'll sleep in the carriage, thank you. And as for inns and guest-houses you can forget them.'

I sighed. 'Fair enough, it was just a thought. We'll do the trip in a oner if you like.'

'Liking doesn't come into it.'

Bugger. I'd hoped that the prospect of a bit of sightseeing might've brought down the hackles a tad – Perilla's a total sucker for anything that constitutes local colour, and Capua, at least, has more ancient monuments than you can shake a stick at – but evidently even there we were on a hiding to nothing. Ah, well, when the lady is in that sort of mood you may as well talk to the wall for any good it'll do. Besides, I agreed with her: if we had to go, as we undoubtedly did, then it was best to get the thing over and done with as fast as possible.

Extra holiday nothing: as cases went, this one was turning out to be a real bummer before it got started.

Fuck!

So there we were two days later twiddling our thumbs in the atrium, all packed and ready, waiting in the prelude to what promised to be a grey and overcast dawn for Satrius to show up with the sleeping coach. Me, I'm a morning person, always have been, although getting out of a warm bed half way through the final quarter of the night was pushing things. As for Perilla, she normally doesn't surface until the sun's well clear of the horizon, and where her current mood was concerned *grouchy* didn't even begin to hack it.

In short, all agog with excitement and anticipation about the forthcoming trip was something we were not.

Bathyllus buttled in.

'That's the coach arrived, sir, if you'd care to come out,' he said.

'Fine,' I said. 'Alexis and Meton all set?' We'd put most of the luggage and supplies in one of our own covered carts the night before, and it was parked ready to go in the alleyway behind our garden wall.

'Yes, sir.' A sniff; but this early even one of Bathyllus's disapproving sniffs lacked the usual zip and zing. 'They're on the cart with Phryne.' Phryne was Perilla's maid. 'I'll join them now, if you don't mind.'

'Sure. Go ahead.' I got up off the couch. 'Come on, lady, stir your stumps. Show on the road.'

She fixed me with a look reminiscent of lightly-poached eggs.

'Marcus, dear,' she said. 'If you intend to be insufferably cheerful at this hour then I am going straight back to bed. You can go to bloody Brundisium on your own.'

I grinned; she didn't really mean it. 'You'll be okay when you get into the coach.'

'Really? Define "okay".'

Some people have no sense of adventure. I led the way outside, to where Satrius and a Significant Other had parked in the main drag in front of the house.

'Morning, Corvinus,' he said. 'You ready for the off?'

'Yeah. More or less.' I opened the coach door and stood back while Perilla climbed in.

'This is Felicio, by the way. He'll be doing most of the driving.'

I nodded to the hunched, great-coated and seriously-hatted figure sitting beside him on the coachman's bench. The tip of his nose was showing, but not much else. 'Hi, Felicio. Pleasure to meet you.'

Grunt.

Yeah, well, mysteries to be unravelled there, then. Probably human as opposed to primate, but with Satrius as my only point of comparison I wasn't placing any bets. So long as he (or it, as the case might be) could drive it was none of my business.

I climbed in after Perilla.

I'm no great fan of these monster sleeping coaches – they're comfortable enough, sure, if your definition of comfort stretches to having your back molars shaken out while you're trying to snatch more than an hour's real sleep from the night's twelve – but I had to admit that, here at least, Eutacticus had done us proud: seats with cushions stuffed with lamb's-wool that converted into a couple of proper beds, windows with tight-fitting shutters to keep out the draughts, and a pull-out table with sockets to hold a wine jug and cups. Which, indeed, they were already equipped with. All the necessities, in other words, including, I noticed, the emergency *en suite* facilities provided in case you got caught short during the night and didn't fancy risking the great outdoors. Barring the aforesaid problems when the bugger was actually moving – and until some smart-as-paint Greek comes up with something to counteract the combined effect of iron-rimmed wheels, leather-strap suspension and paving-slabbed road surfaces – not by any means a bad way to travel.

Slow as hell, mark you – arthritic snails come to mind – but you can't have everything.

Perilla was already ensconced under a pile of blankets and snoring softly. I settled down opposite her, pulled my own blankets up to my chin, and joined her.

There was a sudden lurch and off we went.

Oh, the joys.

I must've managed to doze off, because the next thing I knew it was full daylight. I glanced through the open shutters to check out the position of the sun. Still inside of the first hour, and not a bad morning after all, weather-wise; the covering clouds and threat of rain had gone, and it looked as if it was turning into a very respectable early-autumn day. We were clear of the city itself, but judging by the number of tombs bordering the road not by all that much. Which, of course, given that our top speed was practically walking pace, wasn't surprising.

Perilla was still snoring away in her cocoon of blankets. I stuck my head out of the window.

'Hey, Felicio!' I shouted. 'You want to pull up for a moment? Comfort break.'

Grunt.

The coach slowed and stopped. Yeah, well, we'd established communication, at least; basic as you get, but still.

I got out, stretched, and pissed into the roadside ditch. I noticed that the male members, as it were, of our luggage cart were doing the same, while Phryne disappeared behind one of the roadside tombs. You can't be too squeamish on these long trips, and when there isn't much actual ground cover – as on this stretch there wasn't – the options are pretty limited. Felicio and Satrius had stayed where they were. Either gorillas had cast-iron bladders or, more likely, they'd had their personal comfort breaks earlier while I was still asleep.

'So how far have we come?' I asked Satrius while we waited for Phryne to reappear.

'We're doing good. Just passed the fifth milestone.'

'Uh-huh. Far as that, right?' Like I said, your expectations where sleeping coaches are concerned need to be set pretty low: at this rate if we were lucky we might be in Brundisium by the Winter Festival. 'You fancy walking for a bit? Fill me in on a few details?'

'Bugger off, Corvinus.'

'Pretty please?'

He scowled, then shrugged and climbed down. 'Okay. What d'you want to know?'

Phryne reappeared, gave me a nod and rejoined the lads on the cart. Felicio clicked his tongue and shook the reins, the mules took the strain, and the coach resumed its headlong career.

'That would be just about everything, pal,' I said, matching the pace. Not a particularly difficult feat, in the circumstances. 'Your boss wasn't exactly communicative.'

'What did you expect? A full fucking narrative epic?'

I kept my temper. 'No. Just a bit more than I got, that's all. So give. Start with this deputy of his, that I'll be seeing a lot of. What was his name? Cluvius, right?'

'Quintus Cluvius. Yeah.' He fell into step beside me. 'Him and Marcius, they'd been together for years. They was practically brothers.'

'You've met him?'

'Oh, yeah. Me, I'm through to Brundisium on the boss's business fairly regular, three or four times a year at least. He's okay, like the boss said your typical old school operator, same as Marcius himself was. You can trust Cluvius. His son, now, Marcus' – he spat into the ditch – 'that one's a real bastard.'

'Even by your standards?'

He stopped and faced me. 'Look, Corvinus,' he said. 'Let's get one thing straight. I do what I'm told because that's my fucking job and it has to be done, right? Doesn't mean to say I always enjoy doing it. Marcus Cluvius, he's just evil. You watch him when you meet him. I'm not kidding here.'

'Uh-huh.' Oh, whoopee; just what I needed. Anyone that Titus Satrius categorised as 'evil' would definitely not be a joy to know.

'Him and Marcius's second son – Aulus – they're an item.' I shot him a startled, sideways glance and he chuckled. 'Nah, not like that. They've got a thing of their own going.'

'How do you mean, a thing?'

'A sideline to the business. In areas that their dads wouldn't've touched with gloves and a fucking barge-pole.' He spat again. 'The heavy stuff. Protection rackets, intimidation, GBH; worse, if the price is right.'

'You mean the same sort of thing you do for Eutacticus?'

He stopped again. This time his hand snaked out and grabbed me by the throat. I froze.

'I won't tell you again, friend,' he said quietly. 'For me it's a job, nothing more. And the guys I get heavy with usually either deserve it or would do worse to me if they got the chance. For those bastards it's a pleasure, and more often than not the poor sods on the receiving end are just ordinary punters trying to make an honest living. So cut the snide sanctimonious crap, right?'

He let me go. We walked on in silence for a bit while I massaged my crushed larynx.

'So,' I said when I could finally trust myself to speak without sounding like a whispering bullfrog. 'I assume their fathers know what's going on. Knew, in Marcius's case.'

'Sure they knew. That doesn't mean to say they could do anything about it, does it? Yeah, old Marcius is already dead, but if he wasn't how long would he've had left? Active life, I mean. Five years? Ten? And Cluvius is the same. Then the youngsters'd be in charge and calling the shots in any case. Their daddies knew it, they know it. More to the point, all the lads on the payroll know it. When push comes to shove which way are they going to jump?'

Encouraging, yes? I was really, *really* beginning to look forward to this job. Thank you, Sempronius bloody Eutacticus. 'You said Aulus was Marcius's second son. What about the elder?'

Satrius snorted. 'Titus Junior. Right. He doesn't figure, Corvinus, or not much. A long, useless streak of piss that even his father had given up on. Nah, now the old man's gone Aulus'll be the one to step into his sandals. Although my bet is that his pal will still be running things on that side. Aulus is jackal to Marcus's wolf. He'd love to be the top dog, sure, but where him and Marcus are concerned he's not in the same class.'

'Fair enough.' I filed all that for later consideration. 'Moving on. What about the other family? The Pettii?'

'Old Lucius Pettius...well, the boss told you about him. He's from the same mould as Marcius and Quintus Cluvius, and just as straight by his lights. Oh, sure, him and Marcius've been in opposite corners of the ring practically all their lives, but business aside they've rubbed along okay. Like the boss said, you live and let live, don't shove too hard and you won't get shoved back.'

'Who suggested the wedding originally? Him or Marcius?'

'That was Marcius. Mind you, Pettius, he was all for it from the first. No surprises there: when you came down to it the three of them, Pettius, Marcius and Cluvius, they thought pretty much alike. Old school values, old school ways of doing things.'

'Uh-huh. And the prospective fiancé? Pettius's son?'

'Sextus.' Satrius frowned. 'Yeah, well, I can't say I take to Sextus much, myself. Able as hell, sure, best of the young bunch, easy, but he's a cold-blooded bastard at root. Listen hard and you can hear his fucking brain ticking. Me, I'm never comfortable with guys like that.'

Yeah, that I could understand, Satrius being the towering intellect that he was. Mind you, I had to admit that he'd given me a pretty good run-down of the various personalities involved here. Plenty of food for thought, certainly.

'How about–?' I began.

'Marcus? What time is it?'

I glanced through the coach window. Perilla was obviously surfacing; early for her, sure, but travelling always throws your sleeping pattern out of kilter. Not to mention leather-strap suspension and a road that's mostly bumps.

'Morning, lady,' I said. 'Second hour, or near enough. We're about six miles from Rome.'

'Oh.' She yawned. 'Stop the coach, please. I need to freshen up.' A euphemism, of course. Felicio drew up opposite a convenient tomb and we waited until she'd got the freshening up over and done with.

It took us fourteen days to get to Brundisium. Don't ask. Enough said.

3.

The house we'd be staying in for the duration, so it transpired, was just inside the town's western gate, where the Appian Road ended up. Which, in accommodation terms, was a definite plus: Brundisium has been Rome's main port for the east for centuries, with the result that the town itself isn't all that much more than an appendage to the harbour complex. There are full-time locals, sure, of course there are, a good few thousand of them, but the place takes its character from the temporary population: travellers coming or going, or stuck waiting for the wind to change, sailors on shore leave while their ships are taking on cargo or unloading it, marines and squaddies from the local garrison, plus the whole supporting infrastructure that you get in places like that, cheap lodging-houses, cookshops and wine bars, brothels (often simply a sideline service offered by all three of the former) and a retail network that caters for the tastes of practically every ethnic group in the empire. Genteel, sober-living middle-class cake-and-honey-wine klatsch territory it isn't, not even in what you would've thought would be the more upmarket areas furthest away from the docks.

The perfect town, in other words, for entrepreneurial businessmen like the Marcii and the Petii.

So there we were, half way through the fifteenth day since leaving Rome, easing our stiff, travel-shattered, stale-smelling bodies from, as appropriate, the coach and the luggage cart. Our absent host had left a skeleton staff behind, and while me, Perilla, Satrius and Phryne went inside Bathyllus, with Alexis's assistance, saw to the unloading of the baggage. Meton, meanwhile, clutching his set of knives close to his bosom, had already disappeared, as was his wont, to his bolt-hole in the kitchen.

We went through the lobby to the atrium. A bit poky, and the artwork on the walls drew a disapproving sniff from Perilla – whoever the erstwhile owner was, the guy clearly favoured the boobs-and-buttocks school of contemporary mural painting – but it was still a hell of a lot better than what we'd had to put up with for the last half month. And at least we had it to ourselves: Satrius, it transpired, had an ongoing arrangement with a lady of a certain age whose husband was away most of the year, so he was happily fixed up already.

'Okay, Corvinus.' The lad himself turned to go. 'That's you delivered. I'll leave you to get settled in and come back tomorrow morning to take you to Cluvius.'

'Hang on, pal,' I said. 'As you were, first things first. This place come equipped with a bath suite?'

He chuckled. 'Want it with jam on, don't you, boy? Nah, you'll just have to slum it at one of the public set in town like the rest of us plebs. There's a good place just inside the gates that should be open till sunset.'

'Fair enough,' I said. 'It cater for women, do you know?' Oh, sure, despite Perilla's declared intention we'd stopped off for a wash-and-brush-up a few times en route, but small-town establishments are often either men-only or have fixed separate bathing times for male and female clients. The last proper steam we'd both had had been two days before, in Tarentum.

'Uh-huh. You want to go over there now? I can get Felicio to drop us off.'
'Great. Great.' I paused. 'So, ah, you'll be coming too, will you?'
'Yeah. I may as well.' He grinned evilly. 'We can scrape each other's backs.'
'Fine,' I said. Oh, the heady joy of anticipation. 'Lead on, pal.'
We picked up Alexis and Phryne on the way and re-embarked on the coach.

The bath-house wasn't up to the standard of the Agrippan in Rome, but it was easily as good as anything since Capua; plus, as Satrius had said, it had a women's section. Not too far from home, either, less than a ten-minute walk away, in fact, and we'd passed a likely-looking wine-shop on the way that I'd be checking out later. All in all, considering that we'd only been in Brundisium for five minutes I reckoned we were doing none too badly.

I sent Alexis off to find a litter rank and arrange for Perilla and Phryne to be collected when they came back out, paid my copper coin entrance fee plus another for towel, oil-flask and the hire of a scraper, and went in, with Satrius tagging along behind.

The place, when we'd stripped off in the changing room and gone through for our steam, turned out to be heaving, most of the punters by the look and the sound of them being plain-mantle or pleb-tunic locals done with work for the day and relaxing before they went home to their wives and dinners. Satrius, fortunately, spotted a bosom crony of his who looked like he was in much the same business, and the two of them hived off in a corner next to the door to compare maiming techniques. I moved further in and squeezed between what turned out to be, from their conversations with their neighbours on the other side, a pork-butcher and a haberdasher, closed my eyes and settled down for a much-needed soak.

I gave it half an hour or so then headed for the cold plunge and recreation area. That last, in a pillared courtyard walled off from the street outside, was pretty busy too, with a fivesome playing pass-the-ball in the middle and a small crowd of less energetic punters engaged in more sedentary pursuits on the fringes. I found an unoccupied pillar next to a couple of oldsters engrossed in a needle-match game of Robbers, sat down with my back against it and watched the ball-throwers.

After the sun had moved on another couple of notches I was on the point of calling it a day, getting dressed and checking out the interesting wine-shop. At which point a big guy with serious muscles came through from the bath suite proper, stopped behind one of the Robber-playing granddads and poked him hard in the back with his finger. The old man winced and turned round. Under the circumstances I'd expected him to give the bastard an earful, at the very least, but he didn't. Instead, he froze, and so did his partner. Both of them were staring at chummie like mice that'd come face to face with the local badass cat.

Uh-huh. Street theatre. And the interesting thing was that most of the surrounding punters, after casting brief covert glances at what was going on, either decided to move elsewhere or succumbed simultaneously to an attack of blindness, deafness and complete lack of interest.

I settled back against my pillar to observe developments.

'Been avoiding me, have you, Pops?' The guy clicked his tongue. 'Bad idea. Bad, bad idea.' The old guy swallowed and said nothing. His face was grey as a well-used dishrag. Chummie grinned and gave him another prod, in the ribs this time. 'Only, the boss can get very peeved when people do that.'

The oldster cleared his throat. 'Honest,' he said, 'I was just–'

'Don't come it. You was just nothing.' Another prod; the grin widened. 'Five days late with a payment isn't good, is it? Not good at all. And not sensible, the line you're in. Accidents happen, and a bakery, well, it's a natural fire risk, isn't it, all that flour dust? One spark from an oven out of place and suddenly you're in real schtook.' A third prod. 'No more business. And it could be even worse than that, if you take my meaning. We wouldn't want that to happen, now, would we?'

'The gods be my witness, Brinnius!' The old man's voice was shaking. 'I never meant to–'

'Yeah, right. So long as you bear it in mind. Tomorrow at the latest, you get me? And that's payment in full, cash on the nail. Otherwise I guarantee that things will turn nasty.'

Okay, enough was enough; bugger this for a lark. I stood up. 'Uh...excuse me, pal,' I said politely, 'but I couldn't help overhearing your conversation there. Why don't you just let this gentleman finish his game in peace?'

That got me a long, disbelieving stare ending in a scowl. Finally:

'And why don't you, *pal*, just butt out?' he said. 'Because it is none of your fucking business.'

I shrugged. 'True. Even so.'

'Fair enough. Suit yourself.' He bunched his fist. 'Last chance. You can either walk away peaceable or–'

'Having problems, Corvinus?'

I turned. Satrius and his mate had come up behind me.

'Yeah. Just a tad,' I said.

'Uh-huh. You leave it to me.' He switched his attention to Chummie. 'Okay, sunshine, now I'll give you a choice. You can piss off yourself and we'll say no more about it or I can send you back to Cluvius on a stretcher. Your decision, no hurry, count of three.' Their eyes locked. 'One two three.'

The big guy gave me a glare and stalked off. I glanced at Satrius.

'Uh...Cluvius?' I said. '*My* Cluvius?'

'Nah, not the old man.' Satrius watched Chummie go and spat neatly into the gutter at the base of the portico. 'His son. I told you about him and Aulus Marcius sidelining. That bastard there's their chief muscle, name of Titus Brinnius. Not that he's worth a fart matched against anything but old-timers and women. With a bit of luck even you could've taken him.'

'Gee, thanks.' I looked for the baker and his mate, but the two of them were long gone.

'You're welcome. This is Carpus, incidentally. Now he *does* work for Cluvius Senior.'

'Hi.' I nodded at the other guy, who nodded back. Carpus, right? *Carver.* Either a nickname or the profession went way, way back in the family. 'Good start. From the look I got I doubt if I'm flavour of the month with the family's hired help. Their younger branch, anyway.'

Satrius chuckled. 'Don't you worry about Brinnius, boy; I can handle him. Marcus Cluvius neither. You just do your job, the way the boss told you, and everything'll be hunky-dory.' He glanced up at the sun. 'Getting on towards my dinner time. And the lady doesn't like to be kept waiting. Pick you up tomorrow, Corvinus, like I told you.'

He sloped off, leaving me with Carpus. Who, it had transpired, worked for Cluvius the Elder. Joy in the morning; some gift horses you don't even *think* about looking in the mouth.

'You fancy a cup of wine, pal?' I said. 'My treat.'

The wine shop I'd noticed earlier, being practically next door to a public bathhouse, was pretty much packed out at this time of day, but fortunately one of the tables in the far corner was still free. I sent Carpus over to scare off any potential rival claimants while I went to get the drinks in at the counter.

The barman finished serving a couple of punters further along the row and came over.

'Yes, sir. What can I get you?'

I'd been checking out the board while I waited. Nothing particularly interesting, at first sight, at least: this being Brundisium Greek wines featured more than they normally would, and me, I'm not a great fan. Unless you know where you are with them – which I don't – half of the time it's like drinking perfume and the other half they take the lining off your throat on the way down. So best avoided altogether.

'You got any recommendations?' I said. 'Italian, not Greek.'

'The Tarentine's good. Or I've a decent red from my cousin's vineyard just down the road.' He half-filled a cup from a jug on the counter and pushed it over. 'You like to try some of that first?'

'Sure.' Good sign; barmen who sucker strangers into buying rotgut don't offer freebies. I picked up the cup and took a sip. Not bad, not bad at all; not Campanian standard by any means, but it held its own on its home ground, easy. 'Fine. Make it a jug, would you?' If I was going to seriously bend Carpus's ear – which I was – we might need the mileage that a full jug would give us.

I paid and took the jug, plus a couple of cups, over to where Carpus was waiting at the corner table.

'There we go, pal.' I sat and poured for us both. 'Get that down you. Cheers.'

'Cheers.' He emptied the cup in a oner and refilled it. Evidently getting the whole jug had been a smart move. Maybe I should've made it two.

'So,' I said. 'You worked for old Titus Marcius before he died, right?'

'S'right, gods rest him. Cryin' shame, that was, him being stiffed an' all.' He took another swallow. 'My dad, he got me the job when I was a nipper. Pers'nal recommendation, like. Him an' Master Marcius, they was close as fish sauce on beans, practic'ly since they was both nippers themselves. He was a good man, was Master Marcius.'

'So what was he like? As a person, I mean?'

'He was straight. Straight as a fuckin' yardstick. He told you somethin', that's how it was, exac'ly how it was, or how it was goin' t' be 'f it was an order. No argument, no faffin' around. An' he expected you to be straight with him back, by the gods he did. Lads on the payroll, friends, fam'ly, business 'sociates, din't matter who they was, they'd be up front with him or there was hell to pay. No second chances, first offence an' that was it, far as he was concerned. Out on your ear, you were, right off.'

'Uh-huh.' I sipped my own wine and offered up a silent thank-you prayer to Mercury, god of eloquence: evidently in Carpus the old guy had landed me a talker. 'Must've made him quite a few enemies, did it, that sort of attitude?'

'One or two, sure, in his time.' Carpus drained his cup, and reached for the jug. 'What'd you expect? That's life, in't it? Me, I'd a lot of time for him. Most people in the business did, friend or foe. Like I said, you always knew where you was with Master Marcius, good or bad, an' that's worth a lot in this town.'

'You care to be more specific about the enemies?' His brow furrowed. 'Ah...give me a few names? Anyone you think might really want him dead?'

'Nah. No one like that.'

'Oh, come on, pal! There must be someone! You've just told me–'

'Look, Corvinus, that's not how it works, okay? The boss had enemies, sure he did, ev'ryone does. More than most, even, no arguments there. You're in the business he was in – we're all in – you're makin' them all the time, every fuckin' day of your life, just to get by. Nothin' special, right? So you learn to give an' take, shrug things off. Oh, sure, first chance you get you'll do the bastard down serious an' whistle while you do it, 'course you will. But no killing, not ever, not unless you've a hell of a good reason for it. An' I *mean* hell of a good. You kill at the old boss's level, even at second hand, an' you've crossed the line, you're a dead man walking sure as if you'd cut your own throat. No rights or wrongs, no excuses, no escape, today, tomorrow, the next day, the next year, it don't matter: you're dead an' burned, finish. You get me?'

'Yeah, I get you.'

'It wouldn't stop there, neither. You've got a brother or a son or a good friend, any fuckin' attachment you like, an' he's going to go full-tilt after the guy who killed you, for the same reasons. Has to, no option. So it all happens again, an' before you know it you've got a fuckin' full-scale gang war on your hands.' He took another swig of the wine. 'No one wants that, right? So what I'm saying is, unless whoever stiffed old Master Marcius was a complete headbanger or din't understand the rules he must've had a fuckin' peach of a reason. An' that sort don't come easy. Clear?'

'Uh-huh.'

'Good. You just remember, then.' He sank the rest of his wine and refilled the cup.

'Yeah. I'll do that.' I took a hefty swig from my own cup and topped it up while there were still refills in the jug to be had. 'Moving on. Tell me about this marriage business.'

'Pass.' Carpus shrugged. ''S way out of my league, that. Between-the-bosses stuff. All I know is, it's goin' to happen come December. Least, that was the plan.'

'You mean it's been called off?'

'Fuck knows. Not as far as I know, sure, but the way things are your guess is as good as mine. Better, because you're in with the nobs.'

'Okay. But what would it mean as far as you're concerned? Any changes?'

'Bound to be. Bury the hatchet with the Pettii an' we're in a whole new ball-game, 'specially with the old man dead.'

'So who'll be in charge? Of your side of things, I mean?'

'Yeah, well, that's the big question, in't it? By rights it should be young Master Titus, him bein' the old man's eldest an' all, but–' He stopped.

'But Titus couldn't hack it, yes?'

He frowned. 'You said it, man, I didn't. Not my place. But I wouldn't argue with you. Master Titus, he's OK in himself, a nice enough bloke, clever as they come, 'specially with figures, but if it's a matter of filling dead man's sandals then no way. If it'd been that wife of his, mind, that'd be another story.'

'His wife?'

'Septimia. Name's Septimia. She's a proper hard nut that one, an' not a healthy bitch to cross, neither. She'd have the mileage, easy. For all she's a looker, me, I don't envy the poor bugger.'

'Uh-huh.' I made a mental note. 'So if not Titus what about the other son? Aulus, isn't it?'

'Aulus, right. Yeah, well, you know about him already, don't you, or so Satrius tells me. Oh, sure, he's tough enough for the job, or thinks he is, but he's not a patch on his father for brains an' he's a real bastard into the bargain. Okay, there's a fair number of the lads would be happy to see him take over 'stead of Master Titus, that's true enough, but I'd be sorry for it myself. An' I'm not the only one, neither.'

'Yeah? How so?'

'I told you. Because he's a thoroughgoing five-star bastard. Plus, he's got sod all in the bank far as having what it takes to be a boss goes. Oh, sure, he's fine when it comes to twisting arms or punching heads, but that's about his limit, an' that's not a boss's job. Me, I wouldn't trust him to run a pastry-shop without his pal Marcus calling the shots. Which 'f he was in charge is what'd happen, sure as daylight.'

'That's Marcus Cluvius, right? The son of the deputy? Brinnius's boss?'

'Yeah. Satrius tell you about him?'

'More or less. He said he was pure evil.'

'Right.' Carpus emptied his cup. 'I'd go along with that. They're bastards, the pair of them, but young Cluvius, he's something special, he's smart with it, really smart. Evil does it nicely.'

'You think Aulus will take over?'

Another shrug. ''S possible, sure. Like I said, he has quite a few of the lads behind him already, an' that counts.'

'With Marcus Cluvius in the background pulling the strings?'

'Maybe. But then that's none of my business, is it?' He set down the empty cup. 'Look, Corvinus, I'm just another grunt on the payroll, okay? I do what I'm told, when I'm told. Finish, end of story. If that's how it turns out then like it or not that's how it is.'

'Fair enough.' I finished the wine in my cup and poured for us both, which after the rate he'd been knocking it back finished the jug. 'This marriage wouldn't affect things, then?'

That got me a sharp look. 'Come again?'

'According to Satrius the groom's a pretty high flier. If he's married to old Marcius's daughter – which he should be, in a month and a half's time – he'll be one of the family, yes?'

'Yeah, I s'pose.' Grudging as hell. 'So?'

'So what are the chances of him squeezing both of the sons out of the running? Titus and Aulus both?'

'Zilch. He's a fuckin' Pettius, pal. We'd work with him, sure, but not for him. If the old Master had still been alive an' given it the okay, put his weight behind the guy, then maybe that would've been different.' He drained his cup and set it down. 'An' granted, from all I've heard he'd make a pretty good boss, sure, no argument, better than either of those two buggers. Only that's not going to happen now, is it?'

Right. Seemingly it wasn't. Which was an interesting point in itself.

Altogether, food for thought right enough.

4.

I was awake late next morning, although not as late as Perilla, who true to form was still flat out and dead to the world when I finally padded downstairs in search of breakfast on the terrace.

Where, it transpired, Satrius was already ensconced and digging into the last of a plateful of upside-down egg pancakes while Bathyllus hovered to one side radiating white-hot disapproval.

'Hey, Corvinus. How's the lad this morning?' Satrius reached for the honey pot and spooned on a generous dollop.

'All the better for seeing your smiling face, pal.' I sat down opposite. 'So. First stop Cluvius's place, right?'

'Marcius's.' He divided the pancake, crammed half of it into his mouth, chewed, and swallowed. 'Cluvius sent a message to say he'll see us there instead.'

'Suits me,' I said , breaking a piece of bread from the loaf and dipping it in olive oil.

'Fine.' The other half pancake followed the first. He stood up and wiped his mouth with my napkin. 'We'd best be getting off, then.'

I paused mid-dip. '*What?*'

'Second hour, Cluvius said. It's almost that now.'

Bloody hell! 'Come on, Satrius! I haven't had my sodding breakfast yet!'

He shrugged and tossed the napkin onto the table. 'And that's my problem how? You want to lie in bed till all hours, boy, that's up to you. We're working to a schedule here.'

'You're winding me up, aren't you?'

'Could be. Or maybe not. You want to place any bets?'

Bugger. Well, I was never much one for breakfast anyway. I finished dipping the crust, popped it in, and tore off the rest of the loaf section to eat on the way. 'Just tell me what the arrangements are in advance next time,' I said. 'Little things like that are good to know.'

He grinned. 'You only had to ask, Corvinus. And don't worry. Far as the investigation goes, after the introductions you're on your own. I've got better things to do with my time than play nursemaid to a fucking purple-striper.'

Yeah, well, thank the gods for that, at least. Just the thought of having that bastard at my shoulder all the time made me shudder. 'Fair enough,' I said. 'Lead on, pal.'

We left.

Like I said, Brundisium's not your average city. It comes fully-equipped with all the usual amenities, main square, temples, baths, public buildings, markets and such, sure, but despite all that it has the feel of a transit camp; as if any moment a large chunk of the inhabitants will up sticks, leave the place to its own devices, and move on to wherever they were going to originally. Or maybe it's just me.

That's not to say it isn't heaving, mind, quite the reverse. At that hour, in Rome, the streets would've been packed with punters going about their lawful (or otherwise) business, with particular emphasis on the archetypal working-class matron equipped with net shopping bag, serious elbows, and a single-minded take-no-prisoners attitude to forward progress that would have a legionary cohort faced with her quaking in its hobnailed boots. You got them, sure – I don't think there's a city, town or hamlet in the empire where you can walk the length of a downtown street without being shoved aside or mown down by one of those human juggernauts – but pedestrians in Brundisium are a lot more of a mixture There's the shipping business element for a start, of course, both on the customer and the service-provider side, easterners for the most part, naturally, but that said inside of a dozen yards you're rubbing shoulders (literally) with more races, colours and creeds than you can shake a stick at. Yeah, okay, you'd get the same in Ostia and Puteoli, sure, but your average punter in Rome tends to be home-grown or several-generations-naturalised, and the chances are that he's never been near the sea in his life. Then there's the military. As well as being a port, Brundisium's also the lead-in to Italy's soft underbelly, the natural landing place of choice for any self-respecting invader from the east, which means that there's a heavy military presence, naval and army both, with the result that you can add a fair sprinkling of off-and on-duty marines and auxiliary squaddies to the mix.

The Marcius property turned out to be in the southern part of town's upmarket residential area, not quite at the Sempronius Eutacticus level but getting there: access via an ornamented doorway in an impressively long stretch of boundary wall, with cast-iron torch cressets either side and a solid-looking door-slave in lime green livery sitting guard on a stool out front.

'Morning, Brunellus.' Satrius gave him a wave, and he stood up. 'Marcus Valerius Corvinus. To see the boss.'

The man grunted and opened up. We went inside.

Sizeable lobby, good mosaic of the standard 'Beware of the Dog' type on the floor, whacking great mural all the way along one wall showing – presumably – the ex-master of the house accompanied by the god Hermes whispering sweet nothings in his ear and watching while his minions unloaded a merchant ship of its cargo, while off to one side his tame accountant sat at a desk totting up the profits from the voyage. Yeah, well, if you've got it, flaunt it. The fact that, knowing what I already did about old Titus Marcius, said cargo had probably fallen off the back of some other bugger's merchant ship to begin with, or was in the process of doing so, was clearly irrelevant.

'Come on, Corvinus,' Satrius said. 'We haven't got all day.'

The atrium beyond was part and parcel with the lobby, pricey and showy. It was empty apart from another couple of green-liveried slaves on statue-buffing duty who barely glanced in our direction before getting on with the job. Satrius led the way straight through and down the short corridor beyond. He stopped at an oak-panelled door, knocked and pushed it open.

The main study, obviously, and a working one at that: document-cubbies occupying most of three of its walls, the fourth being largely taken up by an open folding door leading out onto a portico and small rose garden with a dolphin-fountain. In the centre of the room was a huge oak desk flanked by bronze candelabra.

The guy sitting behind the desk looked up as we came in.

'You got here, then,' he said to me.

Just that. And he didn't seem exactly over the moon about it, either. Hardly the all-smiles-and-welcome-to-Brundisium speech I'd been expecting. Mind you, he didn't exactly look the welcoming speeches type to begin with: mid- to late-sixties, pure Ostia bruiser, with a face like the back end of a mule and a patch covering his right eye.

'Yeah,' I said. 'So it seems. You'd be Quintus Cluvius, right?'

'Right. Pull up a stool and sit down. Satrius, you can bugger off.' Satrius gave me a grin and left. There was a stool next to the open folding door. I carried it over and sat. 'Fine. So let's get this over with, shall we?'

Like I say, hardly encouraging. And since the journey had taken a half-month slice out of my life when I could've been sitting outside a wineshop in Castrimoenium getting happily stewed it was a bit on the thick side.

'Look, pal,' I said. 'Before we do that let's just get one thing straight, okay? This wasn't my idea. You want to take it out on someone, take it out on Sempronius Eutacticus. He's the one who arranged it. And you, presumably, went along with the idea or I wouldn't be fucking well here in the first place, now, would I?'

Cluvius's face darkened. Then he gave a shrug. 'Fair enough,' he said. 'Even so I'm telling you now that you're neither wanted nor needed. Oh, we'll be as helpful and co-operative as you like, don't you worry on that score: Eutacticus is no man to cross, and if he wants to send one of his fancy Roman friends down to dig the dirt instead of leaving us to handle things ourselves in our own way like we've always done then that's that. Only don't expect us to like it.'

'Gee, thanks,' I said. 'Always a pleasure to be appreciated.'

That got me a one-eyed glare. 'Just so as we both know where we stand. Let's get started. What do you know already?'

'About the old man's death? Practically nothing, barring the fact that he was found floating in the harbour a month ago. Why would that have been, do you think? Any particular reason, that you can think of?'

'If I knew of one, Corvinus, or who might've been responsible then you wouldn't be sitting there asking stupid fucking questions, now would you?'

Prickly as hell. But then I wasn't, by this stage, expecting much else. Oh, the joys.

'Right. Right,' I said. 'So nothing to do with the guy's, ah, business activities, then?'

'Absolutely not. To my certain knowledge. That's not the way we do things.'

I remembered my recent conversation with Carpus. 'Yeah, so I've heard. Okay, leave it, for the present at least. Moving on. I understand there's about to be a new partnership arrangement, sealed with a marriage alliance.'

Cluvius's mouth set. 'That's true. So?'

'You think there might be a connection somewhere there?'

'How do you mean?'

'Search me. I'm just asking the questions; I don't have the answers. Only I'd've thought the coincidence needed looking at, myself.'

'That's all it is. A coincidence. Look.' He frowned. 'The arrangement has nothing to do with Titus's death. It's in everybody's interests, for a start. Us and the Pettii, we've been in competition for years, and that doesn't make sense any more for either of us, not the way things look to be going. Titus knew that, Lucius Pettius knows that, everyone in both camps knows that. And before you ask, there's no third player in town who might have the nerve to throw a spanner in the works because a) like I said it's just not done or worth the risk and b) the deal would be going ahead come December whether Titus was around or not. Clear?'

'Okay. So who's the new boss?'

His single eye blinked. 'Come again?'

'There must've been a will, for a start. Who's the old man's heir?'

'Unfortunately it's not that simple.'

'Really? And why would that be?'

'There was a will, certainly, and it's clear enough. A tenth of the estate to the widow, a few smaller bequests amounting to another tenth, and the rest split equally between the two sons. Fifty-fifty, cash and property both, straight down the middle.'

'Uh-huh. So what you're telling me is that, as far as the business is concerned, Marcius didn't specify a clear successor at all?'

'Yes.'

'You know why?'

'He hadn't decided himself. Under normal circumstances the elder – Titus Junior – should've got the lion's share. Or it could've gone the other way, with Aulus being heir in the first degree. Problem was–'

'The old guy didn't think either of them was prime leadership material.'

Cluvius scowled: obviously I'd cut too near the bone for his liking. 'He had his reservations, sure,' he said. 'About both of them, for different reasons. But that is none of your fucking business.'

The hell with that. 'Look,' I said. 'It's completely my business, okay? You're telling me that someone bashes the boss's head in leaving the top job open just when you're moving into a completely new ball game, and there's no connection between the two events?' I waited, but he didn't answer. 'Okay. Did either or both of them – Titus or Aulus – know the contents of the will in advance?'

'No. Not of the most recent will, anyway.'

'You mean there'd been an earlier one?'

'There had. Made about fifteen years back.'

'And that said what?'

'It named Titus as the principal heir, but with a full quarter of the estate going to Aulus.'

'Titus knew this?'

'Sure. Everyone did. Why not? It was the usual arrangement: the bulk of the estate going to the elder son, the younger getting a fair slice of the pie. Neither of them could complain that they'd been short-changed.'

'So when did Marcius decide to change the terms?'

'Two months ago. A month before he died. That was when the deal was finalised with Pettius.'

'And everyone knew he'd done it? Made a new will?'

'No. He kept that to himself. First I knew of it – first anyone knew of it, to my knowledge – was when it was read out the day after the funeral.'

'Why would he do that, do you know? Make such a secret of it?'

'Probably because it was it was only supposed to be temporary, until he saw how things panned out over the next year or so.' He shrugged. 'That's pure guesswork, sure, but I knew Titus Marcius better than anyone. He wouldn't've cared a fig about hurting anyone's feelings, but he was smart, and had his head screwed on tight. That was what made him boss and kept him there.'

'So as far as Titus Junior was concerned at the time the old man was murdered he was the clear favourite for the top spot, right?'

Cluvius shook his head. 'No; like I said, it doesn't quite work like that. In this business it doesn't so much matter who you are as how you shape up. But if Titus had had what amounted to the old boss's vote then he'd've had a better chance of being accepted.' He gave me a sudden, sharp look. 'Hold on! If you're suggesting–'

'Uh-uh,' I said firmly. 'No suggestions, no pointing fingers. Just gathering facts at present.'

'Fuck that!' He was glaring at me. 'You think Titus killed him? Murdered his own father?'

Bugger. Well, we'd best get this sorted out right at the start or I'd be pussy-footing around until the Winter Festival. 'No,' I said calmly. 'But it's a possibility, in theory at least. One of several.' The glare didn't falter. 'Come on, pal! You said yourself that no outsider could've been behind the old man's murder. Okay, fine, I'll take your word for it, for the present, at least. But the converse is that we're looking for someone on the inside, and *that* means family and close associates. Now if you don't like that then tough, because that's how it is.'

His big hands, resting on the desk in front of him, curled into fists. 'Close associates?' he said quietly. 'That mean you're putting me on the list as well?'

'Unless you can give me a cast-iron, no arguments reason why not, and up to the time when I'm convinced you don't belong there, then yeah, of course I am. Like I say, it's a theoretical possibility like any other. You have a problem with that?'

I wondered, from the look on his face, if I'd gone too far with the candid approach. He was just getting to his feet, fists clenched, to smite me to atoms, and I'd tensed to block the inevitable punch, when the door opened and a woman came in.

She couldn't have been more than twenty, tops, and she was a real looker. The granddaughter, obviously, the one due to be married to Pettius Junior in a couple of months' time. If so then he was getting a bargain.

'I'm sorry, Quintus,' she said. 'I didn't realise you had company.'

'That's all right.' Cluvius was mastering himself with difficulty. 'This is Valerius Corvinus. The...gentleman Sempronius Eutacticus has sent from Rome. Corvinus, this is Titus's wife Atia.'

So not the granddaughter after all. And I was sure Carpus had said that Titus Junior's wife's name was Septimia. Nevertheless. I stood up.

'Pleased to meet you, Atia,' I said. 'I'm terribly sorry about your father-in-law.'

'What?' She looked fazed for a moment. Then she shook her head. 'Oh. Oh, no. Titus was my husband. I'm the widow.'

I blinked. Yeah, well, an age gap between husband and wife is fairly normal, but one of almost fifty years is seriously pushing things. And, of course, it opened up a whole new field of possibilities...

'I think Corvinus and I are done for now in any case,' Cluvius said, and I could just hear his teeth grinding together. 'Perhaps you'd like to take him elsewhere.' *And preferably lose him down the nearest sink-hole,* his tone and body language added. So. No long-lasting bond of friendship forged in that direction, then. Still, I was buggered if I'd let the guy hamstring the investigation right from the outset. And a certain amount of cage-rattling never does any harm.

'Suits me,' I said.

'We'll go to my sitting-room,' she said. 'It gets the morning sunshine.'

I nodded to Cluvius, getting barely an acknowledging grunt in return, and followed her out and a half dozen yards or so along the corridor.

'Here we are,' she said, opening a door. 'Come in, please.'

There was another of the lime-tuniced slaves in the room, a woman this time, dusting the shelves of a small cupboard full of knick-knacks. She gave Atia a nervous glance and the duster caught against a small bronze figurine, which fell to the floor.

'Pick it up,' Atia snapped. The slave did, and put it back on the shelf.

'It's not damaged, madam,' she said. I could see that she was shaking.

'That's very fortunate. See me later.'

The woman ducked her head and slipped out of the room behind us, closing the door as she left.

'They're clumsy beasts, aren't they?' Atia said. 'Sit down. Make yourself comfortable.'

She'd been right about the room catching the morning sun. Like the study, it opened out onto a small formal garden, only this time it was properly south-facing, and the autumn sunlight brightened the whole space. There were a couple of wicker chairs either side of the central table. I pulled the nearer one up and sat.

'Now,' Atia sat down and arranged the folds of her perfectly-cut mourning mantle. 'What can I tell you that Quintus hasn't already?'

'That'd be practically everything, lady,' I said.

She laughed. 'He's not the most communicative of men, is he? And he didn't really want you here to begin with.'

'Yeah, I sort of got that impression early on. While you do?'

'I wouldn't say that. Not at all. Personally I couldn't care less who killed Titus. Or indeed why.'

Said without a smidgeon of altered tone. 'Ah...is that so, now?' I said cautiously. 'You care to explain?'

'Certainly. My husband was an arrogant, overbearing, egotistical boor with the manners and personal charm of a pig. If that isn't an insult to the pig. I never liked him, let alone loved him.'

Well, that was straight enough. Comprehensively and graphically put, what was more. 'So, uh, how long had you been married?'

'Three months, five days and...let me see...fourteen hours. That's up to the time a month ago when he was found floating in the harbour.'

'And why did it happen in the first place? The marriage, I mean?'

'I was sold, Valerius Corvinus.' She shrugged. 'Nothing new or surprising there, of course. Daddy's a leading light of the local mercantile community. Ships' chandlery. Only he has ambitions, and getting a foot on the local political ladder isn't cheap. My marriage paid for his aedileship very nicely. The fact that his new son-in-law was twenty years older than he is and an out-and-out crook was only a minor drawback.'

'Uh-huh. And your mother – didn't she have anything to say about the arrangement?'

'Oh, Mummy had lots to say. Mainly on the theme of how lucky I was to get Titus and how I should stop complaining and show a bit of gratitude.' She smiled. 'But we're straying from the subject rather. You want to know about Titus and how he died.'

'A bit more of the background would be useful, yeah.'

'As to that, I'm afraid I can't be all that much help. Marcus came over to break the bad news about the second hour, just after the body was discovered. That's Quintus's son, Marcus Cluvius. I wasn't even dressed, at least not properly. They'd taken Titus directly from the harbour to the undertakers. He was...the back of his head was quite a mess, or so Marcus said. Beaten to a pulp.' For the first time, the smile slipped and the bright tone faltered. 'Marcus thought it ought to be...put to rights before he was properly laid out for viewing. As far as that was possible, at least.'

'So Marcus Cluvius was the one who found the body?'

'Oh, no. That was one of the local fishermen. He noticed it bumping up against his boat as he was getting ready to go out, tipped it over with his steering oar and saw who it was; Titus, of course, was quite a prominent local figure. It just so happened that Marcus's house was the closest, so that's where he went.'

'Where was this, exactly?'

'On the west side of the Neck, three or four hundred yards from the town centre end.'

'"The Neck"?'

'That's the local name for the inlet that runs inland from the junction of the Big and Little Harbours. Most of the smaller fishing boats are anchored there.'

'Uh-huh. And the body was found just after dawn?'

'Or possibly a little before. I don't know exactly.'

'He'd been out all night? Your husband?'

'Probably. At least, the door-slave said he'd unlocked the door for him about the tenth hour and that was the last anyone saw of him.'

The tenth hour, eh? Late to be going out, sure, with only two hours of daylight left. But all the same, he would've had those two hours to play with, if whatever reason he'd had for going out in the first place demanded natural light. 'He tell the door-slave where he was going? Or anyone else? You, for example?'

'No. Nor how long he'd be. And I would have been the last person he'd have chosen to tell.'

'Did he make a habit of that? Going out late without any explanation, I mean?'

She shrugged. 'He did it occasionally Not very often, certainly not on a regular basis. But sometimes yes, and sometimes he stayed out all night. It was none of my concern.'

'No? Not as his wife?'

She laughed. 'Oh, please, sir! Spare my blushes! Titus was sixty-eight years old. Any tomcatting he might manage he was welcome to, as would the lady in question have been. And if his reasons were other than sexual then that was his business. Myself, I couldn't have cared less.'

'Fair enough. Marcus Cluvius. You say he lives near where the body was found.'

'That's right. Only a block or so away. The family own a tenement building near the Temple of Saturn, and he has a flat on the first floor.'

'A tenement flat? That's a tad downmarket, isn't it?'

She shrugged again. 'His father has never been particularly generous where allowances are concerned, any more than Titus was with his sons. And it's quite a few years since Marcus decided that he'd rather not live cheek by jowl in the family house any longer, thank you. It is an extremely nice flat, mind, and it does take up the entire first floor. He likes it, and it serves his purposes.' Bland as hell. 'That's all that's important, surely.'

'You've seen it, then? From the inside?'

'Naturally I have. On several occasions. In company or decently chaperoned, of course.'

'He isn't married, then?'

'Marcus?' A twitch of the lips that didn't quite make it as far as a smile. 'No, as it happens. Or rather, not any more. He was, but he got bored with her and they divorced. That was long before my time; I don't even know the woman's name or what happened to her afterwards. Anyway, he seems to be quite happy to stay as he is at present.'

Yeah, well. Me, I'd pay good money to know if our sweet little Atia was a significant factor there. Oh, sure, maybe it was what Perilla would call my lubricious imagination and overly-suspicious mind-set working overtime, but all the signs pointed to it being a definite possibility. For a good-looking twenty-year-old married lady with a sexagenarian husband whom she can't stand to be in close proximity to a youngish unmarried man-about-town on a daily basis is a situation that just begs a jump to certain conclusions. Still, that was something to be kept in its place for now. Leave it and move on.

'Since we're on the subject of families,' I said, 'tell me a bit about your husband's sons.'

Did she relax slightly? Maybe not; it could simply have been said imagination kicking in again. Even so...

'Titus Junior and Aulus.' She frowned. 'Of course. What do you want to know?'

'Anything you like. Basic general background first, how old they are, wives and kids if any, that sort of thing.'

'Titus is thirty-nine. He's married to Septimia and their daughter is Marcia, who's marrying Sextus Pettius in two months' time. Aulus is two years younger. His wife's name is Gellia. Two children, both boys, aged six and four. Nasty little brutes, the pair of them.'

'Uh-huh. Septimia I already know something about.' Like I said, I remembered her from my wineshop conversation with Carpus the day before: the hard nut that it wasn't healthy to cross, and the driving force of the partnership. 'What's Gellia like?'

'Actually, I get on rather well with her, although she can be rather wet at times as well as being a complete–' She stopped. 'No, I think I'll let you find that part out for yourself if and when you meet her. She and Aulus aren't exactly soulmates, which again will be obvious; goodness knows why he married her in the first place. Oh, except of course her daddy was one of the local landowning toffs who could give chapter and verse on his ancestors back a dozen or so generations. That probably went a long way to persuading him.'

Sour as hell. 'And Aulus himself?' I said. 'What do you think of him?'

'I call him the Conger Eel. Not to his face, of course. He's cold and slimy and savage, a brute like his father but without the saving grace of Titus's intelligence.' I must've winced, because she added coolly: 'You did ask. And I am being truthful.'

'What about Titus Junior? The consensus seems to be that he's not much cop.'

'Yes, I'd say that was a very fair assessment. Oh, he's a nice enough man, but "nice" rather sums him up. He always gives me the impression that he'd rather not have been born into what, let's face it, is a family of crooks, thieves and swindlers and that at base he despises them. Certainly if so then it's mutual: Titus – my Titus – hadn't much time for him, called him the Human Cipher. And Aulus can't stand him, which on consideration is a point in his favour rather than not. Still, he is the elder son. And he has Septimia behind him, even if she is twisting his arm up his back.'

'So who do you think will take over the firm?'

Atia laughed. '"The firm",' she said. 'I like that; it has such overtones of honesty, worth and respectability. Well, we have to call it something, I suppose, so that will do as well as anything else. I haven't the slightest idea, and as I said I don't really care. It's none of my business.'

'What will you do now, yourself? Stay on? Go back to live with your parents?'

She shuddered. 'Not that, at any rate. Never that. Would you, under the circumstances?'

'No, I don't suppose I would. But then I'm not a young woman with limited options.'

'True. Frankly, though, neither of those alternatives offers any attraction whatsoever. We'll just have to see how things go, won't we?' She stood up suddenly. 'Corvinus, we are getting far too serious, and off the subject at that. If you've finished interrogating me, for the moment, at least, and don't feel that you're being dragged from pillar to post I'll introduce you to Marcia.'

'She's here?'

'Not as such, no. At least, not in this house. But Titus and Septimia have a house of their own a little further down the street. I'll take you round and make the introductions. Titus himself won't be there, not at this time of day, and I know for a fact that Septimia has an appointment for a dress fitting this morning, so she won't be around either. You'll have Marcia all to yourself. That please you?'

I stood up myself. 'Yeah. That'd be great.'

Atia smiled. 'It's all quite exciting, really,' she said. 'But honestly, whoever did it, I really hope you don't catch him.'

5.

On the way out I had a quiet word with the door-slave: like Atia had said, Marcius had left the house two hours before sunset, without mentioning where he was going or if or when he'd be back. The guy closed the door behind us.

Atia had watched the exchange in silence with a quiet smile.

'Are you always so suspicious, Valerius Corvinus?' she said. 'Turn left, by the way.'

I did. 'Just checking I have the facts right,' I said. 'And yeah, I suppose I am. Don't take it personally.'

She laughed. 'I don't lie, you know. Not unless I have a very good reason to, which believe me I don't where Titus's death is concerned. But I should warn you that when I do I'm extremely good at it.'

'I'll bear that in mind, lady.'

'Do that. It's the third house along on the right. The one with the blue door.'

The porter in attendance got quickly to his feet and had the door open before we were within two yards of it. I gave the man a nod in passing, but Atia ignored him.

'Just go straight through,' she said to me.

There was an oldish guy standing in the atrium, with 'Serious Major-domo' written all over him. He bowed.

'We want to see the young mistress, Neon,' Atia said. 'At least, Valerius Corvinus here does. Is she at home?'

'Yes, madam. In her rooms.' He gave me a speculative glance. 'Shall I fetch her for you?'

'No. We'll go up.'

She brushed past him and led the way through to the family part of the house and up a staircase to the first floor.

'Don't expect too much,' she said. 'Marcia's a dear in many ways, but she's a terrible frump. If he weren't so obnoxious himself I could almost feel sorry for Sextus Pettius.' She stopped outside a door. 'Here we are. The inner sanctum.' She shot me a sly glance. 'That's not a facetious choice of phrase, incidentally. As you'll see.' She knocked, turned the handle and went in. 'Good morning, Marcia.'

The room smelled strongly of incense. A young girl was sitting near the open window reading a book, and a much older woman – she must've been the same generation as the girl's dead grandfather – was in the chair opposite her, stitching what looked like a sampler. If the old guy downstairs had been an obvious major-domo this woman radiated Childhood Nursemaid. She barely glanced at Atia and went back to her needlework.

The girl looked up. 'Good morning, Atia,' she said. Not much expression there, just the bare acknowledgement. Then she saw me coming in behind and her eyes narrowed. 'Who's this?'

'Valerius Corvinus. He's travelled all the way from Rome to look into your grandfather's death. Wasn't that kind?' Atia turned back to me. 'I'll leave you to find out all about each other, Corvinus. For the brief time that that will require, in Marcia's case. Enjoy.'

And with a last smile she was gone, closing the door behind her and leaving the two of us – the slave's eyes hadn't lifted again from the sampler – staring at each other.

'You mustn't mind Atia,' Marcia said at last, setting the book aside. 'She's a bitch.'

I blinked. *Not* an expression I would've expected from someone of Marcia's appearance: mousey verging on plain, quietly-spoken verging on inaudible, and with a general air, even here on her home patch, of being happy to blend into the background.

'Ah...right. Right,' I said.

'Sit down, please. Capra, would you mind?'

Without a word, the old woman got up and went over to a stool in the corner. I noticed that she was wearing what must have been a good half dozen amulets round her neck or attached to her belt, which jangled together as she moved. Marcia had a good two or three herself, or at least I could see the laces they'd be attached to at her throat and disappearing under the top of her tunic. Next to the stool was a small shrine with a marble statuette of Isis and the smoking incense burner.

Inner sanctum. Right. Got it. Yeah, well, I'm not particularly religious myself, beyond your basic traditional 'I give so you may give' level, and nor is Perilla, for all her interest in temples, but I could see how things spiritual might have an attraction for someone like Marcia, particularly if she'd been brought up under the influence of Capra here. Or maybe I was stereotyping. After all, I'd only just set eyes on the girl, and that 'bitch' had come as a definite surprise.

'I knew you were coming, of course,' she said as I took Capra's place. 'Everyone did. Not that anyone wants you here. I've never seen Uncle Quintus look so angry as when he got the letter from grandfather's colleague in Rome. And Sextus Pettius was absolutely livid.' Interesting: not just plain 'Sextus', like I'd've expected from a young girl talking about her fiancé, but the more formal full name. I tucked that away for consideration. 'So. What can I do for you? Not very much, I'm afraid.'

'Actually, lady,' I said, 'what would be really useful is if you could tell me a bit about this ring that's gone missing.' With all the hoo-hah about the murder that aspect of things seemed to have slipped between the cracks. Natural enough, sure, under the circumstances, but it didn't mean it wasn't important, or possibly important. Far from it. 'If you don't mind, of course.'

She frowned. 'Oh,' she said. 'I'd almost forgotten about that, with everything else happening. So you know about the ring as well, do you?'

'Yeah. Not much, only that it's worth a packet and your grandfather bought it for you to give to your fiancé the day you got married. You think you can fill in the gaps for me?'

'There isn't much to tell. Grandfather gave it to me a few days before he died and I put it into one of the drawers in my dressing table. That was the last I saw of it.'

From her offhand tone she might as well have been talking about a piece of jewellery bought in the local market for a few sesterces. 'You, uh, don't think that was taking a bit of a risk?' I said.

'No. Why should it have been?'

'The drawer has a lock?'

'Of course it does. I'm not stupid, and grandfather had told me how valuable the ring was. I really should have given it to father to put in the safe straight away, I know, but that's thinking with hindsight, isn't it?'

'Fair enough.' The gods protect me from poor little rich girls! 'So when did you realise it was missing?'

'That was three days later.'

'Three *days?*'

'Yes. I don't use that drawer for anything else, you see, and although the lock had been forced it had been done very carefully, so there was almost no damage. I only found out that the ring had gone when I went to have a proper look at it.'

'You have any idea who could've been responsible?'

'None whatsoever.'

'That's pretty definite.'

'Yes. It was meant to be. Father questioned the servants, of course.' I gave her a sharp look, and her lips twisted. 'That's "questioned", as in "talked to": I know the normal procedure in these circumstances would be to employ torture, just to make sure they tell the truth, but all our slaves have been with us as long as I can remember, and they're very loyal. Mother was in favour of using it in any case, but both I and my father objected, so that was that.' She smiled. 'Besides, there's a big difference between appropriating a trinket worth only a few coppers that's been left lying about in the open and stealing a valuable ring from a locked drawer, isn't there? That's not something your average domestic slave would do. The risk would be far too great, and how on earth would they go about selling it?'

True, all of it. Which raised some interesting questions, not least where the bubble-headed poor little rich girl scenario was concerned. We might as well cover all the bases, mind.

'Okay,' I said. 'So if it wasn't one of the servants who took it' – and me, I wouldn't dismiss that explanation altogether out of hand, just on her say-so – 'then who could it have been, and how did they do it?'

'I've been thinking about that. It was probably a burglar. Someone from outside.'

'Who managed to sneak into a strange house through a locked front door with a doorkeeper on guard and find their way upstairs without being seen to a room they didn't know was empty. Who then decided there might possibly be something worth stealing in the locked drawer of an ordinary dressing table. And who finally managed to retrace their steps and get clean away, still without being spotted. Yeah, right, that would work.' I grinned.

She didn't smile back. Instead, she stood up.

'Come over here,' she said. 'Look out of the window.'

I did. We were on the first floor, sure, but the room overlooked the garden, and the roof of the portico on the house wall side was no more than a couple of feet below the sill.

'There's an espaliered apple tree at the far end that's practically a ladder,' she said. 'In fact, I used to climb up here from the garden myself when I was younger, when no-one was watching.' She shot me a sideways look that had nothing mousey about it. 'Girls aren't supposed to do that sort of thing, you know.'

'Fair enough,' I said. 'But whoever it was would still have to get into the garden itself, up the apple tree and a full dozen yards along the portico roof, all without anyone noticing. That's a pretty tall order, don't you think?'

'The back gate opens onto an alleyway, and it's never locked. We have a gardener, of course, but he's getting on a bit; he spends most of his time in his shed. No one else uses the garden much at this time of year, the rooms on this floor with windows overlooking are all bedrooms, and as a family we tend to stay up quite late in the evenings. Which means we're downstairs until well after sunset, usually in the dining-room on the other side of the house. So you see it wouldn't be all that difficult.'

'Provided the thief knew all of that already, of course.'

She shrugged. 'Of course. But if he knew of the ring's existence and intended to steal it from the start he'd have planned things very carefully in advance. There's nothing there he couldn't have found out himself without too much trouble. And if any risk was involved then surely the potential rewards justified it.'

Yeah, well, I had to admit I couldn't fault her reasoning, particularly since, like she said, we were dealing with a major heist here, which pointed to the professional side of the trade. Forget the bubble-head completely; what we had here was an extremely smart cookie. Still, I'd keep an open mind, myself: a scenario involving a top-notch professional burglar, given the surrounding circumstances of the new partnership arrangements and Marcius's subsequent death, plausible or not, was just too much of a coincidence for me to swallow. Besides, the phantom cat-burglar wasn't the only game in town.

We'd have to move delicately on this one, mind.

'Uh...just out of interest,' I said. 'Apart from the servants who else would've had access to the room in the three days between you getting the ring and it going missing?'

She frowned. 'I don't understand.'

'You and your maid, obviously.' I glanced over at Capra, who was still studiously working away at her stitching and paying us no attention. 'Your parents, presumably.'

She was still looking puzzled. 'I suppose so, yes, of course they would. But neither mother nor father would have any reason to come in here, certainly not if I was elsewhere. Still, even if they did then why should it matter?'

'Humour me, okay? I'm just going through the possibilities.'

'If you're suggesting that–'

'Uh-uh,' I said quickly. 'No suggestions. None at all; like I said, I'm just being thorough. Okay, parents. How about visitors, over the three days? Any of them, that you know of?'

'Valerius Corvinus, I really don't think–'

'Please. Just for information.'

'Very well. That's easy. Grandfather himself and Atia. Uncle Quintus. My proper uncle, Uncle Aulus, and his wife. Sextus Pettius, of course, but he comes round most days. Oh, and Uncle Quintus's son Marcus; he came with his father. I think that's everyone.'

Gods, she wasn't kidding! Unless there was someone I hadn't heard of yet that was the whole sodding boiling!

'That more or less how it usually goes?' I said.

'Oh, no. The day after grandfather gave me the ring was my mother's birthday. We always have a party in the afternoon to celebrate, so the whole family was here together from noon to dinner time.'

I groaned, mentally. Bugger! And a party, what was more! That'd mean that no one would be keeping a check on anyone else's whereabouts. And no doubt visits to the latrine would have featured, so even a prolonged absence wouldn't've been commented on.

'Fair enough,' I said. 'We'll leave it at that for now. Incidentally, just how important is this ring, in actual fact?'

'It's very valuable. You know that. Of course it's important.'

'That's not what I meant. How does it being out of the picture affect the wedding arrangements? If at all?'

'Oh. I see.' She frowned again. 'Well, it was an agreed part of my dowry, certainly. Quite a large part, in fact, financially speaking. I suppose that might mean, if it isn't recovered, that our side have to make up the shortfall in actual cash or property. And that wouldn't be easy to arrange, certainly not at this short notice.'

'Meaning that if it stays missing the wedding gets called off? Or at least postponed until either it turns up or both families agree on a new settlement?'

'Yes. Yes, I suppose it does. The second, anyway, almost certainly. I really didn't think of that.'

'You don't sound too concerned.'

She shrugged. 'No, I'm not, as it happens. I don't particularly relish the prospect of being married to Sextus Pettius.'

'Is that so, now? You care to tell me why not?'

'You haven't met him yet. Or have you?' I shook my head. 'Then let's just say he isn't a very likeable man. To put it mildly. To be fair, mind, I don't much want to be married to anyone, and if I have to be then it may as well be to him as to someone else. A dreadful admission to make, I know, but there we are. You did ask.'

'So what *do* you want to do?'

'To be honest, I'd be quite happy to stay a virgin for the rest of my life. All this sex and babies business is just so messy. And probably overrated.'

'Right. Right.' Jupiter! Still, I appreciated her frankness. If, indeed, she was being frank and not spinning me a line; at this point in the case I couldn't take anything for granted. 'One last thing, and I'll leave you in peace. Can you give me a description? Of the ring, I mean?'

'Not really. I told you, I didn't have it for long. Not in any real sense.'

'Even so, you must've had a good look at it when your grandfather first gave it to you.' I paused; nothing; her expression had gone blank. 'Never mind. Quintus Cluvius will know. I'll ask him. Thanks for all your help, Marcia.' I turned to go.

'No, wait.' I stopped. 'It was a man's signet ring, an antique. Gold, with a carved stone, an amethyst, I think. And the design was a rayed star.' She sat down again and picked up her book. 'Now that's really all I can tell you.'

'Yeah, well. Thanks again,' I said. 'I'm very grateful.'

No answer. I left.

Okay, so where to now? I still had half the morning to kill, but I reckoned I'd had my whack of knocking on doors for one day, while barring a talk with the two sons, one of whom at least was away from home, there was only the Pettii side of things to cover at this initial stage. Which, because I didn't have an address at present, was a non-starter. Time, then, for a bit of a walkabout; make my way back towards the centre of town and check out the place where Cluvius's body had been found. Not that there would be anything particular to see there, probably, but then you never knew your luck.

So that was what I did.

One thing about Brundisium, on top of what I've already mentioned, is that you're never far from the sight and smell of the sea. The city's two main harbours, Big and Little, account for three of its four available sides, while the narrow inlet that Atia had called the Neck – barely more than half a cable's length in width and only about six feet deep – stretches back from where they meet almost as far as the main square. Add to which that, unlike in Rome, you're dealing with a grid-patterned street system, and finding your way around is easy-peasy.

The west side of the inlet, three or four hundred yards from the town centre end, Atia had said. Fair enough.

That stretch, it transpired when I got there, was home to the main fish market, and it was heaving, mostly with the local equivalent of the Roman bag-lady. I walked along the quay, keeping a leery eye out for incoming net bags of crustaceans, until I reckoned I was about the right distance along, then chose one of the stalls at random.

'You want to talk to Felicia, love,' the woman behind the stall said when I asked her. 'Fourth one further on. It was her Quintus found it, poor soul. Gave him quite a turn, it did. His stomach's never been strong.'

I thanked her, moved on down the line, and stopped at the fourth stall, where the saleswoman was decanting a fresh supply of whelks.

'Excuse me,' I said. 'Felicia?'

She upended the sack, shook it to dislodge the remainder, and gave me a suspicious look.

'That's me,' she said. 'What d'you want?'

'I think your husband pulled a body out of the water a month ago. Man by the name of Titus Marcius. Would that be right?'

'It would.' She dropped the empty sack on top of the others. 'So?'

'I was just wondering if he – you – could tell me any more about it, that's all.'

'Nothing more to tell.' She started arranging the shellfish into a neat pile. 'What's your interest?'

'I've been sent down from Rome to look into his death.'

The suspicious look disappeared, and her eyes flicked towards the purple stripe on my tunic. 'Official sent from Rome, are you?' she said. 'Well, fancy that, now! There's grand!' She finished spreading the whelks out and wiped her hands on her apron. 'You know that he was a crook, I suppose?'

'Yeah. Yeah, it has been mentioned.'

'Not that I've anything against crooks, mind, so long as they're honest.'

'Ah...right. Right. So this was, what, about an hour after dawn, yes?'

'More or less. My Quintus likes a good breakfast before he goes out. And the baker isn't open until first light.'

'And his boat was moored here?'

'That's his spot. Just behind the stall. He was getting into it when he saw the corpus bumping along the wall of the quay, no more than a yard away, with the back of its head stove in. When he turned it over he saw it was old Marcius. That was after he'd spewed his guts out, of course, poor lamb. Waste of a bloody breakfast, that was.'

'"Bumping along the quay"?'

'That's right. There's a current first thing in the morning, right to left, out towards the sea.'

'Uh-huh.' Interesting; so wherever Marcius had been, his body had probably been dumped in the water somewhere along the stretch between where it was found and the inlet's town centre end. 'I was told that when he recognised Marcius your husband reported the death to a guy called Marcus Cluvius. That so?'

'He did. It made sense: Quintus knew where he lived, and it was fairly close by. Plus he'd a day's fishing ahead of him. He needs all the hours the gods send, this late in the year.'

'You happen to know where it is, exactly? Marcus Cluvius's place?'

'Back that way.' She nodded towards the centre. 'Two streets in and three or four blocks down, just before the temple. The first floor flat, over the cookshop.'

Possibly worth, if not an actual visit, a walk past just to check the place's exact whereabouts. 'Thanks, lady,' I said, turning to go. 'You've been a help.'

'Funny thing, though,' she said.

I turned back. 'Yeah? What would that be, now?'

'Quintus told me afterwards that he'd seen the old man just the night before, right as rain.'

'*What?*'

'That's why finding him like he did gave him such a turn.'

'Where was this?'

'Up at his old offices.' She gave another nod, towards the centre again. 'Quintus was passing them on his way down here – he takes the boat out to set night-lines when there's a decent moon – when he sees Marcius outside the door unlocking it'

'"Old offices"?'

'Where they was before they was moved a year or two back. They were there for donkey's years, long as I can remember, anyway.'

'Is that so, now? What time was this?'

'Tenth, eleventh hour. Maybe a bit earlier or later.'

'And you didn't mention this to anyone, either of you, when the body was collected?'

'No fear. It was none of our business, and that sort of thing only leads to trouble.'

'Uh-huh.' There spoke the *vox populi*. It would've been the same in Rome, mind, or anywhere else, for that matter: if you saw or heard or knew about anything dubious, you kept schtum. It was safer that way. 'Did your husband see anyone else?' I said.

'No. Just the old man. He did wonder, mind, what he was doing down here at that time of the evening. Any time of day at all, for that matter; for all he used to be a familiar face it's been a good while now since he upped sticks to the family's new place nearer the harbour, and we hadn't seen him since.'

'Right. Thanks again, lady. Like I said, you've been a great help.'

Too right she had! Jupiter!

I found the place she'd meant no problem: an old, run-down, two-storey property with shuttered windows on both the ground and upper floors and a stout oak door which, when I tried it, proved to be firmly locked. Otherwise, there wasn't much to see: the building stood alone, with nothing to either side, and it backed directly onto the quay. The object of a future visit, obviously, and pretty damn soon, at that: if it was still in the family's possession – and given that Marcius, according to Felicia, had had a key that was more than likely – I could apply to Cluvius for access. Me, I'd lay good odds that, whatever reason the old man had had for going there in the first place, that was where he'd been murdered, and the body subsequently dropped over the quayside to drift down-current. This late in the day, of course, there probably wouldn't be any signs of the murder itself, but just to have a look round might well spark off a few ideas.

So. Check out the exact location of Marcus Cluvius's flat over the cookshop for future reference, then call it a day and head for home.

Again, Felicia's directions were spot on. And yes, it would've taken her husband ten minutes max to get there from where he'd found the body.

I didn't hang around, though, and I'd no intention, at this point, anyway, of knocking up Marcus Cluvius and introducing myself. Not that he'd probably be in at this time of day in any case. There was a likely-looking wineshop just across the road, but I'd had enough of traipsing around for the present. I headed in what I thought was the most likely direction for the city's west gate and home.

6.

Bathyllus was waiting for me in the atrium with the wine tray. I unfastened my cloak, tossed it onto one of the couches, and took a large swallow from the cup he handed me. Wonderful.

'The mistress around?' I said.

'No, sir. She said to tell you she and Phryne had gone to look round the local shops.'

I grinned; that was her for the rest of the day, then. 'Fair enough.' I held the cup out for a refill.

'You do, however, have a visitor.' Bathyllus had his frigid face on. Not a good sign.

'Yeah?' I said. 'Who's that?'

'Titus Satrius, sir.' Oh, bugger. 'He arrived half an hour ago. He is, at my insistence, waiting for you in the garden.'

And probably, given the change in the weather over the past couple of hours, freezing his nuts off in the process. Bathyllus could be an evil-minded little sod when he chose, and he was the arch-snob's arch-snob.

See me weep.

I went through to the porticoed garden at the back of the house. Satrius was sitting, none too comfortably, on one of the marble benches.

'You took your time, Corvinus,' he said. Snarled.

'You'll get piles, pal. Come inside and be comfortable. I'll square it with Bathyllus.' I led the way back to the atrium. 'What do you mean, "took my time"? It's hardly the middle of the afternoon yet, and I've been running around like a blue-arsed fly.'

'Yeah, well, I thought I'd better check up on you, see how you were doing. Everything going okay?'

We'd reached the atrium by this time. I lay down on the couch while a tight-lipped Bathyllus brought up a stool, ostentatiously spread one of his polishing dusters on top, and exited the room. Satrius removed the duster and sat.

'Fine,' I said. 'Why shouldn't it be?'

'You talked to Cluvius, I know. You see anyone else?' Casual as hell.

'The widow, Atia. And Marcia, the granddaughter, the one who's getting married. Or not, as the case may be.' I paused, then said innocently: 'She told me all about the missing ring.'

I'd done it deliberately to see what his reaction might be, and it was all I'd hoped for. He looked, suddenly, shifty.

'Is that so, now?' he said. 'That's good. How do you mean, "all", exactly?'

'Just the circumstances of its disappearance,' I said. 'Oh, and she gave me a description, of course.'

'A description?' His expression was so wooden you could've hammered nails in.

'"A man's antique gold signet ring with an amethyst bezel cut in the shape of a rayed star",' I quoted. 'That was about it.'

He relaxed, visibly. 'Yeah,' he said. 'Yeah, that's it, all right. I take it back. You've been a busy little bunny after all.'

'Gee, thanks.' I wasn't going to tell him about my conversation with Felicia of the Whelks, no way: candour, or rather the lack of it, went in both directions. 'Incidentally, now you're here you can give me a couple more addresses. Cluvius's actual office, or wherever it is that I'd find him most of the time, and ditto the Pettius place.'

'Cluvius is in one of the big commercial properties facing the quay of the Big Harbour, about half way along. Ask anyone for the Marcius building. The Pettii are at the Little Harbour just beyond the mouth of the Neck. You with me?'

'Sure. I'll find them. No need for you to tag along this time, incidentally. I'm a big boy now; I can get around on my own.'

He scowled. 'I told you yesterday, Corvinus. I've got better things to do than play nursemaid to a fucking purple-striper.' Yeah, I thought, so how come you're here now twiddling your thumbs on my garden bench waiting for me to get back, then, pal? But I let it go at that. 'Here on in, you're on your own.'

'Fine. Suits me. Oh, except that I'll need to know how to get in touch with you if necessary.'

'The hell with that!'

'Come on, Satrius! Pretty please! Just for emergencies. And I doubt if Eutacticus'd be exactly over the moon to discover you'd bunked off first chance you got, just so's you could spend more time canoodling – euphemism – with this secret girlfriend of yours. Or am I wrong?'

'Okay! Okay!' I waited. 'There's a women's lingerie shop just off the main square, right? Half way up the street from the temple of Rome and Augustus, on the left hand side, opposite a wineshop. Ask for Porcia and leave a message. And if you do and it's not a fucking five star gold plated emergency then I will kill you, you get me? That's a promise.'

He stood up. I was grinning. 'Lingerie shop, eh?' I said. 'Deal. I'll see you around.'

'One more thing. If her husband's there – little weedy bald-headed guy with buck teeth – make yourself scarce and go back later.'

'Will do. Cross my heart.'

He left.

Bathyllus oozed back in with the rest of the jug. I held out the cup for another refill.

'Everything okay your end, Bathyllus?' I said as he poured.

'Oh, yes, sir. The house staff are a bit hairy in the hoof, but we'll soon have them licked into shape.'

Spoken like old Gaius Marius contemplating his major restructuring of the Roman legions. He'd do it, too; I reckoned the poor bastards below stairs were still reeling from the shock. Which reminded me.

'Meton settling in as well?'

A tightening of the lips. If our major-domo had had his way our anarchic chef would've been pitched out of the cart before we'd passed through the Capena Gate. As it was, the kitchen skivvies were probably still deciding which particular branch of the primate species he belonged to, and getting it wrong. 'So I believe. He was off at first light for a tour of the local markets. I haven't seen him since.'

'Good, good.' Well, that was promising, and not totally unexpected: a market-fixated Meton is a happy Meton. With any luck he'd found his way over to the Neck, and we could expect a fish dinner. 'That's all great, little guy,' I said. 'I'll let you get on.' He turned to go. 'Oh, one more thing. Tell Alexis I want a word. No hurry, just when he's free.'

'Certainly, sir.'

He buttled out.

I'd just settled down with the remainder of the wine when Perilla got back.

'Hello, Marcus,' she said, taking off her cloak for Bathyllus to hang up. 'Successful day?'

'Pretty good,' I said. 'You? Bathyllus said you and Phryne had gone on a shopping binge.'

She lay down on the couch opposite. '"Binge" is hardly the word for it, dear. Brundisium is *not* the shopping capital of the empire, although we did find a couple of interesting places.'

'Not a lingerie shop in the street up from the temple of Rome and Augustus, by any chance?'

'Pardon?'

I grinned. 'Sorry. Private joke. Forget it.'

'Actually, I did have one success. We were looking at jewellery and I got into conversation with another browser who turned out to be a local.'

'That so, now?' I poured the remains of the jug into my cup.

'Her name's Sentia. Anyway, we've arranged to meet tomorrow.'

'That's great.' It was: if you're a woman the trouble with being outside your usual stamping ground is that, unless you have local connections, you're effectively stuck at a pretty loose end. Oh, sure, we'd been in Brundisium before, several times, but only as long as it took to rendezvous with an eastbound ship, and of course I'd been around all the time. 'You can–'

'You wanted to see me, sir?'

I looked round. Alexis had come in from the portico side of the atrium and was standing by the connecting door.

'Yeah.' Alexis, like I say, is the smartest of our bought help, which is why I'd added him to the team when we came down from Rome. 'I've got a job for you, pal.'

He looked wary. 'What kind of a job?'

'Nothing too strenuous, physically or mentally.' I reached into my belt-pouch, pulled out a handful of coins, and counted out five silver pieces' worth. 'Although I'm afraid it'll probably mean hanging out in wineshops a lot of the time. You think you can manage that?'

The wary look was replaced by a broad grin. 'Yes, sir,' he said.

'Excellent.' I passed over the cash. 'There's more if and when you need it. Basically, I want you to find out all you can about our two families, the Marcii and the Pettii, preferably on the dirty linen side. Oh, and about the Cluvii as well, father and son. Only don't make it too obvious, and certainly don't mention me, or we're all in schtook. Possible?'

'I'll try my best, sir. Are you looking for anything specific?'

'No.' I thought for a moment. 'Actually, yes. See if you can make friends with Marcius's door-slave. His name's Brunellus.' I gave him directions to the house. 'I'd be interested to know about the widow's comings and goings, if you can manage that without making the guy suspicious, but anything you can get. Otherwise, it's just a general remit. You start as of now. Off you go, spit-spot.'

He left, grinning.

'So, dear,' Perilla said.

I gave her the rundown. 'Where *cui bono*'s concerned we've candidates by the bucket-load, for one reason or another. The elder son, Titus Junior, for one. By all accounts he sounds pretty unlikely, sure, but at the time he was the clear favourite to succeed his father, officially, anyway, so at least he has motive of a kind.'

'You mean he isn't now? The leading contender, I mean?'

'Apparently not.' I told her about the will. 'So where that aspect of things goes the brothers are running neck and neck. I'd take out a side bet on old Cluvius, what's more, will or no will.'

'Quintus Cluvius? The deputy?' She frowned. 'How so?'

'He has his feet well under the table already, for a start. He'd been Marcius's deputy and sidekick for the past twenty years to my certain knowledge, probably a lot longer, and despite the fact that the old man's been dead for over a month he's still running the business.'

'You're certain of that?'

'When Satrius told the door-slave who we'd come to see he referred to him as "the boss". Maybe just a slip, sure, but that has to mean something. *Does* mean something, the way the company's hired help use the word.' I was remembering my talk with Carpus. 'And he certainly acted like he was in complete charge.'

'Why on earth would Quintus Cluvius want to murder Marcius? Like you said, they've been virtual partners for years. And by all accounts they got on well together.'

I shrugged. 'I've no idea. But it's a possibility, as much as any other, particularly since he clearly doesn't like me interfering. The widow, Atia, now, well, she's obvious. A third of her husband's age, sold into marriage by her parents, a total stunner and, from what I saw of her, a real goer.'

'Marcus!'

'Yeah, well. You didn't meet her. It's a fair objective assessment, believe me. I'll bet she's no kitten, either: she has the bought help running scared, and that's always a sign of a nasty temper. Plus there might be something going on between her and Cluvius's son Marcus.'

'Really? And after only ten minutes' conversation with the girl your evidence for that is what? Since we're being objective.'

I grinned. 'Come on! Give me a chance! We're only at the tossing around ideas stage here. It was just the way she talked about him made me think they might be kindred spirits, or close to it. And she knows all about his flat, inside and out.'

'He's married?'

'Long-time divorced, ex-wife elsewhere and out of the picture. So he's unattached, with a handy little *pied à terre* in the centre of town, well away from the family home. Both family homes, in fact, hers and his.'

'You haven't met him yet?'

'No. But we already knew from Satrius that he's got something going business-wise with the younger son, Aulus, that both their fathers disapproved of. And from bits and pieces I've picked up since, reading between the lines, that's confirmed. There's been a certain amount of friction there, to put it mildly, maybe even the beginnings of a coup. Anyhow, I doubt if either of them would be sorry to see old Marcius dead, at which point young Atia would be a widow; *Is* a widow. Icing on the cake as far as Marcus is concerned, and Atia wouldn't be crying, either.'

'Hmm.' She was twisting a lock of hair. 'What about the granddaughter, Marcia? You say you talked to her?'

'Yeah, that was interesting.' I upended the jug into my cup, and only a dribble came out. Damn. 'I'd be surprised if she had anything to do with Marcius's death, at first or second hand, sure, but unless I'm mistaken that young lady has serious beans to spill.'

'In what way?'

'I don't know exactly. But all the same I'd bet good money.' I frowned. 'When I asked her about the missing ring and how it was stolen she practically bent over backwards to convince me it was an outside job.'

'Could it have been?'

'Oh, yeah, no problems there. The lady has a brain in her head, and she'd worked it all out, the whole *modus operandi*, top to bottom.' I swallowed the last quarter-inch of wine and put down the empty cup. 'Plausibly, too. For all I know at present she might even be right.'

'But?'

'It was all too slick. Added to which, she'd been at pains, when it happened, to make sure none of the servants suffered. Atia, now, she wouldn't've done that. She'd've brought on the thumb-screws straight off, and whistled while she did it. At base, I think Marcia's just a nice kid in a hole.'

'Even so, you think she knows what happened to the ring.'

'I'd lay a pretty hefty bet on it, yeah. Either she knows who took it or she's hiding it herself.'

Perilla gave me a sharp look. 'Why on earth would she do that?'

I shrugged. 'You've got me there. Oh, sure, it'd postpone the marriage – because she was due to hand it over to Sextus Pettius on their wedding day the family will have to take up the slack where the dowry's concerned – but that's all it would do: the betrothal was tied in with the new business alliance, and that's far too important to scrap. No, all she could've hoped for was a couple of extra months' grace, if that, with marriage inevitable at the end of it. The game wouldn't be worth the candle.'

'Very well. Then who else would steal it, and why?'

'That's the rub. As far as opportunity's concerned, you can pick who you like. Marcia didn't notice that it was missing, or so she claims, until three days later, and Septimia – that's the mother – had a birthday party the day after old Marcius handed it over, with the whole family present plus the two Cluvii and young Sextus Pettius. Any one of them could've slipped upstairs, done the job, and come back down again without their absence being noticed. Easy-peasy.'

'Hmm.' She was still twisting the lock of hair.

'Motive, now, that's more tricky. Like I say, if the ring went missing it would've complicated matters where the marriage and the partnership went, but it wouldn't screw either of them up altogether.'

'Do we know who, if anyone, is against either? Apart from Marcia herself, that is.'

'Uh-uh. Not for definite; at least, no one that I'm aware of so far. The elder Cluvius might be – the rivalry, or whatever you like to call it, with the Pettii goes way back, and I'd be surprised if he could swallow the two firms being all pals together all that easily – but he seemed pretty happy with the arrangement. On the surface, anyway. The two sons...well, I haven't met either of them yet, so I can't judge, but come December they'll have Pettius's son Sextus to contend with as a future rival for de facto overall company boss. By all accounts he's a very smart cookie, the best of the three, so they might well be on the list. Still, like I said, all that's academic. The marriage and the deal will go through come December whatever happens. Or early in the new year, at least.'

'Would have gone through.'

I blinked. 'What?'

'Now Marcius is dead you don't know what will happen, dear. Not for certain, particularly since in effect his will left everything in a state of flux. If either Titus or Aulus take over in the interim then surely – in theory, at least – they can cancel both. As, indeed, could Cluvius if he was just giving lip-service to the arrangements.'

I sat back. Shit. She was right, of course; I'd forgotten, none of this was written in stone. Marcius's murder had changed the whole ball game, and the ring disappearing so conveniently would give the future boss, whoever he was, a bit of extra leeway time-wise. 'There's another factor, too,' I said. 'Maybe not connected, but nevertheless.'

'Yes? What's that?'

'There's something screwy about the ring itself.'

'Pardon?'

'It's valuable, granted, everyone's stressed that. No problems there. But when you get right down to it how valuable can a signet ring be, even if it is an antique? Marcia said it was worth a pretty large slice of her dowry. And Eutacticus told me it cost her grandfather more than I took in in a year. Okay, fine, I'm no Lucullus, but even so that's a fair whack; we're talking serious gravy here, half a million plus.'

'I suppose we are.' Perilla was looking thoughtful. 'And yes, you're right. Come to think of it, it is odd.'

'That's not the only thing. Right from the start, everyone's been cagey when it's mentioned. Eutacticus refused point blank to go into any details, Marcia only produced the description I asked for when she thought I could get it from Cluvius in any case, and Titus bloody Satrius came round about an hour ago, specially, I suspect, to check whether the cat's been let out of the bag. Whatever cat it is that we're talking about. Odd doesn't half cover it, lady.'

'So how did Marcia actually describe the ring in the end?'

I repeated what I'd said to Satrius earlier. 'A man's antique gold signet ring with an amethyst bezel cut in the shape of a rayed star.' I paused, watching her. 'Mean anything to you?'

'Nothing I can think of. Is that everything?'

'Not quite. After I'd left Marcia's I went to check out the place the body was found. The woman I spoke to – she was the wife of the guy who pulled it out of the water – said her husband had seen Marcius the evening before further up the quay, going into what turned out to be the old company offices.'

'You think that was where he was killed?'

'It seems a reasonable assumption, yeah. Everything fits, anyway: Atia told me – and the door-slave confirmed it – that the old man had left the house about the tenth hour, the fisherman saw him what was probably not long after, and his body was found the next morning only a couple of hundred yards away. Plus the fact that, if it'd been dumped over the quay like it must have been, according to my female informant there's a current in the Neck that would've carried it the intervening distance.'

'So what was he doing there at that time of night?'

'Fuck knows.'

'*Marcus!*'

'Sorry. Even so, it doesn't make sense, not if the reason was innocent, anyway. Even allowing for the whacky timing, according to Felicia the fisherman's wife the firm moved their headquarters two years back and the building hadn't been used since.'

'Some sort of assignation, then?'

'That'd be the obvious explanation, sure. Marcius would've been the first to arrive, because Quintus – Felicia's husband – didn't see anyone else, and the old man was just unlocking the door.'

'He had a key, then? You think that implies he arranged the meeting himself?'

'Yeah, well, that's the most likely scenario. Unless, of course, the other party had one themselves and it just so happened he was the first to arrive.'

'Who would have another key?'

'Anyone in the firm who rated it, I'd expect. Cluvius, one or both of the sons. Or maybe it was just hanging up on a nail forgotten about somewhere in the company's new offices, in which case it could be anyone. That's something I can check when I go to see Cluvius tomorrow and ask him if I can take a look inside.'

Perilla shook her head. 'I'm sorry, dear,' she said, 'but all this really doesn't make sense. If the meeting was with Cluvius or with either of his sons then why on earth should Marcius go to all that trouble? He could have seen and talked to any of the three of them at any time as a matter of course. Secretly and privately, if that were necessary, although I can't for the life of me imagine why it should be.'

'Agreed. Me neither.' I sighed. 'Still, again it's a possibility. We don't know all the circumstances. We don't know *any* of the sodding circumstances, for that matter. Hell.' I picked up the empty cup and got off the couch. 'Leave it for now. Enough for the day. I'm going to roust out Bathyllus, see what time dinner is.'

Meton had found the fish market, and he did us proud. We had broiled tunny in a lovage and saffron sauce, plus a couple of chargrilled lobsters flanked with oysters, sea urchins and, yes, whelks.

Maybe Brundisium had something going for it after all.

7.

I had a leisurely breakfast next morning and set off across town for the Big Harbour and Marcius's – now, temporarily at least, Cluvius's – offices. I wasn't sure what I was expecting, but what I got was the headquarters of your average sizeable company, with a roomful of clerks busy as little bees making their contribution to Brundisium's reputation as a thriving commercial hub.

The guy on the desk that I gave my name to showed me straight through. Quintus Cluvius was dictating a letter to a secretary. He held up a hand and I waited for him to finish.

'Valerius Corvinus,' he said as the guy went out with his wax tablet and closed the door behind him. 'Good morning. Come in and have a seat.'

Affable as hell, especially considering that when we'd parted company the day before he'd been preparing to rearrange my face. I pulled up a stool and sat.

'I was wondering–' I said.

Cluvius held up a hand. 'Apologies first,' he said. 'I lost my temper yesterday, and I'm sorry for it. We'll start afresh. Agreed?'

Nice as pie, albeit beneath the surface the cheerfulness sounded more than a little forced; in fact, the phrase "drawing teeth" suggested itself. Yeah, well, if he wanted to bury the hatchet anywhere but between my ears then that was perfectly fine with me. Even if it did raise the interesting question of underlying motive.

'Agreed,' I said. 'No bones broken.'

'Good.' He cleared his throat. 'You talked to Atia?'

'Yeah. Marcia too. Atia took me round and introduced me. She told me all about the missing ring.' Was that a flicker in his one remaining eye? Could've been, I wasn't sure, but given the subject's track record I would've laid a substantial bet. Still, I was happy, at this stage, just to let that side of things slide.

'Excellent. So what can I do for you?'

'I was wondering if I could have a look inside your old offices on the Neck,' I said. 'If they still belong to the firm, of course.'

He hesitated. 'As it happens, they do,' he said. 'But they've been empty for almost two years now. What's your interest?'

'It seems that Marcius visited them on the evening he died.' I told him what Felicia had told me. 'You have any idea why he did that?'

'None at all. If it's true, of course. You're sure this man, the fisherman, wasn't mistaken?'

'I didn't talk to him personally, but his wife seemed pretty sure he'd got it right. Anyway, it's worth my having a look, isn't it?'

'If you say so. There'll be nothing to see, mind.' There was a bell on his desk. He picked it up and rang it, and the secretary came back in. 'Decimus, go and ask Euxenus for a key to our old offices on the Neck.' The man nodded and went out again. 'Euxenus is the firm's janitor. He keeps all the duplicate keys in his cupboard, and they're all labelled. It shouldn't take long.'

'Great.' I smiled. 'Organised crime must be more organised than I thought.'

Oops. Mistake: the temperature of the room suddenly plummeted to Riphaean glacier levels. Forget the bonhomie, façade though it might have been; he was looking at me like I was a particularly impressive slug that had just crept out of his salad.

'Ah...joke?' I said.

'Listen,' he said softly. 'Let's get one thing clear, right? We're a legitimate business, import and export, and don't you forget it.'

Really? And I was Cleopatra's grandmother. The hell with this; if he wanted to play Let's Pretend that was up to him, but he could do it on his own. 'Is that so, now?' I said. 'Not that it particularly matters, under the circumstances, because I couldn't care less and it's none of my business, but that's not the impression I got from Sempronius Eutacticus. Certainly not where your dead boss was concerned.' Yeah, well, a slight stretching of the truth, but he wasn't to know that. 'And most of the other people I've talked to, including his widow, seem to have him set down as a crook, pure and simple.'

'Look, Corvinus.' He was still glaring at me. 'That may've been true twenty, thirty years ago, maybe even ten. Not that Titus would've been ashamed to admit it, any more than I am: it was a living, no more no less. You think you bloody Roman aristocrats have the right to criticise?' Yeah, well, he had a point there: where being bent is concerned your average Roman senator could give any ordinary crook a head start and still romp home five lengths ahead of the field; the only difference between them being that, most of the time, said senator keeps within the law. Which isn't all that difficult, because his ancestors and those of his broad-striper pals were the buggers who made said law in the first place. 'But the world's a different place these days, and unfortunately the old rules don't apply. There are crooks and crooks, and some of the modern ones just give crime a bad name.'

I said nothing, just waited. The glare faded, Cluvius's lips twisted, and he shrugged.

'Fine,' he said. 'Okay, I may've exaggerated a tad: the business may not be totally legit. Say two thirds, if you're not too fussy about definitions. That do you?'

'Sure,' I said. 'I told you; it's not my concern.' Except when it turned out to be such, of course, but now was not the time to quibble.

'Good. We'll leave it at that, then.' The door opened and the secretary came back in. 'You get it?'

'Yes, sir.' The man handed him a heavy iron key and he passed it over to me.

'There you are, Corvinus,' Cluvius said. 'Bring it back when you're finished. But I tell you, you're wasting your time. Your fisherman friend must've made a mistake.'

'Yeah, well, maybe.' I stood up. 'If so then there's no harm done. Thanks, pal.'

Now that little heart-to-heart had been very interesting. I thought about the implications all the way to the Neck.

I had problems turning the key in the lock, the hinges creaked when I finally managed to get the door open, and the room beyond – it was the usual outer office, where the clerks are stationed, and took up the whole of the ground floor space – had that damp, musty, close smell that unused rooms always have. There was a line of narrow clerestory openings four feet above my head, above the shuttered windows themselves and immediately below the high ceiling, and in the light from them and the open door I could see another set of shutters in the back wall, the one on the harbour side. That made sense; when the place had been a functioning office having plenty of natural light in the clerks' room for as much of the day as possible would've been a necessity. The desks and document-cubbies were still in place, sure, but most of the former had been piled together every which way, and there was a lot of stuff that had obviously come from elsewhere in the building. Why, when the company had moved offices, they hadn't taken the existing furniture along, I didn't know. Maybe with the move upmarket they'd simply decided to upgrade to new and impress the clients. Or maybe, because most of it looked pretty old and rickety, it just hadn't been worth the bother.

Yeah, well; it looked like Cluvius had been right after all, and no one had been in here since the move.

Still, I might as well do things properly. I was just heading across the room to let in more light when my foot caught against something that went skittering across the floor. I carried on to the far wall, opened the shutters, and looked out across the harbour. I'd been expecting a stretch of quayside, but the rear of the building went down sheer to the Neck.

Now the light was better I turned back to see what my foot had caught on. It turned out to be a two-foot length of heavy wood, shaped like a club, rounded at one end, the thickness of my clenched fist, and tapering regularly almost to the width of two fingers at the other. I took it over to the window for a closer look.

'Club' was right. That purpose might not have been what it was originally made for – and made for something specific it must have been, although I'd no idea what that was – but the crust of dried blood and hair at the business end left no doubts on that score. I'd found my murder weapon. And, by extension, the place where it'd been used.

So. Back to Marcius and Sons' company office and another word with Quintus Cluvius.

'It's a belaying pin,' he said.
'A which?'
'A belaying pin. They slot into holes on the side-rail of a ship to tie the sail-ropes to.'
'Right. Right.' Uh-huh; I recognised it myself now, the thing itself, anyway, although I couldn't have given it its name; the problem had been that it was totally out of context. 'So what was it doing in your old offices?'
'I've no idea.' He handed it back. 'You're supposed to be the shit-hot investigator. You tell me.'

Sour as hell; evidently I still wasn't the blue-eyed boy as far as Cluvius was concerned.

'Okay,' I said. 'The obvious explanation is that for some reason the killer brought it with him. The question is, why?'

He frowned. 'Why what?'

'Why a belaying pin? Oh, sure, it's perfect for the purpose, no arguments, but it's not something your ordinary punter keeps in his broom cupboard, let alone carries around with him. So why should the killer choose it to do his business for him?'

The frown became a scowl. 'Come on, Corvinus!' he said. 'The answer to that question isn't exactly difficult, is it? Marcius was killed next to a harbour, where there are plenty of boats around. Maybe whoever did it was connected with one of them.'

'Maybe.' If you were into theories involving flying pigs. On the other hand, who was I to say he wasn't right? We were only five minutes into the case, and all the options were open. Also, like he said, where better to find a standard item of ship's equipment lying around just waiting to be picked up and used than on a quayside?

Still, slice things how you will, they still felt wrong, because a belaying pin per se just didn't belong in the clerks' room of a company's office building. If whoever had killed Marcius had knifed him and tossed him into the Neck, framing a scenario would've posed no problem: the killer had come prepared with malice aforethought and the murder had gone ahead as planned. End of story. Or if, given Marcius's head had been beaten in, the murder weapon had turned out to be a wooden stool or the leg of a broken desk, the result would've been the same, only with the odds on a killing that was unpremeditated. In the normal scheme of things, though, pre-planned murder with a belaying pin, or unplanned murder ditto, made no sense at all. Which, ipso facto, meant that whoever had killed the guy, whether he had brought the thing with him all the way from home or not, had chosen it deliberately.

The real bugger, of course, was explaining why.

Not that I was going to put all that to Cluvius, mind. Certainly not until I was damn sure he was completely off the suspect list.

'I have to hand it to you, though, Corvinus,' he was saying. 'At least now we know where it was done, and how. As to the why, and what Titus was doing there in the first place' – he shrugged – 'that's still got me foxed. So what are your plans now?'

'I thought I might have a word with either Titus Junior or Aulus. If either or both of them are around.'

'Aulus, no; I know that for a fact. Titus, I'm not sure. But I can get Decimus to take you to his room, if you like.'

'No, that's okay.' I had another, intermediate, call to make, that I didn't particularly want Cluvius to know about. And he hadn't asked me for the key back, either, which was the perfect excuse for making it. 'I'll find him.'

'As you like. Keep in touch.'

I went back through to the clerks' room and buttonholed the nearest one.

'Excuse me,' I said. 'Where can I find Euxenus?'

'The janitor?' He pointed. 'His cubby's down that corridor, sir. Last room along.'

'Fine. Thanks.' I half-turned. 'Oh. One more thing, pal. You happen to know if Titus Marcius is around at present?'

'Master Titus? Yes, he is. Upstairs, first door on the left at the top.'

'Thanks again.' I took the key out of my belt, headed for the janitor's cubby, knocked on the door, and went in.

'Cubby' was right: if you'd put your arms out either side and turned round you would've been touching the walls all the way round, except for the grilled window that let in the light. There was a big cupboard that took up most of the available space, and the old man in a freedman's cap snoozing in a chair accounted for most of what was left.

I cleared my throat. No response. I prodded him gently, and he woke up. 'Euxenus?'

'That's me, sir. What can I do for you?' His eyes went to the stripe on my tunic. 'Ah. You'll be the gentleman from Rome who wanted the key to the old offices.'

'Yeah, that's right,' I said. 'Valerius Corvinus. I was just returning it.' I held it up.

'That's good of you.' He took it, got to his feet and opened the cupboard door. 'There was no hurry, though.'

I looked. The back wall of the cupboard was lined with hooks, all neatly labelled, all of which held keys, either singly or as bunches. Euxenus hung the key from an empty hook and closed the cupboard door. There was, I noticed, no lock.

'It's there if you need it again,' he said.

'Uh...it's the only one, right?' I said.

'That I've got at present, yes, sir.' He went back to his chair and sat down.

'So there are more?'

'Surely. Four, all told, including the spare.'

'Who had the others? Do you know?'

He gave me an odd look, but he answered readily enough. 'The old master, him that's dead, sir, he had one of them. He kept one of all the keys. Master Quintus, of course, he'd another. Then there was the senior clerk, that opened up in the mornings, he handed his in after the move. And mine, that was the spare, that made four.'

'Hang on. Master Quintus, you say. You mean Quintus Cluvius? He has his own key?'

'Naturally he does, at least he did when the place was in use. About now, I can't tell you. All I know is he hasn't given it to me.'

'How about the old master's two sons? Did they have copies?'

'No, sir. They didn't need them, or not when the offices was open, as it were. Although Calippus's, that's the senior clerk, I did give that to Master Aulus, right enough. That's why there's only one left on the hook.'

Uh-huh. 'When was that, exactly?' I said casually. 'Do you remember?'

'Of course. Nothing wrong with my memory, sir, where keys is concerned. The Nones of September, it was, or a day or so either side.'

Ten days before Marcius had been killed, in other words. Shit! 'Did Master Aulus give you a reason why he wanted it?' I said.

'No, sir. Why should he?'

'No reason. I just wondered. And he didn't return it?'

'No.'

Gods! Oh, sure, from the actual murder point of view the keys weren't all that crucial – Felicia's Quintus had seen the old man unlocking the door himself, after all – but all the same I'd've paid good money to know why Aulus Marcius had wanted to get into a set of offices that'd been abandoned for years and which ten days later had hosted his father's murder. Also why, if he had a key of his own, Quintus Cluvius hadn't volunteered it. Or at least mentioned the fact.

'Thanks, Euxenus,' I said. 'If I need the key again I know where to come.'

'You're welcome, sir. Any time.'

I went to talk to Titus.

Like the clerk had said, his room – office – was on the first floor. I knocked, and pushed it open.

Titus – presumably Titus – was sitting at his desk talking to an elderly freedman. He glanced at me and made a 'wait a moment' move with his hand. I closed the door, put my back against it, and waited.

The room, I noticed, was the real executive type, big, with couches and a low table in addition to the usual desk and document-cubbies, a set of windows overlooking the harbour, and even a couple of bronze nymphs holding up a set of lamps, plus a small still-life mural on the far wall. A lot snazzier than Cluvius's place downstairs, that had been completely functional. Mind you, the very fact that the latter *was* downstairs, right next to the clerks' room at the business hub of the building, might well say something in itself: I'd guess that, if either of the two offices had been Marcius's it would've been the one Cluvius was using. Which, again, was interesting.

'It will work,' Titus was saying. 'Trust me.'

The old freedman – I'd guess, from the quality of his tunic and his whole body language that he was the firm's chief clerk – shook his head. 'Look, sir,' he said. 'However you work it, you can't get past the fact that out of every three gallons that the customer orders we'd only be paid for two. I'm sorry, but that makes no sense.'

'On the contrary, it makes perfect sense.' I could hear the exasperation in the guy's voice. 'Look. We over-ordered in the first place, yes?'

'Admitted, but–'

'Just bear with me, please. The stuff is perishable; it won't keep indefinitely. So even allowing for a peak in sales before the Winter Festival come the end of the year, or let's say by early February at the latest, we'll either be selling at a loss or pouring it down the drain.'

'Agreed. All the same–'

'Now. My way, what happens is that both we and the customer profit from the arrangement. He gets a bargain, three for two, so he increases his order to take advantage of it; we sell him two gallons where before he'd only have been buying one. You see?'

'Yes, but we'd be giving a third gallon away! Sir, I'm sorry, but I still don't understand–'

'We would probably, at the end of the day, have been left with that one gallon in any case,' Titus said patiently. 'As it is, we get the cash up front, more of it than we would have done previously, we clear much-needed warehouse space for new deliveries, and we net a substantial amount of goodwill which will hopefully result in future orders. Don't forget, this is new ground for us; we're trying to break into an already-oversubscribed market, and we have plenty of competitors.' He patted the man on the shoulder. 'Believe me, Callippus, I know what I'm doing. And I have cleared it with Master Cluvius.'

'Then I suppose there's nothing more to be said, sir.' The guy didn't look any happier, though. 'I'll make the necessary provisions.'

'Thank you.'

I stood aside, and the old freedman – with a brief, sideways glance at me in passing – went out, closing the door behind him.

'I'm sorry,' Titus said. 'You'll be Valerius Corvinus, come down from Rome.'

'Yeah. That's me,' I said.

'Pull up a stool. Or would you rather sit on the couch?'

'No, a stool's fine.' There was one beside the desk. I moved it over and sat. 'That was very interesting. I didn't understand a word of it, but it sounded impressive.'

'A consignment of fish sauce. I'm trying to bring the more long-established members of the firm round to a different view of how a commercial company is organised these days, but it's an uphill struggle. Especially when there's no actual criminal element involved. That they find very difficult to get their heads round, and to be frank they see it as quite insulting. Or demeaning, anyway.' He must've seen the look on my face, because he laughed. 'Don't worry, Corvinus. I quite appreciate that up to now – indeed, including now, to a certain degree – this company has not operated totally within the law, to say the least, and I won't pretend otherwise. Just because I'm my father's son doesn't mean to say I approve. Far from it.'

'I heard you tell your freedman – Callippus, was it? – that you had Cluvius's backing. Is that so, or were you just spinning a line?'

'No, it was true enough. Like Callippus, Cluvius is one of the old guard – in fact, if you don't count my father, he *is* the old guard – but although "backing" is too strong a term at least he's open to new ideas. *Legitimate* ideas.' He stressed the word. 'However. You're not interested in the business side of things, are you? You're here to find out who killed my father.'

'True.' Not that that little exchange with Callippus hadn't been informative. Quite the reverse.

'Well, I can't really see how I'd be of much help, but if you have any questions for me then ask away.'

'Your daughter is marrying Sextus Pettius,' I said.

He frowned. 'Yes. And?'

'You approve?'

He hesitated. 'Not altogether, no, to be honest. It was completely my father's idea.'

'But you agreed to it, you and presumably your wife.'

'You didn't gainsay my father, Corvinus. You never met him, so you won't appreciate how true that statement is, but I assure you it's absolutely accurate. And if you've talked to Marcia, which I think you have, she'll have told you she isn't totally against the arrangement.'

Yeah, well, I wouldn't have put it quite as strongly as that myself from what I remembered of the conversation, but maybe she had given her parents the edited version. 'You got on well with your father?' I said.

Another hesitation. 'Not particularly. We were chalk and cheese, character-wise: he didn't understand me, and I didn't understand him. A pity, at least I think so, but there you are.'

'How about your brother?

'I'm not with you. Do you mean, did Aulus get on well with our father, or did I – do I – get on with Aulus?'

'Both, if you like.'

'Very well. The answer to the first is not at all, at least latterly. I suspect that was because they were so similar. Even as a boy, Aulus always was the hot-headed type who liked to get his own way and would have no scruples about how he managed it. None whatsoever. Father...well, to be fair, he had the scruples, of a sort – he'd his own code, and by and large he kept to it, whatever the consequences – but they didn't carry him very far, and in his way he was just as bloody-minded and ruthless as my brother. When they clashed, as they did a lot these last few years, neither of them would back down, and it caused a lot of bad blood. Then of course – you probably know this already – Aulus got in thick with Cluvius's son Marcus, and that made matters worse where father was concerned. You've talked to Marcus?'

'No. Not yet.'

'A pleasure in store, then. I won't prejudice you.'

'All right. You and your brother.'

He smiled. 'As you'll have guessed, we're not close. The phrase "at daggers drawn" springs to mind: he despises me, I despise him. You think that's dreadful.' A statement, not a question.

'Uh-uh,' I said. 'Not if it's honest.'

'Oh, it's honest enough. He'd tell you the same, although possibly not the second part: I doubt if he's even noticed my opinion of him, and even if he has he certainly doesn't care a straw for it.'

'Cluvius told me about your father's will. The new one.'

'Did he indeed?'

'What did you think about that?'

'What should I have thought?'

'You weren't surprised that you'd been passed over?'

'I wasn't "passed over", I was just made equal with Aulus. It didn't come as a great surprise; I've been telling you, neither of us was particularly the blue-eyed boy. As Cluvius probably explained, father was simply playing his usual game of watching events before committing himself to designating a successor. He was good at that, very good. It was one of his strengths.'

'So if as you say he had reservations about both of you, albeit for different reasons, then who was in the running? Sextus Pettius?'

'It's a possibility, yes.' Titus didn't seem too fazed – or, for that matter, too surprised – by the question. Which was interesting. 'On the face of it he shouldn't be a candidate: he's a Pettius, after all, and whatever's happening now the two families have been bitter rivals for the past twenty-odd years. On the other hand, by father's reckoning, he was – is – excellent successor material.'

'But not by yours.'

'What I think didn't and doesn't matter. Please remember that. He's your archetypal successful crook: clever, inventive, cautious, devoid of principles but not overly greedy, ruthless when he has to be but not for any pleasure it gives him. So yes, as I say, in my father's estimation he was by far the best bet going. In fact, I wouldn't be surprised if bringing him in hadn't been the old man's intention from the very beginning, and the marriage with my daughter the first stage.'

'Would the firm have accepted him? I mean the rank and file?' I was thinking of my conversation with Carpus.

'I don't know. Not to begin with, of course, but perhaps in time, given he possesses the qualities I've mentioned. It would certainly have been far more likely had father been around to ease him into the role.'

Yeah, that's what I was thinking, too. And it was interesting to hear it from Titus. 'Fair enough,' I said. 'Leave it for the moment. This ring your father gave your daughter to give to young Pettius. What can you tell me about that?'

I'd sprung the question on him intentionally, and I wasn't disappointed. His face went blank.

'What should I be able to tell you?' he said. 'It was part of the dowry, only it came from father, not from us. Someone appears to have stolen it – no doubt Marcia gave you a full account of the circumstances – and it's still missing. That's about all I know.'

'Where did your father get it from in the first place?'

'I really can't say.'

Uh-huh: a double-tongued answer if ever I heard one. 'Something as expensive as that seems to be, well, I'd be surprised if it just came out of nowhere. He bought it, presumably?'

'Of course he bought it!'

'Okay. It was an antique, from all accounts. So what was its history? The seller must've told your father something.'

'I really–' he began.

The door opened, and I looked round. A woman in her mid- to late thirties, handsome rather than good-looking, and done up to the nines.

'Titus,' she said. 'I need some money, please.' She'd completely ignored me, but something obviously registered because now she gave me a dazzling smile. 'Ah. You must be Valerius Corvinus. Marcia said you'd called round yesterday. I'm pleased to meet you.'

'Septimia,' Titus said. His voice was expressionless. 'My wife.'

Yeah, well, I'd already worked that one out. 'Delighted to meet you,' I said, getting up.

'No, don't go on my account,' she said, closing the door and moving over to the couch.

I hadn't been planning to, but saying so might've damaged the blossoming cosy atmosphere, so I didn't. I sat down instead, repositioning the stool so I didn't have my back turned to her.

There are some people you dislike on sight, for no obvious reason whatsoever. Septimia was beginning to qualify in spades.

'Marcia said you'd had quite a chat,' she said, sitting down and arranging the folds of her mantle.

'Yeah. Yeah, we did.'

We exchanged insincere smiles. I was damned if I was going to speak first.

'Interesting?' she said at last.

'Yeah. Yes, it was. Very. We talked about the missing ring, mostly.'

Her smile faded, just for a moment. Then it was back, even brighter than before. 'Did you indeed?' she said. '*Such* a mystery. We think the thief must have come in from outside, through the garden and across the portico roof.'

'While you were all downstairs partying. Yeah. Marcia tried to sell me that theory.'

'You don't believe it?'

I shrugged. 'I wouldn't say that. It's as good an explanation as any, at present. After all, what's the alternative? That someone sneaked upstairs during the party, broke into the drawer, and had the thing away. Or of course at any other time during the three days between the time your father-in-law gave her it and when she discovered it was missing.'

'Who on earth would want to do that?' There was no smile now.

'Pass. Maybe you can tell me.'

'We know nothing whatsoever about the ring, Corvinus, apart from the fact that it existed and was stolen,' Titus said. 'Take my word for it.'

'So you were saying when your wife came in.' I turned back to Septimia. 'Perhaps you can help with that, lady.'

'No, I'm afraid I can't.'

'An antique signet ring, gold, with an amethyst cut in the shape of a star.' I was watching her face closely. She was better than her husband in that respect, at least: there wasn't even the twitch of an eyelash. 'Sound familiar?'

'If that's the description Marcia gave you then I suppose it's accurate enough,' she said. 'It was my father-in-law's gift to her, and he gave it to her personally. I never saw it myself.'

Right. Believe that if you will. Still, there was no sense in flogging a dead horse, or antagonising the pair of them more than I had done already. I got up.

'Fine,' I said. 'I'll be getting on. Thanks for your help.' I nodded to Septimia in passing on my way to the door, then paused and turned.

'Oh. By the way,' I said to Titus. 'You wouldn't've had any cause to visit the company's old offices, would you? The ones by the Neck?'

He frowned. 'No, of course not. Why do you ask?'

'No particular reason. It's just that it turns out that's where your father was killed.'

'*What?*'

'Not a problem. I was only checking, in case you had and you'd noticed anything out of the way.' I opened the door. 'Thanks again. I'll see you around.'

I went downstairs. Now *that* had been a surprise. When I'd mentioned the offices Titus hadn't reacted with anything but what looked like genuine puzzlement. I'd been watching him primarily, sure, but I'd also caught Septimia's reaction.

Forget the twitching eyelash; that had been pure and simple shock.

8.

Okay, so now for the opposition. Or whatever the Pettii were, nowadays.

Satrius had told me that their offices were facing onto the Little Harbour, just beyond the mouth of the Neck. Not far from where I was at present in actual distance, sure, but there was a hundred-yard stretch of water between me and them, and going the long way round by land towards the city centre and back would've taken me the best part of an hour. However, I'd checked with one of the clerks on my way out and there were several small boats that operated a ferry service back and forth across the Neck itself and along the length of the two harbours. So I took one of these.

The Pettius offices proved to be older and a tad more down market than the Marcius ones; presumably, I supposed, because instead of upgrading at some point during the twenty-odd years that he'd been in business Lucius Pettius had preferred to stay put. Or, of course, it could've been that Marcius had been the more successful of the two.

I went inside and asked to see the boss.

'Your name and business, sir?' The freedman manning the front desk was eyeing me with suspicion.

'Valerius Corvinus,' I said. 'I'm looking into Titus Marcius's murder.'

The suspicious look didn't shift. 'Then you're in the wrong place,' he said. 'The Marcius building is on the other side of the Neck, half way down Big Harbour quayside.'

'Yeah, I know that, pal,' I said patiently. 'I've just come from there. All the same, I need to talk to Lucius Pettius. Or his son Sextus, if the father isn't around this morning. That possible, do you think?'

'Wait here. I'll go and ask.'

He disappeared, leaving me to twiddle my thumbs. Yeah, well, I was clearly not flavour of the month this side of the water, either, certainly not as far as the paid help was concerned. Not that that was too surprising, mind: if the two firms were long-time rivals the fact that the other side's top man had been found floating in the harbour with his head bashed in was probably an occasion for putting out the flags.

The guy came back. He didn't look quite so hostile as before, sure, but he wasn't one big welcoming smile, either.

'The boss says he'll see you,' he said. His tone suggested that, if that was the executive decision, he didn't think much of it. 'This way.'

I followed him past the line of stony-faced clerks to the screened-off section at the rear. He stopped at one of the doors, knocked, and opened it.

I went in. The old guy sitting behind the desk didn't look too friendly either.

'Corvinus, wasn't it?' he said.

'Yeah. Valerius Corvinus. I'm–'

'My clerk told me who you are. And why you're here, or here in Brundisium, at least. Why you need to talk to me I don't know.' He gestured towards the stool in front of me. 'Sit down.'

I sat. 'Your son is marrying the dead man's granddaughter and you're going into partnership with the Marcius family,' I said. 'Me, I'd say that was reason enough.'

'Partnership's wrong, at least for the present. We've agreed to co-operate in certain areas of business, that's all. But if either arrangement has anything to do with Marcius's death then I can't see it. Unless, of course, you coming here means you think I or any of my people were directly responsible, in which case you can–'

I held up a hand. 'Whoa! Hold on! No accusations, pal; all I want is a friendly chat, okay?'

He was scowling. 'I've got no time for so-called "friendly chats",' he said. 'Say what you want to say, or ask what you want to ask, and then get out.'

Gods! This was real uphill work, and no mistake. Mind you, gratuitous rudeness aside, by his own lights the guy had a valid point: the murder was the concern of the Marcius family alone, no one else. Even Eutacticus, as far as I knew, wasn't a factor where the Pettii were concerned. Unless, of course, they *were* involved at the sharp end, although in that case they were hardly likely to feel the need to co-operate either.

'Fair enough,' I said. 'First off: the, ah, arrangement, the marriage, and so on. That was Marcius's idea originally, wasn't it?'

'It was.'

'It come as any sort of surprise to you?'

'What do you think?'

'I don't know,' I said patiently. 'That's why I'm asking. Straight question.'

'All right.' He frowned. 'We'd been business rivals for over twenty years, we hadn't met, let alone spoken in all that time except by accident and in company, and our families – by which I mean families in the business sense, employees and so on – have followed our lead and had nothing to do with each other. That do you?'

'So why did he suggest it?'

'How should I know? I'm no mind-reader.' I waited. 'Fair enough. The reason he gave me was, things are changing. The competition's harder, and staying ahead of the game is a lot tougher now than it used to be. Simple as that. He thought it was about time for a truce, and when he put it to me I agreed.'

'Just like that? After over twenty years?'

'We dickered for a while over the details, yes, and there were compromises on both sides, but that was all minor stuff. The deal went through because it suited us both and it made sense. End of story.'

'Uh-huh.' Well, all that was more or less what Eutacticus had told me originally, but it'd been worth checking up on. 'So what does your son think of all this?' I said. 'He quite happy to be burying the hatchet and marrying into the Marcius family?'

'Why shouldn't he be? The deal goes both ways. Marcia will be my daughter-in-law and their children will be my grandchildren. Plus they'll have my name, so I reckon we'll come out ahead.'

'Your son thinks the same?'

'Naturally he does; Sextus is no fool. But you can ask him yourself. His office is next door.'

'That'd be good.' It would, at that: I'd been hoping to have a word with the prospective groom. 'Just one more question, if you don't mind. Marcius's death. Does it change things in any way?'

'No. Not as far as I'm concerned. A deal's a deal, and we made it with the family as a whole. They want to break it, fine; it'd be a shame, sure, in my opinion, but that'd be up to them.'

'You think that's likely?'

That got me a long, slow, considering look. Finally: 'I don't think, Corvinus,' he said. 'If it happens we'll take it from there. That'll be time enough. But they'd be fools if they did.' He stood up. 'Okay. We're finished here, and if you've no more questions I have work to do.'

'Suits me.' I stood too. 'Oh. One more thing, nothing to do with the murder or the deal, I'm just curious. Quintus Cluvius, Marcius's deputy, is missing an eye. You know how that happened?'

'He lost it in a fight. In his younger days.'

'Yeah? What kind of a fight?'

'Turf war. If the phrase has any meaning for you. Now if that's all I'll introduce you to Sextus.'

I could see the resemblance between father and son straight off: same heavy build, nose you could've used to split logs, black – not just dark – curly hair that pointed to African blood somewhere in the mix, and a look that could've skewered a rhino. I got that last one point blank as I came through the door.

Pettius Senior was close behind me. 'Sextus, this is Valerius Corvinus,' he said. 'He's here about the murder. Can you spare ten minutes?'

'Make it five.' I was still getting that cold, hard stare that lifted the hairs on the back of my neck. This one wasn't one to play around with, I could see that now. 'Sit down, Corvinus.'

I did, on the obligatory visitor's stool. Pettius left, closing the door behind him.

'So.' Sextus wrote something on the flimsy that he'd been reading and laid it on top of the pile in his out-tray. 'To save us a bit of time I'll tell you now: first I heard the old man was dead was the day after the body was found, when I called in at Marcia's. Nothing before, nothing since. That's the sum of it. Will that do you?'

'You're round there often? At Marcia's?'

'As often as I can spare the time, yes. That's the usual procedure for the fiancé in the circumstances, isn't it?'

'True. So you're looking forward to the wedding?'

'I haven't given it much thought. It makes practical sense, certainly.'

'So you're happy with the arrangement?'

'Happy doesn't come into it. This is business and I'm marrying the girl as part of the deal. That's all that needs to be said.'

'What about the rest of the family?' I said. 'You okay with them?'

'You want an honest answer?'

'Sure. No point in giving me the other kind.'

'Fine. Let's see. Titus Junior and wife. He's a canting bore with the backbone of a jellyfish and an abacus for a brain, she's a pushy bitch who thinks she's the gods' gift to men, which she isn't. Not that any of that matters, of course, because I'm marrying the daughter, gods help me, not the parents.' He frowned. 'Brother Aulus, now, Aulus is solid bone between the ears, and he thinks with his prick. When he bothers to think at all, that is. His wife Gellia...well, all I can tell you about Gellia, Corvinus, is that I haven't really noticed her enough to form an opinion. That do you?'

Gods! I was thinking of Satrius's assessment of him – 'able as hell but a cold-blooded bastard at root' – and Marcia's own 'unlikeable, to put it mildly'. On present showing I'd go for both of these, in spades.

'How about the widow?' I said.

'Young Atia? There's a sore need there, and I'd imagine she's done something about it in the three months she was married to the old man. But in case you're wondering, she hasn't done it with me.' His lips twitched. 'Or has she? Your call. You can choose whichever answer suits.'

'Okay,' I said. 'Leave it there. Let's move on to the business side of the arrangement, shall we?'

'If you like.'

'Marcius's death must've changed things for you, surely?'

'Not particularly. I'd be his granddaughter's husband, granted, but the two companies would still be completely separate.'

'Yeah, that's what your father said. Even so, with the old man gone and no clear successor named in his will there's a lot of uncertainty there, isn't there?'

'Ah. So you know about the new will?'

'Uh-huh. That be of any interest to you, by any chance?'

He shook his head. 'Not in the slightest. Why should it be? Look, Corvinus, let's get this straight. I've told you, my father's told you, that the firms of Marcius and Pettius are separate companies. That won't change. You've got that through your skull?'

'Yeah.'

'Well done. Congratulations. Added to which, as long as I can remember – longer – our two families have either steered clear of each other or they've fought like cats. So if you think that, as a result of Titus Marcius's murder, I or my father or both of us together can somehow sneak in and take over his company from the inside then you're fantasising. Before the Marcii would accept him or me as boss hell would freeze solid. Understand? Theorise about the old man's death all you want, that's your job, seemingly. But leave us the fuck out of things: we had nothing to do with it and we can't possibly profit from it. Clear?'

'Yeah, clear,' I said. I stood up. 'Thanks for your time.' I paused. 'One more thing, before I go.'

He was reaching for another flimsy. His hand paused. 'So long as it's quick. You've had your five minutes and more.'

'That ring. The one Marcia was supposed to give you at the wedding ceremony but went missing. Can you tell me anything more about it?'

'No. All I know is that it was worth a small fortune. The old man must've had a sentimental streak somewhere in his makeup.'

'You think it was a family treasure he was passing on, then? An heirloom?'

'I don't think anything. Never saw it, never wanted to. Now push off. Close the door behind you.'

I left.

I walked the short distance along the quayside to the mouth of the Neck.

Okay; so what did I make of all that? Oh, sure, on the surface, in the light of what I already knew, what Pettius and his son had said sounded perfectly reasonable: the two companies were separate entities with a long history of mutual loathing and distrust, and you don't sweep that under the carpet in five minutes. If anything, the murder hadn't done them any favours in that direction: given – and I was beginning to think that the theory was on the probable side of possible – that the old man's secret motive in setting up the deal in the first place had been to get Sextus Pettius's feet under the corporate table, and so replace the two other possible candidates, neither of whom, in his eyes, could cut the mustard, with a decent successor, for them to have stiffed the guy made no sense whatsoever. What they had needed, if that was their aim as well as his, was time, and time was just the thing that now, thanks to the murder, they didn't have.

On the other hand...

First off, Sextus had known about the new will. Considering that, at his own and his father's insistence, the two firms were completely separate, with no mutual contact barring at the most basic level, that was *really* interesting. Oh, sure, he could've got the information from Marcia, but somehow I doubted it: given her lukewarm, at best, attitude to her fiancé, plus what I'd seen of the girl herself, I couldn't imagine her slipping that particular detail into their whispered exchanges on the atrium couch. And if he hadn't got it from Marcia then where had he got it?

Second, he obviously had no illusions about the competition, if competition you could call it: he'd dismissed both sons, Titus and Aulus, with complete contempt. And the corollary of *that* was, deny it until he was blue in the face though he might, he believed there was a potential gap at the head of the Marcius company that, *a fortiori*, he was qualified to fill.

Third...well, third was just the general feel of the guy. That sort, if they see a chance to claw their way up the greasy pole then they take it. They may claim that they're not interested, sure, but that's been the politician's ploy since Romulus sucked the she-wolf's tits: 'I have no ambitions in that direction, but if the people wish it then in all humility I will accept.' And somehow, eventually, it happens.

No, I wasn't about to cross either of the Pettii off the suspect list. Far from it.

I'd reached the end of the harbour by now. There were two or three small boats touting for business, so I got the guy in the nearest one to ferry me over to the west bank of the Neck.

'Just out of interest, pal,' I said as he pushed off from the quay. 'This go on all night?'

'What's that, sir?' he said.

'You take passengers at all hours? I mean, let's say I turned up a couple of hours shy of midnight. Would you still be operating?'

'Depends on the season and the moon, sir. In summer, sure, all being equal. No problem; good weather, light evenings, there's plenty of punters around.' He pulled on the sculling-oar. 'Winter, nah; evenings are slack, in winter.'

'This time of year? Tonight, for example?'

'Ninth, tenth hour at the latest. Mind you, that's just me, I pack in early, get back to the wife and my supper. There's a couple of the other lads'll hang on longer, just on the off-chance of a fare.'

'And if I wanted to go back, when I'd finished whatever I was doing on the other side? Say midnight, maybe even a bit later?'

'Then you wouldn't have a hope of a boat, sir. Not as a rule. 'cept of course if you'd arranged things with the man beforehand, paid up front, like. Well over the odds, sure, but that's how things go. Depends where you was coming from and going to, mind. A silver piece on top of the usual, well, given you can afford it and it saves you a half-hour's walk in bad weather that'd be worthwhile, wouldn't it?'

'Yeah,' I said. 'Yeah, it would.'

I didn't know at present where either of the Pettii actually lived, as opposed to worked, but the information was good to have. I filed it for future reference.

We docked.

'Thanks, pal,' I said, handing over my copper piece. 'Enjoy the rest of your day.' He put the coin in his belt-pouch and picked up his sculling-oar. 'Oh. Just out of interest. The lads who work the night shift. Can you give me any names?'

'Well now, let's see, sir.' He leaned on the oar. 'That's tricky. A couple I said, and a couple at most it is, this late in the year. Gaffer Barrio, he used to work all hours just to get out of the house, but his back's been giving him gyp these last few months and the damp night air sets it off terrible. There was Boy Titus, but since he got married in the summer nights're his busiest time, as it were.' He frowned. 'Your best bet, maybe your only one, that's Gaius Milvius.'

'Where would I find him?'

'When he's not out on the water he's got a lean-to at the mooring he uses. Further on that way' – he nodded towards the sea end of the Neck – 'a tad past the shrine. But you won't see him today, sir, if you were thinking to do it. His eldest was married yesterday and he'll be sleeping it off.'

'No problem. Another time will do,' I said. 'Thanks again, pal.'

'You're very welcome.'

I turned to go. So; where to now? I still had the egregious Aulus and Marcus Cluvius to see, but the first hadn't been at the Marcius offices when I'd been there earlier, and I doubted, this early or late in the day, if Cluvius Junior would be at his flat. Perhaps I might just–

'Valerius Corvinus?'

I turned. Two beefy auxiliary squaddies had come up behind me.

'Yeah,' I said. 'Yeah, that's me. Is there a problem?'

'No problem, sir,' one of them said. 'None at all. But the prefect would like a word with you.'

'Really? What about?'

'That I couldn't say, sir. All I know is, general instructions was we was to look out for a Roman purple-striper name of Valerius Corvinus and ask him if he'd drop in to headquarters whenever he was free.'

'Uh-huh. Headquarters being where?'

'Citadel, sir.'

Oh. Right; I should've guessed that. I hadn't actually been up that far yet, but I'd seen it in the distance: a fortress built into the angle of the town walls overlooking the Big Harbour. Yeah, well, at least I was on the right side of the Neck. 'And you've no idea at all what he wants?'

'No, sir. Sorry, sir.'

Shit. The auxiliary prefect, being commander of the military garrison, represented the law in Brundisium: *was* the law, for all practical purposes. My conscience was completely clear, sure, but it was still worrying.

'Fine,' I said. 'I'll go along there now. That be all right, do you think?'

'Perfectly, sir. But like I said, there's no hurry.'

He saluted, and the pair of them strolled off.

Yeah, well, that was my afternoon sorted for me, wasn't it?

Bugger!

There was a sentry on duty outside the citadel gate. I gave my name, told him the prefect had asked to see me, and he passed me through to one of his mates who took me the rest of the way. We stopped at a heavy door with a military clerk on duty outside. The squaddie knocked and waited.

'Come in.'

He opened the door and stood aside for me to pass. 'Valerius Corvinus, sir.'

'Ah, excellent. You can go.' The squaddie saluted and exited, closing the door behind him and leaving me facing a man in a military tunic sitting behind a desk. He stood up and came towards me, hand held out. 'My dear chap. Apologies. Julius Montanus.' We shook. 'Sit yourself down. Wine?'

'Yeah.' I said cautiously. 'Yeah, that'd be great.'

'Pull up that chair, then, and make yourself comfortable.' He went over to a table in the corner with a jug and cups, poured for us both and brought my cup over. 'Here you go. Cheers.'

'Cheers.' Yeah, well, at least I'd got a drink out of this meeting. Up to now as far as the case had been concerned the hospitality trolley had been conspicuous by its absence. I sat down. 'Ah...don't think I'm being pushy, but why exactly am I here?'

'Your wife seems to have taken up with mine at present. That's how I knew you were in town.'

Oh; right, I'd forgotten. Perilla had mentioned that she'd met up with one of the local ladies in a jeweller's and that they'd arranged to go around together. So her new pal was the wife of the garrison commander, was she?

Bugger! Double bugger!

'Uh...got you,' I said. 'Sentia, wasn't it?'

'That's right. Your wife told you?'

'She mentioned it yesterday. They met shopping.'

'Indeed.' He'd gone back to his own chair behind the desk. 'Anyway, Sentia tells me that...Perilla, is it?' – I nodded – 'Perilla told her something of your business here in Brundisium, so I thought we'd better have a little chat asap.'

Fuck; I would *kill* that lady! 'Is that so, now?' I said.

He laughed. 'Don't look so worried, man! And I have no intention whatsoever of interfering.' Well, that was a relief to hear, anyway. 'I simply wanted to make absolutely sure you know what kind of people you're involved with.'

'I've got a pretty good idea of that already, pal. Thanks all the same.'

'"*Absolutely* sure", I said. You know that they're out and out crooks, I suppose?'

'That had impinged on my mental horizon, yes.'

'Mm. I suppose it had, at that.' He frowned. 'Possibly, though, not in any detail. Gambling rackets, organised pimping and prostitution, handling of stolen goods, various scams connected with the building, construction, agricultural and shipping trades, in the town itself and other centres within a thirty mile radius – that do you for starters?'

'Look, Montanus,' I said. 'None of that is any of my concern. Perilla will have told your wife that all I'm doing here is investigating the murder last month of Titus Marcius. Who may well have been a crook, sure, but whatever he was he didn't deserve to end up in the harbour with half his skull missing. Okay?' I set the wine cup down and got to my feet. 'Now if you don't mind I have places to be.'

'Sit down. Please.' Said quietly, but an order nevertheless. I sat; when the guy you're talking to has five hundred squaddies on hand ready to clap you in irons at one word from him then you do what you're told. 'I meant what I said: I have no intention of getting in your way. None. Whatever my private feelings on the subject are.'

'Uh-huh. And what exactly are these then? You didn't think to look into the murder yourself, I suppose?'

'No, I didn't. For one thing it wasn't reported, and without an official complaint I'm not obliged to interfere. For another, I honestly can't see why I should agonise over the death of a known long-term criminal. My only regret is that it wasn't the younger son or his associate. Now either of those two I would gladly see put out of the way permanently.'

'You have your reasons? Specific reasons?'

'Specific? Well, let's see now.' He leaned back in his chair, inspected the ceiling, and closed his eyes. 'Gaius Vecilius, occupation carter, found in an alleyway with three broken ribs, a crushed larynx and various internal injuries from which he later died. Messia Postuma, common prostitute, slashed across the face with a razor to her permanent disfigurement and the loss of an eye. Turia Gemella, no profession in that she was aged two years and seven months, died of burns along with her parents when their pastry-shop was torched in the small hours. Specific enough for you? That's only within the past two months, you understand. I could go further back if you like.' He opened his eyes again and leaned forwards again. 'But of course none of that is your concern.'

I felt sick. 'Okay,' I said. 'Point made. I'm sorry. Even so, I'm a private citizen, I've no authority, either here or in Rome, and so far I've never so much as met either of the guys. As the military commander in Brundisium you're empowered to make arrests. If you know they were responsible then why the hell don't you nail them?'

'The usual reason. I may know, but I can't prove. You ask questions, no one's seen anything, no one knows anything.'

Yeah; I'd been there myself, time and time again. And I knew exactly how he felt. Frustration isn't the half of it.

Two years and seven months old. Sweet holy gods!

'Fine,' I said. 'So just what – *specifically* – do you expect me to do about that?'

'If it turns out that either of them were behind Marcius's murder, and you can prove it, then report it directly to me and we'll have the bastard shuffled off before you can say "noose". If, while you're nosing around, you find anything on them that'll do the job equally well, again let me know and the same thing will happen. If you don't, well, there's nothing lost. In return, I'll give you any help you need with your side of things.'

'So in other words you want me to be a sort of spy.'

'Not at all. I'm not asking you to do my job for me, Corvinus, As you say, you're a private citizen and I don't have the right. But if you're willing to make a deal on those terms I'd be very grateful.'

Well, he couldn't say fairer than that, and if Aulus Marcius and Marcus Cluvius were the sadistic bastards he claimed – and what I'd heard so far about Cluvius, at least, certainly backed it up – then I'd pull the rug out from under them in a second, and whistle while I did it. Plus knowing I had the full armoured might of the empire behind me, or at least an auxiliary cohort's worth of it, was a comforting thought.

I put out my hand. 'Deal.'

'Deal it is. Thank you.' We shook. 'So. Business done. How are you liking Brundisium in general?'

'It's okay. I haven't really had a chance to see round properly yet.'

'You've been here before?'

'Not as such. Just when passing through on our way to somewhere else.' I took a sip from my wine cup. Not bad, not bad at all. 'How about you? You been stationed here long?'

'Five years. Before that I was a tribune with the Larks.' He smiled. 'The Fifth Gallic, to you non-military types. My family has an estate near Aquae Sextiae.' Yeah, well, with a name like Julius Montanus the likelihood of his being Gaulish-born had been pretty high, and Gaul, as the legion's formal name implied, was the Larks' prime recruiting ground. 'That's our wine you're drinking. My brother sends me over a few jars every year.'

'It's good.'

'Leave your address with my clerk and I'll send you some.'

'That'd be great. Thank you.' I could take a hint when it was given, and the guy was obviously busy. I drained the cup, set it down on the desk, and stood up. 'Nice to meet you, Montanus. I'll be in touch.'

'I sincerely hope so.' He hesitated. 'I'd ask you and your wife to dinner while you're here, but perhaps that wouldn't be a very good idea under the circumstances.'

I grinned. 'No, I don't think it would, at that. No problem, pal.'

'Perhaps when it's all over.'

'Yeah. If I'm still persona grata hereabouts, which I suspect however things pan out will be pretty unlikely.'

'Indeed. Well, if you do need to contact me before then you can do it through Sentia.'

A thought struck me. 'Oh...before I go,' I said. 'You mentioned a prostitute who'd been badly cut up and survived.'

'Messia Postuma. Yes. So?'

'You happen to have an address for her?'

'Not offhand, no. But I can easily find it, if you think it's important.'

'It might be,' I said. 'I don't know. But it'd be useful to have just in case.'

'Then I'll look it out and send the information to you with the wine.'

'Perfect. Thanks again.'

I stopped on my way out to give the location of the house we were staying in and headed back there myself.

'The mistress back yet?' I asked Bathyllus while I handed him my cloak.

'No, sir.' He folded it neatly over his arm. 'But Alexis would like a word with you, if you have a moment.'

Hey! Great! 'Sure,' I lay down out on the atrium couch. 'Wheel him in.'

He did, along with the much-needed wine jug and cup.

'You have something for me already, Alexis?' I said.

'Yes, sir.'

'That is really fast work, pal. Congratulations.' I sipped. 'Okay. Go ahead.'

'You asked me to strike up a conversation with the Marcius family's door-slave.'

'Brunellus? Yeah. And?'

'Actually, I went one better. I assume you were interested in the Lady Atia?'

'That's right. I am.' I sat up.

'Only when I was coming round the corner into the street I saw a young woman leaving the house with her maid. Shortish? Slim? Fair hair?'

'That's her, yeah.'

'So I followed them. The lady put her hood up and they walked towards the town centre.'

I felt the first prickle of excitement. Oh, sure, there was no reason why a trip to the centre shouldn't be completely innocent, but then Alexis would hardly be reporting back re a simple shopping expedition, now, would he? And I already knew that Marcus Cluvius's flat lay in that direction...

'Go on,' I said.

'They turned right at Market Square and walked towards the vegetable market. There's an alleyway just before it on the left that gives out onto a small square with a public water fountain in the middle and houses all the way round. The lady knocks on the door of the one with the potted bay tree outside and–'

'Hang on, Alexis,' I said. 'So we're not talking about a tenement flat above a cookshop here?'

He frowned. 'No, sir. Should we be?'

'No. I'm sorry I interrupted. Forget it. You go ahead.'

'Anyway, she knocks on the door, a woman opens it and she goes inside.'

'With her maid?'

'Yes, sir. I hung around, naturally, waiting for them to come out again. That was about an hour later.'

'And she went straight back home?'

'That I don't know. I didn't follow her. I thought you'd prefer to know something about the place where she'd been.'

'Absolutely.'

'It's a rooming-house, sir, half a dozen long-term tenants, all single working men. The woman's the owner, seemingly. Her name's Fulgentia.'

'You spoke to her yourself?'

'No, sir, of course not. But there was a girl sitting on the bench next to the fountain. We got chatting and I asked her.'

He'd gone slightly pink. I grinned to myself. 'Got chatting', eh? And she'd just happened to be sitting there doing nothing while he was hanging around kicking his heels a few feet away. Alexis may be smart as a whip, as he'd just proved, but where women are concerned he's a complete non-starter. 'That is absolutely brilliant, pal,' I said. 'Nice work.'

'You want me to carry on gathering information, sir?'

'Sure. Forget the Brunellus side of things, for the time being, at least, but the wineshop angle, certainly. You still in funds?'

'Of course. I haven't done anything in that way at all yet.'

'That's good, then. Make a start. Like I said, if you need any more cash come and tell me.'

He went out.

Okay. Where did that leave us?

With one theory shot to hell, that's where: whoever Atia had been visiting, it hadn't been Marcus Cluvius. And from Alexis's description of the venue it didn't sound like a place of assignation, either. Plus the fact that her maid had gone inside with her and hadn't come back out before she had herself. So the obvious sexual explanation was looking pretty unlikely.

Bugger.

The problem was, if you discounted a clandestine affair then where did it leave you? Atia hadn't exactly struck me as the altruistic type, so the theory that she was engaged in some form of charitable good works involving, say, an ex-servant or company employee was so unlikely that it slotted into the flying pigs category. Plus according to Alexis the rooming-house catered exclusively for males, so maid or not we were back onto sexual ground...

Ah, hell. Leave it. Clearly not a mystery that I was going to solve sitting on my beam end and theorising; I'd simply have to go round to the place tomorrow and check it out for myself.

'Hello, Marcus. Good day?'

I looked up. Perilla, back from her tryst with Sentia.

'Not bad,' I said. 'It would've been a lot better if my loud-mouthed wife hadn't broadcast to all and sundry what I was doing in Brundisium.'

She was handing her cloak to Bathyllus, who had buttled in behind her. 'I beg your pardon?'

'Your new pal's husband just happens to be the auxiliary prefect. He had his squaddies out scouring the town for me.'

'Really?' She sat down on the couch opposite. 'Why on earth would he do that?'

'He wants me to blow the whistle on Aulus Marcius and Marcus Cluvius.' I gave her a run-down of the conversation. 'That's absolutely fine with me, particularly after what he told me about what the bastards are up to. But it's an added complication, and that's something I could've done without. Next time before you decide to get friendly with someone while you're out shopping just check up on what her husband does for a living first, okay?'

'That's hardly fair, dear. And how was I to know that he'd take an interest?'

'Even so.'

'You haven't met either of them yet, have you? Aulus or Marcus?'

'Uh-uh.' A pleasure yet in store. 'But before Montanus's lads tracked me down I did manage to talk to Titus Junior and the two Pettii. Oh, and best for last we have the scene of the crime.' I told her about my visit to the old company offices. 'We already knew that Marcius had gone there that evening, sure, so it was always a probability, but finding the murder weapon makes it definite. My guess is that after the murder the killer simply tipped the body out of the window directly into the Neck.'

'The ship's equipment aspect of things seems rather odd, doesn't it? The...what did you call it?'

'The belaying pin. Maybe; I thought that myself at the time, sure, but on consideration why not? If the killing wasn't absolutely premeditated from the start as such it's something chummie could've picked up readily enough locally, if only at the last minute as a sort of insurance policy.'

'Mm.' She frowned. 'What about a suspect list? Have you got that far yet?'

'Come on, Perilla, give me a chance! We've only been here five minutes!'

'Yes, I know that. Nevertheless, you've met most of the people involved now. You must've formed at least some impressions. Perhaps it might be a good idea to talk things through, see what we have.'

'Fair enough. One proviso, though.'

'Yes? What's that?'

'All this is work in progress, right? So no sniffs, no withering remarks, no downers. Comments, yeah, sure, they're fair game, but keep them positive.'

'If you say so, dear. But when have I ever–?'

'Frequently. In fact, every time. So just can it for the duration. Agreed?'

'Very well.' A sniff, barely caught. 'Agreed.'

'Good. Just keep it in mind.' I took a fortifying swallow of wine. 'Okay. Before we get down to possible suspects, I reckon we need to think about the new will. I mentioned that, yes?'

'Of course you did. Replacing Titus as principal heir with him and his brother as equal beneficiaries.'

'Right. Only that's just half the story. According to Cluvius, the old man had kept it secret, and the first anyone knew of the change was when it was read out the day after the funeral. Correct?'

'Yes. So?'

'So what if that wasn't the case?'

'Pardon?'

'Look. A will has to be drafted so that it's watertight, it has to be witnessed, and it has to be kept somewhere until the time comes to open it. Yes?'

'Of course. All of that. So?'

'So keeping it a total secret is pretty difficult. People other than the guy who makes it are involved, maybe a proper lawyer to do the checking and certainly a witness – two witnesses – to sign it. Even if they don't know the actual contents at least they'll know the thing exists. You with me?'

'Yes, I suppose I am. In theory, at least. But–'

'Plus, where was it kept? In Marcius's own safe at home or the company's one? How secure was either? Did – could – anyone else have access?'

'Marcus, all this is pure sophistry. If Quintus Cluvius told you categorically that it came as a surprise to everyone then–'

I held up a finger. 'Ah? Positive, remember? Come on, lady! Sake of argument!'

She sighed. 'Very well. So what you're saying is that someone – specifically the killer – knew the terms of the will in advance, yes?'

I shook my head. 'Uh-uh. Not exactly. What I'm saying is we have a split. In some cases *but not in all* knowing the terms in advance could be a motive for murder. Fair enough?'

'No. *Not* fair enough. I'm sorry to sound negative after all, dear, but I really am afraid that you're over-complicating matters.'

'Yeah, well, maybe I'm not explaining it properly. Or on the other hand maybe you're just being thick.'

'*Marcus!*'

I grinned. 'Trust me. It makes sense, and it's relevant. You want to do the bit with the suspect list now, see how they shape up? No particular rank order, just as they come.'

'Very well.' Now that was *definitely* a sniff! 'Go on.'

'Okay. Let's start with Titus. Me, I'd taken the general consensus of opinion about the guy at face value, which was understandable because it's pretty much universal. Satrius described him as a long, useless streak of piss; his mate Carpus was kinder, sure, but he obviously still didn't rate him, and nor did Atia, when I talked to her. His father – again, by general agreement – actively despised him. As, seemingly, does his brother and, from what I'd guess, his own wife. The problem is, it doesn't stand up. His only fault, as far as I can see now I've met him, is that he's not a crook.'

'I beg your pardon?'

'The guy's a very switched-on businessman, in the proper, legitimate sense. I don't think his father understood the value of that, nor do dyed-in-the-wool professionals like Satrius and Carpus. And Atia's opinion, that he was just too nice, tells you more about her than it does about him.'

'And all this relates to his being a viable suspect how, exactly?'

Sarky as hell, but I ignored it; that crack about being thick had definitely rankled. 'This is where the business of the will comes in. For that to work, everything has to be on the square, with the contents coming as a surprise. As far as Titus was concerned at the time of the murder he was Marcius's heir. Okay, scenario. Titus knows that he may not be particularly popular with his father, but nevertheless that if and when the old man keels over then he inherits. Problem is, Marcius suddenly decides to change the whole setup. The twenty-odd-year feud with the Pettii will be scrapped, the two families will work together in future, and the deal will be cemented by a marriage between Pettius Junior and Titus's daughter. Titus is no fool; he knows that if the old man gets his way, Sextus – as his granddaughter's husband – might well squeeze him out.'

'Why should he do that? When all's said and done Titus is direct family, which Sextus wouldn't be. Besides, he's a Pettius, with all that means. You told me yourself, dear, he'd never be accepted.'

'Never's a long time, and Sextus has everything going for him. In the old man's eyes unlike either of the sons he's alpha successor material, and from what I know already about Marcius that would count above everything else. Give the guy a couple of years to prove himself – as he would – and with Marcius backing him chances are when the time came he'd walk it. Not only that, but with Sextus Pettius at the helm as far as the company's potential Honest Trader status went you could kiss that side of things goodbye.' I took another sip of wine. 'So. Titus is faced with the prospect of all his plans for betterment going down the tubes in less than three months' time. What does he do?'

'You're going to say that he murders his father before any of it can happen. Obviously.'

'*Could have*, lady; *could have*. It's just one scenario, it isn't fact.'

'I thought you said Titus wasn't a crook.'

'He isn't. That's the point. It doesn't mean he's not a murderer, though.'

'*That* is pure sophistry. Again.'

I grinned. 'Have it your own way. But if Titus is our perp then it explains the theft of the ring as well.'

'How so?'

'Come on, Perilla! You made that particular point yourself. The fact that the ring had been stolen might not have affected things in the long term while Marcius was still alive, but with him dead it was another matter: it would give Titus – and remember, he still thinks that he's the old man's heir nem. con. – a bit of extra breathing space, during which time he could call the whole thing off. And I know for a fact, because he virtually told me, marrying his daughter to Sextus Pettius was no more to his liking than it was to hers. So that part of it would be a bonus.'

'Hmm.' She was tugging at a lock of her hair: always a good sign. 'Very well. Leave Titus for the time being. Let's have the next possibility.'

'Okay. Quintus Cluvius.'

She stopped tugging. '*Cluvius?* I've asked you this before, dear, and I'll ask it again: why on earth would Cluvius want to–?' I held up the warning finger again. 'All right. Carry on. Tell me. Why Cluvius?'

'To start with, he was Marcius's long-standing deputy, he's used to running things, he's currently in charge, and as far as street cred goes he has it in spades.'

Perilla sighed. 'Marcus, this is old ground. I'm sorry, but true as it may be it is *not* an argument for him being the murderer. I mean, for goodness' sake!'

'Just wait, lady. I hadn't finished. This is where the question of the will comes in. When I talked to him, second time around, what he said – and more, how he said it – was interesting. Surprising, too.'

'In what way?'

'As far as the future's concerned unlike his ex-boss Cluvius can see past the nose on his face. Oh, sure, they were kindred spirits, no argument, but I think where they differed was that Cluvius had – has – a lot of time for Titus and what he's trying to do with the company.'

She was twisting the strand of hair again. 'Go on.'

'This time round we'll take the other branch: that Cluvius, at least, knew nothing whatsoever about the new will and its contents before it was opened. That point's crucial. Okay?'

'If you say so.'

Hardly wetting her pants with enthusiasm. Still... 'So as far as he knows if and when Marcius dies Titus will succeed. Only before that happens the old man will have handed the firm over to the Pettii, Titus will be out on his ear and it'll be back to the dodgy business ethic, only now with a Pettius in charge.'

'So to stop that happening he murders his long-time associate and close friend out of pure altruism. Brilliant, dear.'

Gods! 'Possibilities, right?' I said. 'I'm only trying to cover all the angles. And how possible it is depends on where his prime loyalty lay, with Marcius or with the company. Me, I can't answer that question, and until I can I'm not ruling the guy out. Fair enough?'

'I suppose so. Yes.'

'Good. We'll leave things there. Moving on. Next in line, Aulus Marcius, with a side order of his crony Cluvius Junior.'

'Now that is more like it.'

'Maybe so, lady, but just because according to your pal's husband they happen to be a pair of out-and-out sadistic, psychopathic thugs doesn't mean they're any more firmly in the frame than anyone else, does it?'

'Marcus, do you actually *listen* to yourself when you make a statement like that?'

'Even so. I haven't met either of them yet. I'll reserve judgement until I do.' I glanced round; Bathyllus had buttled in. 'Yes, Bathyllus. What can I do for you?'

'Meton says dinner is in fifteen minutes, sir. If that's satisfactory.'

I grinned. The last bit was a tactful add-on, I knew: if Meton said fifteen minutes then what he meant was, be in the dining-room, bibs on and spoons poised, in fourteen minutes flat. 'Yeah, okay, little guy,' I said. 'Message delivered. Fifteen minutes it is.' A sudden thought struck me. 'Hang on a second.'

He turned back. 'Yes, sir?'

'Ask around among your local skivvies for Aulus Marcius's address. Can you do that?'

'Certainly, sir.'

'Oh, and addresses for the two Pettii as well, if that's possible.'

'I'll do my best, sir.' He exited.

'Okay, then.' I re-settled on the couch. 'Where were we?'

'Aulus and Marcus Cluvius.'

'Right. Maybe I'm wrong to think of them in pair terms, but we'll let that ride at present. Not that it's unreasonable, mind, because at least from what I've heard of them they're pretty much joined at the hip as far as villainy's concerned, with Marcus being the dominant partner. Suit you, lady?'

'You have the floor, dear. Treat them however you like.'

From the tone we were in seriously-put-upon mode here. I ignored it.

'Fine,' I said. 'I'm working on the assumption that if they are our perps their ultimate aim was the equivalent of a palace coup. They'd already done the groundwork by striking off on their own, independent of both their fathers, and gaining a lot of street cred with the firm's rank and file in the process. Fair?'

'For the sake of argument, yes.'

'Thank you. The problem is, it's an uphill job. Marcius might be getting on a bit, but he's still firmly in charge. And even if the old guy were to hand in his lunch pail under the terms of his will Titus would take over. Worse: it turns out that Marcius is going to make peace with the Pettii and bring Lucius Pettius's shit-hot son into the family, so now he has another rival to contend with.'

'At which point, you're going to say, he finds out about the new will.'

'You want to take over, lady?' I said sourly. She ducked her head and smiled. 'So. Aulus discovers that, instead of being an also-ran, he's level-pegging with the erstwhile leader; not a perfect arrangement, but it's better than the kick in the teeth that the earlier will handed him, and when the time comes he reckons he can handle Titus. There's the deal with the Pettii in the offing, certainly, but Aulus is in a lot better position to see off a challenge than his brother would be. The only fly in the ointment is his father. Give Marcius a clear two or three years and the bets are he'll have manoeuvred things so that Sextus is ahead of both of them in the succession stakes. On the other hand, put the old man out of the way now and he'd have the edge just when he needed it most.' I swallowed the last of my wine. 'What do you think? Fair assessment?'

'In a suppositional fashion, yes, but–'

'Sod off. Aulus is prime perp material, trust me. Plus there's the circumstantial side of things.'

'Which is?'

'The old offices where Marcius was murdered. It so happens that Aulus has a key. As of, what's more, only ten days previous.'

'Really? And?'

Gods! I didn't deserve this! 'Come on, Perilla! No one's set foot inside the fucking place for the past two years, then ten days before his father gets his head beaten in on the premises Aulus Marcius asks the janitor for the key. Without, note, offering any explanation. You don't think that's significant, maybe?'

'I don't know, dear,' she said calmly. 'His reasons – and he will obviously have them, whether he gave them at the time or not – may be completely innocent. I suggest you ask him first before jumping to unsubstantiated conclusions. And don't swear, please. It goes nowhere towards strengthening your argument.'

'Okay.' I subsided. 'So leave Aulus for the moment. Who else have we got?'

'I would've thought the Pettii myself. You've talked to them, haven't you?'

'Yeah. Them, I'm not sure of. Oh, on the face of it they'd have no cause to wish Marcius dead, none at all, quite the reverse; he brokered the deal in the first place and according to Lucius Pettius everything was sweetness and light. As, indeed, it would've been: hatchet well and truly buried, his son with his feet under the table and Marcius's blue-eyed boy, with the likelihood that in another thirty years' time when the grandchildren grow up there might be a Pettius in charge of both firms. Neither he nor Sextus had the shade of a reason for killing the guy.'

'But?'

I frowned. 'Yeah. Exactly. *But.* There's nothing I can put my finger on, sure, admitted, but it doesn't quite sit right. For a start, Sextus knew about the terms of the new will.'

'So? Wouldn't you have expected him to? He is marrying into the family, after all.'

I shook my head. 'Uh-uh. Don't forget, we're talking of an estrangement – to put it mildly – of twenty-odd years here; you don't get over that hurdle all that easily. And his fiancée wouldn't have told him, no way. Plus, as both Sextus and his father were at pains to point out, the two companies were, are and will be completely separate. The will and its arrangements are the business of the Marcius family, no one else, as is any investigation of the murder; they made it pretty clear that that had zilch to do with them either.'

'Actually, all that seems quite reasonable.'

'Too reasonable. That's the problem; between the pair of them they made too much of it. And you can't tell me that the old man not being around any longer and the succession being in a state of flux doesn't suit their purposes down to the ground.' I shrugged. 'Ah, the hell with it.'

'Is that everyone? You haven't mentioned any of the women. The widow, Atia, for one. Didn't you have her down as a leading contender?'

'Yeah, now that's a strange thing.' I told her what Alexis had told me. 'So scratch an involvement with Marcus Cluvius, on every level. Ditto, for all I can see, given the address, with Aulus or Sextus. And Titus would always have been a non-starter.'

'But she is having a clandestine affair, of some kind?'

'Maybe. Or maybe not. I just don't know. Oh, sure, the way Alexis described it that seems pretty likely, but some parts of it just don't add up. So as far as young Atia's concerned the jury is out for the duration, or at least until I can check out this rooming-house for myself. Which' – I got up – 'I will do first thing tomorrow morning. You have any plans yourself?'

'Actually, yes.' She got up as well. 'Sentia tells me that there's quite a famous painting by Aetion hanging in the Agrippan Porch. She thought we might go and see that, then meet up with some friends of hers for honey wine and cake.'

I shuddered. Well, to each their own. Me, I'd take a visit to the rooming-house over a honey-wine-and-cake klatsch any day.

We went into the dining-room.

9.

I was just finishing breakfast the next morning when Bathyllus came in with what looked like one of the skivvies in tow.

'A messenger, sir,' he said. 'From Titus Marcius.'

'Really?' I sopped the last of the olive oil up with the last of the bread and turned to the slave. 'Go ahead, pal. I'm listening.'

'I was asked to fetch you, sir. To the house.' The guy was looking uncomfortable. 'Straight away, the master said.'

'He say what it was about?'

'No, sir. Just that it was urgent.'

Shit; this did not sound good. And why the secrecy, anyway? Still, there was no point in grilling the messenger, even though I was damn sure he knew the answer perfectly well. Clearly, he had had his orders, and that was it.

'Fair enough,' I said, getting up. 'We'll go round there now.' I paused. 'Oh, yeah. Bathyllus, before I go. Did you manage get those addresses I asked you for yesterday? Aulus's and the Pettii's?'

'Yes and no, sir.' He handed me the cloak he had brought in with him. 'Master Aulus is on the east side of town, near the Julian baths. I'm afraid I haven't yet been able to secure addresses for the other gentlemen. Possibly by the time you return, if that suits.'

'That's okay. No hassle, sunshine.' Now that I was going round to Titus's I could ask there. And of course he would've been able to supply an address for his brother. Mind you, it would've deeply offended Bathyllus's professional sensibilities as the unchallenged fount of all information if I'd cancelled the order, so I didn't. 'Later will be fine.'

Titus was waiting for me in the atrium, pacing the floor and looking distinctly grey about the gills.

'So what's the problem?' I said.

'Marcia has disappeared.'

I stared. '*What?*'

'She and her maid went out yesterday afternoon. They haven't come back.'

Oh, shit. I took off my cloak and sat down on the couch. 'Okay, pal,' I said. 'Sit down. Take a deep breath and tell me from the beginning.'

He sat. 'Seemingly, there's a new dress shop near the market square that she wanted to have a look at. She and Capra – that's the maid – went off after lunch. They weren't back by dinner time, so I sent a slave to look for her. He checked the shop first of all, and she hadn't been in. By the time the lamps were lit she still hadn't come back, and we began to be concerned. Not actually worried, because it was possible that she'd simply decided to visit a friend instead, got chatting and forgotten the time. Only of course she hadn't. I waited up all night, and the door-slave was under strict instructions not to go to bed either, but by first light there was still no sign of her.'

'Uh-huh. This...ah...unusual?' I was careful to keep my voice neutral. 'I mean, if she did go round to a friend's house and forget the time she may just have decided to stay the night and be done with it.'

'No. Marcia wouldn't do that. She doesn't have all that many close friends to begin with. And if she had decided to sleep over then surely she would've sent word.'

Yeah; that was my thought, too. And from what I'd seen of her the girl wasn't exactly the flighty type. Quite the reverse. If her father was worried he had a perfect right to be.

'Okay,' I said. 'So what do you think yourself?'

'I don't *know!* I thought if I told you you might have some ideas.'

Sure I did; but none of them were comfortable ones. If she'd been of a type with, say, Atia I might've guessed some sort of romantic escapade, maybe even – given the imminence of a wedding that she wasn't all that happy with – an outright elopement with an unknown prior attachment, but in Marcia's case neither explanation fitted. And failing a secret boyfriend, where would she run to? If, as Titus said, she had no obvious close female friends then that was out, too. And as a viable explanation for a sixteen-year-old girl from a cloistered background to strike out on her own was a complete non-starter.

Which only left possibilities that were a long way from being pleasant...

'Right,' I said. 'Let's look at the options.' I paused; this was going to be difficult, but it had to be done. 'What about the maid? Capra? She perfectly trustworthy?'

'Absolutely. She's been with the family all her life. She was my mother's maid while she was alive, and she's been with Marcia ever since she was born, first as her nurse and then as her maid. I'd as soon distrust myself.'

'Fair enough. You know of any reason anyone might want to, uh, lift her? Marcia, I mean?'

'Kidnap, you mean?' Yeah, well, I'd chosen the most euphemistic term I could think of, and a simple kidnapping was far and away the best-case scenario, but I was happy, under the circumstances, to start there. 'A ransom, of course. We're not particularly wealthy, but obviously we'd find whatever was asked, and pay it gladly. You think that's the explanation?'

Me, I'd put it up there with the flying pigs: coincidences happen, sure, but if this didn't have something to do with the case then I'd eat my sandals. Still, it wouldn't hurt – given that he genuinely had no idea who was responsible, or why, both of which were on the certain side of probable – to play along with the idea until events proved it wrong. Which I was very much afraid they would. 'There's a good chance of it, yeah,' I said. 'Give it a couple of days. Oh, keep looking, asking around, sure, but my guess is that if you haven't found her and she hasn't turned up of her own accord by then whoever took her will get in touch. After which we'll see what can be done. Meantime, uh, you think I might have a look round her room?'

He frowned. 'What on earth for?'

I shrugged. 'I don't know. But there may be something there, a clue to where she's gone. Do you mind?'

'No, if you think it might help. It's upstairs.'

'Yeah, I've been there before.'

'Of course. I was forgetting; Atia brought you round two days ago, didn't she? Just go up, then. Take all the time you need.'

'Thanks.' I stood up. 'Incidentally, is your wife around?'

'Septimia? No, she's gone out. She'd arranged to meet a friend this morning, and since I'll be staying in all day there seemed no sense in cancelling.'

'Right.' Well, so much for maternal concern. But having met the lady myself I wasn't unduly surprised. 'I'll be as quick as I can. And I won't disturb anything.'

'Disturb what you like, Corvinus. As long as it helps to find my daughter I couldn't care less.'

I went upstairs.

The smell of stale incense hit me as soon as I opened the door. I crossed the room and put back the shutters covering the window.

Okay, so where did we start?

With the dressing table, of course, where Marcia had put the ring.

The drawer was unlocked and empty, with the woodwork between drawer-top and frame showing clear signs of forcing. I checked the other drawers, also unlocked. Cosmetic stuff, not a lot of that, just the basics, and it looked pretty unused; certainly there was none on the table's top. Some bits and pieces obviously left over from childhood, shoved away and forgotten about, including a teething-ring with little silver bells, seriously tarnished. An ivory comb with three of the teeth broken. A few articles of jewellery, nothing that looked very valuable. And that was it.

Damn. I'd been hoping for a diary, or something similar, but Marcia clearly didn't follow the pattern for girls her age in that respect, either.

What about the rest of the room?

The bed was made up and hadn't been slept in. I checked under it: nothing but the obligatory chamber pot, again unused. Nothing between the mattress and the bed-frame, or under the pillow.

Hell's teeth. Didn't the girl have *any* secrets?

The book-cubby, against the wall next to the bed, held nothing of interest either. What book-rolls there were were serious stuff, to do with religion or philosophy. None of the hidden-away steamy Alexandrian romances or dodgy lyric poetry that, again, I would've expected was standard secret reading for a sixteen-year-old.

Clothes chest. Nothing out of the ordinary in there, and I searched it all the way down.

That only left the table with its Isis statuette, its offering-bowl, and its incense burner. I examined all three carefully.

Nothing. Zilch.

Well, that was about it. Barring a loose floorboard – and I checked for one of those, as well, out of sheer desperation – the room was clean as a whistle.

Bugger. A complete waste of time.

Except...

I glanced back at the Isis statuette.

It was certainly worth a go. And, after all, what did I have to lose?

The goddess's temple in Brundisium wasn't exactly swish; certainly nowhere as upmarket as the one in Rome's Mars Field, that Gaius had had built for her. After asking several local punters for directions, and getting in some cases nothing but a blank stare in reply, I tracked it down to an alleyway in a less-than-salubrious quarter near the town's east wall.

I went inside.

Religion, like I say, isn't my bag. Our approach to it I can live with, no problem, because it's completely sensible. Make sure the gods are treated properly, with their rites celebrated bang on time and accurate to the last sacrificed sheep, bird or whatever, say the proper words in the proper order, make sure you don't drop the knife or forget to sprinkle the barley-meal, and everything will be hunky-dory. You fulfil your part of the bargain and you can be certain that the Powers that Be will fulfil theirs. All very civilised and business-like, with no issues on either side.

The whacky eastern variety is another matter. Don't get me wrong: if foreigners want to get stoned on *qef* and lop their own wollocks off in memory of some poor bugger a few thousand years back, or even just shave their heads and dance through the streets shaking rattles, then that's absolutely fine with me, so long as they keep it to themselves and in their own back yard. Getting mixed up with that sort of thing just makes me nervous.

Even so.

I'd barely crossed the threshold when a shaven-headed elderly guy in a white linen nightshirt hobbled across to intercept me.

'I'm sorry, sir,' he said. Quavered. 'The ceremony doesn't begin for another hour.'

'Actually, granddad,' I said, 'I was looking for someone. A friend.'

'Pardon? You'll have to speak up, I'm afraid. I'm a little deaf.'

I put my mouth next to his ear, raised my voice and spoke very clearly and distinctly. 'I'm looking for a friend. A girl. Name of Marcia. She here?'

He shook his head. 'No. Still no good. Not a thing. Come back in an hour.'

Jupiter on wheels! Maybe we could try lip-reading. I faced him square on, pointed to my mouth and then said slowly: 'Is there someone else I could talk to?'

Preferably someone with all their faculties still in working order and who had at least partial use of their aural abilities. If that wasn't too much to ask.

'I'll tell you what,' he said. 'You wait here. There might be someone else you could talk to.'

Gods!

He shuffled off while I twiddled my thumbs and contemplated the twice-life-size statue of the goddess at the other end of the nave.

'Yes? How can I help you?'

I half-turned: a priestess this time, by the looks of her. Well, at least I'd got the right sex for the question. And as an added bonus she was the right side of ninety, although not by much.

'I was looking for a young girl called Marcia,' I said. 'Titus Marcius's daughter. Have you seen her, by any chance?'

Pause; *long* pause. 'And you are?' she said finally.

'Valerius Corvinus. We met a couple of days ago, and I thought she might be here.'

'Hmm. Wait, please.'

She disappeared back the way she'd come, and I twiddled my thumbs for another five minutes. Finally:

'Valerius Corvinus.'

I turned. Marcia had slipped in on my blind side, from the passageway immediately to the left of the main entrance, and like the old guy she was wearing a simple white linen shift. No shaved head, mind; maybe that came later.

'So,' I said. 'You've joined up.'

'Yes.' She fingered the amulet hanging from a leather lace round her neck. 'How did you know?'

'I didn't. Lucky guess. Or maybe not a guess altogether. It was just something worth checking.' I hesitated. 'Is this, uh, permanent?'

'Oh, yes. Yes, it is. And in case you're wondering it wasn't a sudden decision. I've been thinking about it for months.'

'Since the engagement?'

'Yes. I haven't actually been properly initiated yet, but that will happen in a few days' time.' She was absolutely calm. 'It really is the best solution to the problem that I can think of. To become one of the Lady's priestesses.' She glanced at the statue and ducked her head.

'When were you going to tell your father? He's very worried.'

'Yes, he would be. I'm sorry about that, really sorry. But it was unavoidable, and as I say it'll be for the best in the end. You can tell him yourself, if you like. I don't mind, and there's absolutely nothing he or my mother can do about it.'

'He's your father. Your legal guardian.'

'Not any longer. And I doubt if he would risk taking me away by force.'

'Maybe not; but still.'

She frowned. 'Actually, I think he'll be relieved when you tell him, if anything. Whatever he says to the contrary. He didn't want me to marry Sextus, any more than I did myself.'

'And your mother?'

'She can go to hell.'

I blinked; I'd forgotten Marcia could be so forthright. 'You have a reason for saying that?'

'She's sleeping with Uncle Aulus.'

Gods! 'You're sure?'

'Oh, yes. She has been for at least three months now, to my certain knowledge. Probably a lot longer. Father doesn't know, or at least I don't think he does, and I thought it best not to tell him. Not that he'd be too upset, because they don't have very much to do with each other in any case, he and mother, but even so.' She paused. 'Oh, and I'm fairly sure she's sleeping with Sextus as well.'

I goggled. '*What?*'

'It's not really as surprising as you might think. Mother's always been one to hedge her bets, and it looks like Sextus might be the coming thing, where the company is concerned.' She smiled. '*Looked* like, I should have said; past tense. Because of course with the wedding being off now grandfather's deal with the Pettii might not actually happen.'

Jupiter Best and Greatest! 'The affair with Sextus,' I said. 'You know how long that's been going on?'

'No. But not as long as the one with Uncle Aulus, certainly: that came first. He doesn't know about it, though. My uncle. I'm pretty much sure of that.'

All this in a completely matter-of-fact voice: she was being so calm it was eerie. 'And the other way round?' I said. 'Do you think your uncle knows about Sextus?'

'I doubt it. He's a very jealous man, Uncle Aulus. And violent, of course; there would've been blood spilled. Will be, if he ever does find out, which he probably won't. Mother is extremely good at managing these things.'

Yeah, well, she would have to be, wouldn't she? A single adulterous affair would be difficult enough to cover up; running two simultaneously would be a logistical nightmare. Still, if the liaison with Sextus Pettius went back as far as the murder I needn't look any further into the problem of where the guy had got his inside information from. 'There's just one more thing, Marcia,' I said, 'before I leave you in peace.'

'Yes? And what's that?'

'The missing ring. I'll take that now, please.'

There was a long silence. Then she shrugged and half-turned. 'Capra!'

The old woman had obviously been standing just out of sight in the passageway that Marcia had come out of. She stepped forward.

'Yes, miss?' she said.

'The ring, please.'

Capra hesitated, then took off one of the amulets hanging round her neck and gave it to her. I held out my hand, but Marcia shook her head.

'First I need you to swear you'll return it to where it originally came from,' she said.

'And where would that be?'

She told me.

Shit!

'You can manage that?' she said. 'Otherwise I'm sorry, but it stays here, where it's safe.'

'Actually, yeah. Yes I can.' Gods! Valuable was right! 'Strangely enough, I know just the man for the job.'

'Good. Swear it, then, by the Lady.' She smiled. 'I should warn you first, though, that Lady Isis doesn't take kindly to oath-breakers, and she can be very inventive and quite merciless. You must make sure that the ring is returned to its proper owner or death will only be the start of your problems. You do understand that, don't you?'

Still the quiet, matter-of-fact tone. I glanced up at the statue, which stared back at me blank-eyed. The hairs lifted on my neck.

'Yeah, I understand,' I said. 'It'll be put back where it belongs. I so swear.'

'Very well.' She put the ring with its leather lace into my hand. 'Take care of it. Take *very* good care of it.'

I slipped the thong round my neck, tucked the ring beneath the collar of my tunic, and left her to her prayers.

So how did you follow that little episode?

Not with a return visit to the family home; Marcia, I knew, was safe enough and perfectly happy where she was, and I reckoned she deserved a bit of breathing space before having the whistle blown on her. As for her father, well, I'd advised him in the first place to give it a couple of days, so that was how we'd play it. Once the girl was properly initiated she'd be off and running. Besides, it would only have led to awkward questions that I couldn't have answered without lying.

I'd originally planned to spend at least part of the morning on a visit to Alexis's rooming-house to check up on Atia's secret rendezvous. That was still very much on the cards, sure, but since I was in this part of town anyway it seemed sensible to call in at the address that Bathyllus had given me for Aulus. This time of day the guy himself might not be around, but there was a chance his wife would be. If nothing else I could pat myself on the back for ticking another box.

The Julian baths were easy to find – bigger and more upmarket than the ones Satrius and I had been to – and a friendly local pastry-seller directed me to the Marcius house itself. I gave my name to the door-slave outside and waited while he checked if anyone was officially at home.

He reappeared a couple of minutes later.

'The mistress will see you, sir,' he said. 'This way, please.'

I followed him through the formal atrium to a sitting-room overlooking the garden: evidently, from the decor and various knick-knacks on display, Gellia's private space. The lady herself was ensconced in a wickerwork chair next to the portico opening watching two young children climbing an apple tree. I noticed that there was a wine jug and cup on the table beside her.

'They're so boisterous at that age, aren't they?' she said. 'Quite tiring on the eyes.'

'Yeah. Yeah, they are.' I glanced at the wine cup: half full, and from the slight slur in the lady's voice I reckoned it wasn't the first cupful she'd had this morning. Or even the fifth. 'Valerius Corvinus. I'm–'

'Here to investigate my father-in-law's murder,' she said. 'Yes, I know. Aulus is out at present. You're married? You have children?'

'Married, yes. We have an adopted daughter and a grandchild.' I nodded towards the kids in the tree. 'He'll be about their age. Maybe slightly younger.' There was another chair beside me. 'You mind if I sit?'

'Not at all.' The door-slave was still hovering. 'Bring a cup for Valerius Corvinus, Erastus. And fill up this jug.'

'Certainly, madam.' The guy's face was expressionless as he bent to pick up the jug and carried it out with him.

I'd been expecting, from Sextus's appraisal of Aulus Marcius's wife that she'd be fairly nondescript, and as far as the lady's appearance was concerned, at least, that was bang-on. Thin-faced, mousey hair, no make-up that I could see: the phrase 'washed out' came to mind. Oh, she'd been pretty enough in her day, say ten, fifteen years back, but I'd've reckoned that even then it had been an insipid prettiness, with no blood to it.

'He was found with his head beaten in, floating in the harbour, wasn't he?' she said. Her eyes were still on the children.

'That's right,' I said. 'Or so I was told.'

'Do you know, I burned a whole pan of incense on the family shrine when I heard?' She turned to face me. She was smiling. 'Horrible man!'

'You, ah, didn't get on, then?'

'Titus Marcius was a crude, foul-mouthed bully. He fully deserved to die.' The slave came back with the wine. 'Thank you, Erastus. Pour for Valerius Corvinus, please. And I'll have some more myself.' She waited until he had finished and left. 'No, we did not get on. To put it mildly.' She picked up her cup and drank. 'Aulus is out at present. Did I say?'

'Yeah,' I said. 'Yes, you did.'

'If you wanted to talk to him, as I presume you do. Of course, that's not surprising. My husband is seldom *in*.' She turned back to the children and raised her voice. 'Marcus, *do* be careful, dear!' Then, to me: 'He's the spitting image of his father, don't you think?'

'I haven't met your husband yet, I'm afraid.'

'Oh, don't be afraid. Congratulate yourself.' She poured more wine into the cup. 'Spitting image, in character as well as looks. I keep hoping that one of those days the little monster will fall and break his neck, but alas he never does.' I said nothing. 'You have met Septimia, though, I suppose. My sister-in-law.'

'Yes.' I took a sip of the wine. Neat, with not a drop of water added.

'They're the perfect match, don't you think? The mongrel and the bitch.' She smiled again. 'But of course, as you say, you haven't met Aulus, so half of the equation is missing.'

'Uh...maybe I'd better go.' I half rose, but she put out a hand to stop me.

'No. I'm sorry. I'll behave,' she said. 'Was there something you wanted to ask me?'

Frankly, all I wanted to do was to leave her to get stewed. Or rather more stewed than she was at present, which would be saying something. Still...

'So you know about your husband's affair with Septimia?' I said.

She laughed. 'My dear, *everyone* knows about it! Barring poor Titus, of course, although I wouldn't be surprised if he knew too and was just not letting on. The man is a natural cuckold. And Septimia isn't Aulus's first mistress, not by any means. I've known he was a complete shit from before I married him.'

'So why did you, then?'

'None of my doing, darling. It was the usual story: Aulus needed a wife, my father needed the money, Titus Marcius needed the social status the connection with our family would give him, and they all came to an amicable agreement. You've met Atia?' I nodded. 'Same thing, poor girl; well, as far as the money went, anyway, although in her case it was looks and youth as opposed to status. Only she's rid of hers now, she's free to do whatever she wants.' She picked up the wine cup. 'I'm fond of Atia. We talk. I only wish someone would do the same for me.'

'Uh...come again?' I said.

The cup paused half way to her lips. 'I beg your pardon?'

'You said you wished someone would do the same for you.'

'Did I?' She looked puzzled. 'I don't think so, dear. Do what?'

Jupiter! 'You were talking about Atia.'

'Oh, yes. Atia. We get on well together, despite the fact that our backgrounds are so different. Her father is in trade, you know, a ship's chandler. Mine owned an estate about ten miles west of here. Not a particularly profitable one, mind, it was losing money hand over fist, which explained the marriage, but it had been in the family for five generations. And she can't stand Aulus either. That was an added bond.'

'Gellia,' I said patiently. 'You were saying that Atia is free now to do whatever she wants. You know what that is? She have something specific in mind? Some*one*?'

She frowned. 'I don't think that follows,' she said. 'I certainly didn't mean to imply it.' She turned back to the children and raised her voice. 'Marcus! I won't tell you again! That branch is *not* safe! And Titus, that tunic was clean on this morning! Don't you *dare* get it dirty!' She faced me again and smiled. 'They really are dreadful scamps. Is your grandson the same?'

'Uh...yeah. He is. To get back to Atia–'

'Valerius Corvinus, you mustn't think me rude, but I have things to do this afternoon and I must get ready for them. Would you mind terribly if we continued our talk some other time after all?'

Hell's teeth! 'No, that'd be fine.' I stood up. 'I'm pleased to meet you, Gellia. Thanks for your help.'

'It was nothing.' Yeah, well, she could say that again, with knobs on. 'Aulus will be so sorry he missed you. I'll tell him you called.'

'You do that,' I said.

I left.

Bugger!

Alexis had said that the rooming-house was near the market square, down an alleyway between it and the vegetable market. Not all that far, in other words. And after that little conversation with Gellia I had even more reason to check it out.

It was clouding over and beginning to rain. I put up my hood and headed off towards the Square...

'Hey, Corvinus!'

I turned. Brinnius, Marcus Cluvius's hired muscle. He came over.

'I was just waiting for you to come out,' he said. 'Nice chat with the lush?'

'It was okay,' I said guardedly. 'You been following me?'

'Nah, not exactly. I was on my way there myself to pick something up, but that can wait. The boss told me to keep a look out for you. He wants a quiet word.'

Shit, here we went again; shades of Montanus. This time, though, I doubted that a dinner invitation would figure in any form. 'The boss?' I said.

'Don't get smart, boy! You know who I mean. Marcus Cluvius. He wants to talk to you.'

I gave him my best dazzling smile. 'Then that is absolutely fine with me, pal,' I said. 'I've been intending to fit him into my schedule those past couple of days, but you know how things pile up on you. Busy, busy, busy. Not a free moment to call your own.'

He scowled. 'Can it, Corvinus. You're not flavour of the month, I can tell you that now. Keep walking the way you were going, towards the Square.'

I did, and he fell in beside me. 'So where exactly are we heading for?' I said. 'The company offices or the flat?'

'A wineshop on the corner of Saturn Temple Street and the Hinge. The boss told me to meet him there. Nothing to do with you. Business with the owner.'

'Uh-huh.' I didn't pursue the matter; from what Montanus had told me about the guy's business activities a meeting with the owner was unlikely to be a cosy little confab among friends.

We walked on in silence.

The wineshop, when we got there, was the mid-market type, nothing too fancy, probably catering for a clientele of local artisan workers and shopkeepers: your basic counter with a few tables and benches and a range of four or five reasonably-priced wines in the racks. The place was empty of ordinary punters, probably nothing to do with the time of day or the quality of the wines but because of the guy sitting alone at a table in the corner. The owner – obviously the owner; no one else, under the circumstances, would still be hanging around the place, or look that definite shade of grey – was standing behind the bar and trying to look busy with a dishtowel and some wine cups.

'Guess who I bumped into, boss,' Brinnius said as he closed the door behind us and shot the central bolt.

'Valerius Corvinus.' Marcus Cluvius smiled. Or at least that was probably the idea; picture a smiling pike. Otherwise he was pretty nondescript, certainly not a copy of the bruiser his father was, even without the eyepatch. 'Come in. Sit down. Wine?'

'Yeah, that'd be great,' I said: in the end I had hardly touched the cup that Gellia's slave had poured for me, and I reckoned a bit of confidence-bolstering was going to be needed here.

I sat. Brinnius parked himself with his back to the door and folded his arms. The owner hurried over.

'Wine,' Marcus said. 'Two cups.' The man nodded nervously, went back behind the bar and busied himself with filling a jug. Marcus turned back to me. 'Gaius Julius Montanus,' he said. 'Ring any bells?'

Oh, shit. 'Uh...yeah,' I said. 'He commands the auxiliary cohort here. His wife and mine ran into each other in a jeweller's shop a couple of days back, and they've palled up.'

'So why would you choose to call in on him at the barracks yesterday morning?'

I was ready for that one. I shrugged. 'Just a courtesy call,' I said. 'I was in the neighbourhood and I thought I'd drop in, introduce myself. Thank his wife at second hand for her offer to show Perilla around.'

'You were hardly in the neighbourhood, Corvinus. You'd just been over on the other side of the Neck at the Pettii offices.'

Jupiter! The bastard would be telling me when I last changed my underclothes next. And probably how many spare pairs I had left in my clothes chest, as an encore. 'That's right,' I said. 'I'd taken a ferry-boat over and I was on my way home.'

'To the west gate. So the Citadel wasn't exactly on your way, now, was it?'

'It was close enough. And I've just arrived, remember. I wanted to see a bit of the town.' The guy came over with the wine jug and cups. He poured for both of us, and I drank, trying to keep my hand steady.

'Hmm.' Marcus picked up his own cup and held it without drinking. The owner, with a quick glance at me, went back to his polishing. 'Courtesy call, right? So what precisely did you talk about?'

Gods! This wasn't easy, like juggling four plates at once with a meat cleaver thrown in for good measure. And the pike's eyes never wavered. I was beginning to sweat. 'This and that,' I said. 'Nothing important, the usual stuff. He asked how I was liking Brundisium. Then it came out that he was from Aquae Sextiae in southern Gaul. We were out there ourselves, my wife and me, a couple of years back, so we compared notes for a while. That was about it, really. The guy had a busy schedule, so I didn't stay all that long. Fifteen minutes, half an hour, max.'

We locked eyes. Then his shoulders lifted, he swallowed some of the wine, and set the cup down. 'All right,' he said quietly. 'You're off the hook for now. But a word of warning, Corvinus. Snoop around all you like where the old man's death is concerned, that's what you're here for and I can't do anything about it. But our private business is our private business. You stick your nose into that and we'll cut it off for you. And I'm not speaking figuratively; that's a promise. You understand?'

'Yeah.' Jupiter! 'I understand.'

'Good. So relax. Drink your wine.' He took another swallow of his own, set the cup down, and leaned back against the wall. 'How's it going, by the way? The investigation, I mean?'

'Not too badly. Nothing concrete yet, we're still in the early stages.' Assurances of benign neutrality or not, I wasn't going to let Marcus bloody Cluvius into any secrets.

'I was sorry about old Marcius.' His hands toyed with the half full cup, rolling it back and forwards between the palms, and his eyes followed the motion. 'But it was all for the best. Men like him and my father, they were good enough in their day, but that's gone. Things are different now, and there has to be change, right? You have to clear away dead wood to encourage new growth.' The cup paused, and he looked back up at me and smiled. 'Know what I'm saying?'

'You have any idea who killed him, yourself?' I said. 'Just asking, no hassle.'

The smile didn't shift. 'I wouldn't tell you if I had. But they did Aulus and me a big favour. Saved us a lot of trouble, too.' He looked directly at me. 'The way things were going, the old bastard could've hung on for years. Not good, Corvinus; not good.'

Gods! So was he admitting that he and Aulus were behind the killing? Or implying it, rather? Me, I wouldn't have put it past him, either the murder or the implication. I'd met Marcus Cluvius's type before: so bloody confident and full of themselves that they can't pass up the chance to play with whoever they're talking with in the same way as he'd been playing with the wine cup. Backwards and forwards, am I or am I not?

The problem was, if the bastard *was* responsible, or partly responsible, and it looked like I might be able to prove it at any stage, or even that I was getting too close for comfort, then he'd have no compunction about adding me to the tally. That I was certain of, and it wasn't a cheerful thought, even with the deal with Montanus in operation. And on top of what I'd heard about him second hand now that I'd finally met the guy I was beginning to feel even less comfortable about that side of things.

'I mean, look at this business with the Pettii,' he went on. 'Twenty fucking years of hating one another's guts and old Marcius suddenly decides to cosy up to them, even brokers a marriage between his sodding granddaughter and the son and heir. I ask you, how bloody stupid is that?' I didn't answer; not, mind you, that I imagined for an instant that he expected me to. We'd obviously got into full rant mode. 'I'm telling you, Corvinus, if I have anything to do with it now he's dead that's well off the programme.'

'You think you can swing it?' I said.

'Sure. Easy. The younger lads in the firm are all like Brinnius here: they won't take orders from a Pettius, and if the old man's plan goes ahead that's what'll happen. Maybe not in two months' time, when the wedding comes off, but a year, two years, maybe five at most, down the line. Me and Aulus, once we're in charge we'll see it doesn't work like that.'

'Uh-huh.' I was careful. 'So you don't rate Sextus Pettius, then?' I said.

'I've no quarrel with Pettius, so long as he sticks to his own back yard. But the bastard's got no business mixing with us. Marcia can marry someone else; there're plenty of other possibilities closer to home.'

Now *that* was an angle I hadn't thought of. I hoped the sudden interest didn't show on my face.

'Like you, for example?' I said. I'd kept the tone as neutral as I could, but it still netted me a sharp look. 'You're not married yourself, are you?'

'She could do worse. And we'd be keeping things in the family, as it were. My father being who he is.'

'Right. Right.' I drank some of my wine: not bad, but if that was the best they'd got – and I assumed it was – then I wouldn't be visiting this particular wineshop in my off-duty hours. 'I'd sort of got the idea that he was in favour of the marriage. And of the deal.'

'Maybe he is. But like I say, the old guys have had their day; they're not relevant any more. When push comes to shove, which it will, my father'll find himself outvoted.'

'What about Titus? He's co-heir; he'll have a say, at least.'

'Fuck Titus, he's no problem. We could eat him for breakfast.'

'It all depends on some kind of election, then? For the company boss?'

'We're not a democracy, Corvinus. All the same, if it turns out that my father wants a trial of strength he'll find that he's on a loser from the start. Best thing he can do is bow out gracefully before things get heavy.'

'How do you mean, heavy?'

He shrugged. 'Just an expression. And anyway, it's none of your business.' He picked up his wine cup again and drained it. 'Okay, that's all; we're done for now. You go off and do whatever the hell you were on your way to do. But remember, you've had your final and only warning, so be very, very careful. Have a nice day.'

He nodded to Brinnius, who sidled clear of the doorway and slipped the bolt.

I left.

Now *that* had been interesting.

10.

The rooming-house was one of those old buildings that predate everything else around them: what had, a century before, been a snazzy upper-class residence that had gradually gone to seed and moved several steps down market. Places like that, nine times out of ten the current owner either puts in some party walls and divides the space up among sub-tenants or keeps the building as is and runs it as a brothel. I hoped, from what Alexis had said, that his informant wasn't being euphemistic, particularly given the 'single working men' side of things, but I wouldn't have laid any hefty bets: these days Alexis may not exactly be the young innocent he started out as, but smart though he undoubtedly is he still has a naive streak a mile wide.

It would've pushed the theories of what Atia was up to into the realms of fevered speculation, mind.

I'd considered the options on the way over and decided that the direct approach was best. So I knocked on the front door and went straight in.

Yeah, well; if the place was a brothel the decor of the entrance lobby wasn't exactly designed to put the incoming client into a mood of priapic readiness: there was a floor-mosaic and a fresco, sure, but the first was a standard 'Beware of the Dog' with serious cement patching replacing the missing tiles and the second a faded and peeling still life comprising, with startling originality, a bowl of fruit and a dead pigeon. There was a faint but pervasive smell, too, of bad drainage combined with something less immediately identifiable but just as unpleasant.

Right. So we definitely weren't talking des. res. standard here. Far from it.

I carried on through to what would, in the original house, have been the atrium. It was still there, as a smaller version complete with its pool and light-well, but the added party walls had converted it into a second lobby, with doors leading off either side and a staircase at the back.

One of the doors opened and a woman emerged.

'Yes?' she said. 'Can I help you?'

Late middle-aged, and not so much dressed and made up as upholstered and shellacked; perfect madame material, in other words. Maybe I'd been wrong to dismiss the brothel possibility after all.

'I was looking for a lady called Fulgentia,' I said. 'The owner?'

'That is me,' she said. 'But if it's a room you want I'm afraid we've none vacant at present.'

'No, that's okay. Actually, I wanted to ask you about one of your tenants. If you don't mind.'

She smiled, putting her foundation layer in real danger of cracking. 'Oh, I don't mind at all,' she said. 'They might, of course, that depends on your questions, but we'll cross that bridge when we come to it. What was the gentleman's name?'

'Yeah, well, that's the problem,' I said. 'I don't know his name. But I understand a young woman visits him here. Twentyish? Fair hair, very good looking? She comes with her maid.'

'Ah, yes. That would be Gaius Frontius's young lady. Atia.'

Bull's-eye! 'Yeah, that's her,' I said. 'Do you think you could–?'

'Perhaps we should retire to my sitting-room. That will be *far* more private and comfortable.' She turned and paused, her hand on the doorknob of the room she'd just left. 'You *are* fond of cats, I trust?'

'Pardon?'

'Really, young man. I cannot put it any more plainly. Cats. Felines. Do you like them?' She opened the door.

'Not particularly,' I said, following her inside. 'Our neighbour used to have–' I stopped; the phrase 'wall to wall' occurred. Jupiter! Still, it explained the indefinable part of the pervasive smell. 'How many of them have you got in here, lady? Just out of interest?'

'Thirteen at present. *Very* unlucky, of course, but Jocasta had triplets last month and I didn't have the heart to deprive her of one. Have a seat, dear. That couch would be best. Push Theophrastus off if he's too much in the way.'

The seriously-scarred tomcat in part-possession gave me a malevolent glare and didn't budge an inch. I sat beside him, keeping what I hoped was a safe distance. Fulgentia picked up a much more amenable tabby from the cushioned wickerwork chair opposite and settled down with her cradled in her lap.

'Now,' she said. 'What can I tell you?'

'Uh...you don't want to know anything yourself first?' I said cautiously.

'Such as what?'

'The basic stuff. Who I am, why I'm asking. That sort of thing.'

'Oh, no, dear. I never pry; it's not polite. Excuse me.' She raised her voice. 'Aeneas! I've told you before, leave Dido alone! She's not in the mood for you at present!' Her eyes came back to me. 'Now, young man. Where were we?'

Mad as a March hare, that was clear enough. Still...

'Gaius Frontius,' I said.

'Yes, indeed. A lovely boy. Young man, I should say. He was one of my first lodgers. He came five years ago, just after my Lucius ran off with the contortionist.'

'He, ah, wouldn't be around at the moment, would he?'

'Frontius? Bless you, no, none of the young gentlemen are. He doesn't finish work until late in the afternoon. And then he generally stops in at a cookshop on the way back for his dinner. I discourage the gentlemen from bringing cooked food in, it stinks the place out. Onions, especially. I have never been able to come to terms with the smell of fried onions, it turns my stomach right over. My Lucius was the same with fish.'

'So where does he work?' I said.

'In the large chandlery concern facing the Big Harbour, near the mouth of the Neck.'

'*What?*'

She frowned. 'I do wish you wouldn't do that, dear,' she said. 'I expressed myself concisely and with what I know was perfect clarity. Gaius Frontius is a sales assistant in the large chandlery near the entrance to the Big Harbour, which belongs to Atia's father. That, of course, is how the two young things came to meet in the first place.'

'So they're definitely an item, are they?' I said. 'Frontius and Atia?'

'Of course they are. I told you; she's his young lady. She has been for years. It's a shame about her husband, I know, but some things can't be helped.'

Gods! 'You, ah, knew she was married, then?' I said.

'But naturally I did! Why else would they have to meet here in secret on his day off?'

'And you don't mind?'

'Why on earth should I mind? It was the poor lamb's father's doing, not hers, and the husband was more than three times her age. It was a silly arrangement in the first place.' She stroked the cat. 'But I *meant* it was a shame they had to resort to such drastic measures. That's the trouble with young people today, they have no patience.'

I blinked. 'Pardon?'

She sighed. 'Really, young man, you either have a *very* limited cognitive vocabulary or you are developing symptoms of premature deafness. Again, I'm sure I was speaking quite clearly, both in terms of sense and of volume.'

I didn't believe this. 'Hang on, lady,' I said. 'You're telling me that Atia and her boyfriend murdered her husband?'

'Oh, yes. Not that I blame them; it was by far the simplest solution.'

Jupiter Best and Greatest! 'You have any actual proof? Did they tell you, either of them?'

'No, not as such. And as I say, I never pry. But I assume they did; I would have, myself. Certainly they have the wedding all planned. Just as soon as the mourning period is decently over and she has her share of the estate, Atia told me.'

Okay, so let's take this very slowly and carefully. 'Fulgentia, this is important, right?' I said. 'The old man died two days after the September Ides, probably just before midnight. You happen to know if Frontius was out of the house at that time, at all?'

'I really would have no idea whatever the date, dear. The front door is locked after dark, but I hang the key on the nail beside it. And there's another key left under the potted bay tree outside so that the young gentlemen can come back in whenever they like.'

Bugger! Yeah, well, I supposed it had been asking too much, at that. Never mind; I'd got plenty to go on without it. And this Gaius Frontius was definitely someone I needed to talk to.

But not today; I reckoned I didn't owe the case anything for the time being, and it would've meant a longish hike back up to the harbour area. Besides, I'd got this ring practically burning a hole in my tunic. That was really something I had to tell Perilla about.

I made my hasty goodbyes and left.

She was already there when I got home, stretched out on the couch with a book-roll.

'Good! You're back!' she said. She was looking excited. 'I have the most marvellous news!'

'Yeah?' I took off my sodden cloak – the rain had got worse on the way over from the centre – and handed it to the waiting Bathyllus, swapping it for the cup of wine he was holding. 'That makes two of us. Go ahead, lady. You first.'

'Believe it or not I've identified the missing ring.'

'Is that so, now?' I swallowed some of the wine. Not the usual stuff, but instantly recognisable. 'Hey, Bathyllus! Hang on a moment!'

Bathyllus, exiting with the cloak, turned. 'Yes, sir?'

I held up the cup. 'This is from the jar that the cohort commander sent over, right? Julius Montanus?'

'Yes, sir. It came while you were out.'

'Was there a message with it? An address?'

'Indeed there was, sir.' He hesitated, sniffed, and glanced sideways at Perilla. 'The young lady in question works from an establishment in the alleyway behind the Temple of Vulcan. About half way between the market square and the Tarentine Gate, sir. The establishment itself, sir, goes by the name of Calypso's Purse.'

A brothel, obviously, and as such not on the little snob's list of the top ten places for a respectable purple-striper to be seen at in downtown Brundisium. I hadn't missed the implication of the sniff and all those 'sirs', either; nor the 'works from', for that matter. Where thinly-veiled sarcasm was concerned Bathyllus didn't give best to no-one. 'Thanks, Bathyllus,' I said. 'That'll be all.' He left, the back of his bald head radiating disapproval. I turned back to Perilla. 'Sorry, lady, where were we?'

She was looking daggers.

'You were about to tell me how this Calypso's Purse place fits into things, dear,' she said. 'Not to mention Bathyllus's "the young lady in question". Or at least I hope you were.'

.I grinned. 'Come on, Perilla!' I said. 'It's part of a deal I made with Montanus.' I told her what Montanus had told me, about Messia Postuma. 'I thought I might look the girl up, see if I could get anything specific on Aulus and young Cluvius. Nothing to do with the case as far as I know, but still. Let's just leave it to one side for the time being, okay?'

'Very well, Marcus.' She sniffed. 'If you insist.'

'You were saying about the ring. You've found out what it is, right?'

'Oh. Oh, yes.' She frowned. 'It was pure luck, really. You remember my mentioning a painting by Aetion? The one hanging in the Agrippan Porch, that Sentia was taking me to see? Well, it showed the wedding of Alexander to Roxane. And the ring on his finger was–'

'An amethyst with a sixteen-rayed star.'

'That's right! Seemingly, and I got this later from Eudemus of Caria's *Journal*' – she patted the book roll – 'which Sentia was kind enough to borrow for me from the local library, a sixteen-rayed star was the badge of the Macedonian royal house. Which means that–' She stopped. 'Wait a moment. The rays. How did you know there were sixteen of them? That wasn't part of the description you were given originally, was it? Or am I wrong?'

'Uh-uh. It's just that things have moved on a bit since, and I counted.' I pulled the ring attached to its lace out of my tunic-neck and held it up. 'Ta-daa!'

She gaped. '*Marcus!* Where on earth did you find it?'

I lay down on the other couch and told her.

'You mean Marcia had it all along?' she said.

'Yeah. She staged the burglary herself and took it with her when she scarpered. Or rather she gave it to her maid to hang on to, because snitching it was Capra's idea in the first place.'

'But why should she bother? I mean, yes, as we said, the fact that it was missing complicated matters as far as the wedding and the business alliance were concerned, but it didn't necessarily change them to any great extent. And if she intended to duck out of the marriage in any case then from that point of view the presence or absence of the ring was immaterial. Why take the risk of being found out?'

'That was Capra again, at least I assume so. She's seriously superstitious, that lady.'

'What does that have to do with anything? Granted, from the device on it the ring must have belonged at some stage to a Macedonian royal, which explains why it was so valuable, but by definition any antique has to have a past history. It's not as if–' She stopped again. 'Oh. Oh, my. I'm being stupid. It came from a tomb, didn't it?'

'Yeah. Not just any tomb, either. You remember that visit Gaius paid to Alexandria when he had Alexander's tomb opened and half-inched the sword and breastplate? Okay, fine, after the guy was chopped Claudius had them put back, sure; only in the process before the tomb was re-sealed some light-fingered bastard had had it away with the dead king's signet ring.'

'Wait a moment, dear.' She was staring at me wide-eyed. 'Let's be clear about this. You're saying that Marcia's ring was Alexander's? *The* Alexander's?'

'Uhuh. As ever was. At least that's what Marcia told me, and I've no reason to disbelieve her. No wonder everyone was so cagey when it was mentioned.'

'But what on earth do we do with it?'

'That bit's easy. It goes straight in the house safe for the duration, and when we get back to Rome we hand it over to your pal Claudius Caesar. Let him take things from there. And he had sodding well better make sure the job's done properly, because if he doesn't I have it on Marcia's authority that the Goddess Isis will not be a happy bunny.' I tucked the ring back beneath my tunic. 'Now. In other news.'

She was still looking shocked. 'Marcus, you cannot *possibly* top that!'

I grinned. 'I'm not trying. But to be fair the ring has nothing to do with the case, and never did have. On the other hand, there have been developments.'

'Namely?'

'To begin with, we have a completely new suspect.' I reached for the jug Bathyllus had left beside me on the table and re-filled up my wine cup. 'Or rather, the Significant Other to one of the existing ones.' I told her about my conversation with Fulgentia. 'True, the woman's mad as a barrel of ferrets, but I'd bet what she said about the liaison holds good, at any rate.'

'You think this Gaius Frontius was the killer?'

'It would make sense, sure. He predated Marcius, and from the sound of things he was well on his way to tying the knot with Atia before her father buggered things up. They're still very much an item, and have been throughout. As far as motive's concerned, well, that's obvious, isn't it? Apart from the union of childhood sweethearts aspect of things Atia will be a wealthy widow. Or comparatively wealthy, anyway. Plus the convenient circumstantial fact that the guy works in a chandlery shop just up the road from where the murder happened and which, no doubt, stocks enough examples of the murder weapon to outfit half the fleet. Perfect fit. What more could you ask for?' I picked up my wine-cup and took a sip.

'An explanation of why he chose the old offices as the place to commit the murder.'

I set the cup down. 'Pardon?'

'I mean, what connection does he have with them? How does he know that they even exist? Not from Atia, certainly: she'd only been married a few months, and in any case she wasn't involved with Marcius's business affairs.'

'Frontius is local. I said: the shop where he works isn't all that far away, and by all accounts he's been working there for years. Certainly much longer than the offices have been closed up. He'd have known they existed, at least, sure he would.'

'Hmm.' She frowned. 'All right. It still doesn't explain his choice of them as venue, though.'

'Who says the choice was his? Marcius was the one with the key, and he arrived first. Maybe he was the one who arranged the rendezvous.'

'Why?'

'Gods, I don't know, Perilla! Maybe he'd found out that something was going on between Frontius and his wife and arranged a meeting there to have it out in private.'

'That's two maybe's. Come on, dear, be honest. You're floundering. It doesn't work, does it?'

I sighed. No, it didn't. In fact it was a complete no-brainer, because to start with, Marcius being Marcius, if he'd caught anyone fooling around with his wife, particularly a no-name shop assistant like Gaius Frontius, the bugger would've been cat's-meat before you could say 'adultery', with no discussion involved.

'Okay, admitted,' I said. 'But that's just a detail. The rest of it – motive and so on – still fits. The guy's in the frame and he stays there.'

'I'm not arguing, Marcus. You may be right; perhaps he is the killer. You haven't actually talked to him yet?'

'No. I'll do that tomorrow. Go round to the shop.'

'So what were the other developments you mentioned?'

'Mm? Oh. Right. They all have to do with Aulus and Marcus Cluvius.' I told her about my talk with Cluvius Junior; the edited version, of course, with the threats taken out. 'Fair enough, as far as he and Aulus were concerned the old man was an obstacle removed, we knew that already. But he came pretty close to boasting that the murder was all part of the great ongoing master plan. Made a pretty good case for it as well, vis-à-vis support from the rank and file. Me, if I were his father I'd be checking my porridge for rat poison in future. Brother Titus, too.'

She gave me a sharp look. 'You're serious?'

'Half-serious, sure, particularly now I've met him. He has it all planned, and he's certainly ruthless enough. Now the old man, at least, is out of the picture he's even thinking of cancelling the deal with the Pettii, cutting out Sextus, and marrying Marcia himself.'

'You didn't tell him about her defection, then?'

I shook my head. 'Uh-uh, never even considered it. Let the bastard find out for himself in his own time. Mind you, it's an angle we didn't think of when we were talking motive. If he could've swung it a marriage with the ex-boss's granddaughter would've been a huge step forward: unlike Sextus he's practically family as it is, he's got the following already, and marrying into the boss's line would give him official standing even better than his father's. Plus, if we can trust what we've heard, he can wrap Aulus round his little finger, so with Aulus in charge at the end of the day he'd be the de facto head of the firm.'

'Hmm.' She was twisting her lock of hair. 'Very well. So a definite possibility, then? In his own right, I mean, independent of Aulus?'

'Absolutely. Although I'd still bet that, if he is our perp, he and Aulus were working hand-in-glove, with him as the brains.'

'All right. Anything else?'

'Yeah.' I finished off the wine in my cup, reached for the jug, and poured. 'Back to the conversation with Marcia. It seems that Aulus is having an affair with her mother.'

'She told you that?'

'Yeah.' I took a sip and glanced at her over the rim of the cup. 'You don't seem too surprised.'

'I'm not, particularly, considering the description you gave me of Septimia's marriage; in fact, I'd be more surprised to find that she wasn't having an affair with somebody or other. And from your description of him Aulus would seem to be the obvious candidate. Do either of their partners know?'

'Gellia – Aulus's wife – definitely does. She was someone else I talked to today; in fact, it was her who really got me thinking about Atia's boyfriend. She's another one who believes that he's is our perp. Approves, into the bargain.'

'Just believes? Or knows?'

'Only believes, I'm afraid. She's got no more proof than Frontius's landlady has.'

'What about Titus? Does he know that Septimia and Aulus are lovers?'

'Marcia says no, but Gellia seems to think it's possible. So the jury's out on that one. The really interesting thing, though, is that according to Marcia Septimia's also having an affair with Sextus Pettius.'

Perilla sat up straight on the couch. '*What?*'

I grinned. 'Yeah, that was my reaction. Still, once you've finished marvelling at the lady's stamina it makes perfect sense on both sides, and it explains a lot. As Marcia put it, her mother's pretty good at hedging her bets. She's already married to Titus, and if she can establish an in, as it were, with both Aulus and Sextus Pettius she's got all her options covered where an attachment to the future head of firm is concerned; while Sextus, in his turn, gets a direct line to what we'll still call the enemy camp. And *that*, as I said, explains how he came to know about the will and the new succession arrangements. Or lack of them.'

'Do they know about each other? Aulus and Sextus, I mean. That they're...concurrent, as it were?'

'Again according to Marcia, Sextus knows about Aulus, but not the other way about.' I picked up my wine-cup. 'Me, I have to hand it to the lady. She's obviously a logistical genius. Oh, sure, Sextus is a bachelor with a place of his own, so presumably there's no problem there about meeting up. But both she and Aulus are married with home lives of their own. They'd have to arrange somewhere safe and private where they could–' I almost spilled the wine. 'Shit!'

'Marcus?' Perilla was staring at me. 'What on earth–?'

I set the cup down on the table. 'Fool! Total, bloody, sodding *fool!*'

'Marcus...'

'The old offices, right? They're in a two-storey building.'

'So? You've already been there. You told me; they haven't been used for years.'

'Right. But then I only saw the ground floor, didn't I? And there was no internal staircase; that, I *would've* noticed. Meaning?'

'Whatever is on the floor above is completely separate. With its own access.'

'Round the far side of the building, where I didn't bother to go. *Bugger!*'

'Calmly, dear. You weren't to know at the time.'

'Yeah, well, I do now, don't I?' Hell's bloody teeth, it had been staring me in the face! 'What are the bets the first floor is a private flat? It'd be absolutely perfect for them. And we already know that Aulus has a key, that he got from the firm's janitor.'

'Wouldn't he have needed a separate one? After all, if it was a private flat, then–'

'Maybe. I don't know, one way or the other. If so it's a complication and we're screwed, sure, but we'll cross that bridge when we come to it. Meanwhile tomorrow morning I go over to the new company offices and get the spare I had before, check the place out. Only thoroughly, this time.'

I picked up the wine-cup and took a long swallow.

Gods!

So Aulus borrows the key to a building that no one has set foot in for two years, he uses the upstairs flat for his secret meetings with his sister-in-law, and ten days later his father is murdered down below. It couldn't be a coincidence; no *way* could it be a coincidence! And if I was right – and six got you ten, easy, that I was – then we'd just blown the lid off the case.

11.

I was off bright and early the next morning in the direction of the Big Harbour and Atia's father's chandlery.

Yeah, well, we certainly couldn't complain of a shortage of suspects this time around. Except that considering I'd known from the start that we'd be up to our necks in crooks to begin with that shouldn't really come as much of a surprise.

Atia's boyfriend, though, was out on his own. On the face of it, that side of things played like the plot of a romantic pot-boiler: poor-but-honest working lad wins the heart (but definitely nothing more, for the present) of the boss's beautiful daughter, fate in the form of a rich but seriously elderly suitor lands the hapless pair a whammy, parted but still deeply in love they continue their chaste relationship in secret, and finally the goddess Aphrodite or one of her equivalents-stroke-minions shoves her divine oar in to sort everything out. True love triumphs, evil is confounded, and the young couple are joined at last in carefully-expurgated wedded bliss. Only it hadn't happened like that, had it? The oar had turned out to be a belaying pin, the sorting out involved the corpse of said elderly suitor floating in the harbour with his skull bashed in, and whoever our perp was it certainly wasn't Aphrodite. So as far as Lover Boy was concerned I'd be keeping an open mind.

Fulgentia had been right in calling the place a 'concern' rather than a shop. Sure, this being the main harbour of a busy port there were far more establishments catering for the seagoing trade and its offshoots around than you could shake a stick at, but this one took up a respectable slice of the block and spilled over out front onto the quayside itself. For all that Atia had said her father had sold her because he needed the cash to finance his career in local politics, the guy clearly wasn't anywhere near being short of a copper piece or two. Mind you, aedileships don't come cheap, and even when you've landed one that's only the beginning: Atius would still need to keep a high profile, and just to be in there and punching on a long-term basis he'd have to be selling all the clews and hawsers he could shift.

I went inside.

The place wasn't exactly heaving; apart from me and a couple of what looked like idle browsers there was only one actual customer at the desk, discussing the comparative merits of three what looked to me identical and unidentifiable pieces of equipment.

The young man serving just had to be Frontius, and, yes, we were firmly into Alexandrian pot-boiler territory here: mid-to late twenties, tall, dark curly hair, with a face and body that would've had old Praxiteles biting through his chisel. That wasn't all, either: from what I could hear of his voice when he spoke to the customer the guy could've made a fortune in Rome doing poetry recitals at middle-aged matrons' honey-wine klatsches, not to mention from the resulting appointments of a much more private nature. No wonder Atia hadn't wanted to drop him after she'd got hitched. It explained Fulgentia's partisanship, too: aelurophile to her mascara'ed eyebrows the lady might be, but woman of a certain age that she was I'd bet she'd entertained a few private fantasies of her own in that direction.

I was hanging around a display of various types and thicknesses of rope, waiting for the punter to make his choice, pay for it and go, when a little balding guy in a sharp tunic came over from where he'd been chatting to one of the browsers.

'Can I help you, sir?' he said.

Probably, from his prosperous look and his assured manner, the owner himself, and Atia's father. Not that I was going to introduce that connection, mind. Besides, I'd prepared for this eventuality on the way over.

'Well, yes and no,' I said, putting on my best Roman purple-striper cut-glass accent. 'Actually, I was rather hoping to speak to your assistant there. No hurry, just when he's free.'

The little bald-head was looking at me with deep suspicion. Which, under the circumstances, was understandable: I'd bet that, sculptor's dream model that he was, for a single man to come into the shop and ask for a quiet word alone with Gaius Frontius wasn't an unusual occurrence.

'In connection with what?' he said.

'Fact is I'm in the throes of having one of those yacht thingies built,' I said. 'Nothing too grand, just big enough for the wife and me and a few friends to tootle round the islands in next season. Chap I talked to recommended your lad there as a fount of knowledge on the best bibs and bobs to fit it out with.'

'Really?' He still didn't sound too happy. 'Did this chap have a name, by any chance?'

Bugger. 'Of course he did,' I said. 'Told me it himself. Damned if I can remember it, though. I only met him the once, a couple of evenings ago, at one of Gaius Montanus's dinner parties. You know Gaius at all?'

'Julius Montanus? The prefect in command of the garrison?' The suspicious look disappeared and was replaced with a smile. 'Not personally, I'm afraid, sir, but certainly by reputation. The gentleman in question might be Papirius Primus, perhaps? He's one of our regular customers, and very knowledgeable and discriminating.'

'Well done you! Spot on!' I beamed. 'That's the very bunny. Apologies – forget my own head if it wasn't screwed on. Papirius Primus, as ever was. Lovely chap.'

'In that case I'm sure there'll be no objection. We're not too busy this morning – end of the sailing season, you know, that's always a quiet time – so I'm sure I can spare the lad for half an hour or so.'

'That would be excellent. Thank you.'

'You can use my office, if you like. It's quite comfortable.'

'Actually prefer the fresh air myself, if it's all the same to you.' The last thing I wanted was for him to burst in at an inconvenient moment with an armful of samples. 'Doctor's orders. Get the old humours in proper balance again, know what I mean?'

'As you like, sir. Well, I'll leave you to it. A pleasure to meet you. No doubt we'll see you when the time comes.'

'Indeed. Indeed you will.'

He drifted off. I waited until the customer had left and went over to the counter.

'Gaius Frontius?' I said.

He frowned. 'That's right, sir. Who are you?'

'Valerius Corvinus.' Then, quietly: 'I want to talk to you about Titus Marcius.'

'*What?*' He gave me a scared look. I glanced across at his boss, but another customer had come in and luckily his attention was taken.

'No hassle, pal,' I said. 'I guarantee it. But we do need to talk. Outside, and now. You okay with that?'

He nodded dumbly; he looked sick.

'Fine.' I turned and went towards the door, without checking whether he was following.

He was. 'I'd nothing to do with that,' he said when he'd carefully closed the door behind him. 'Gods be my witness. Atia neither.'

I glanced up and down the quay. There was a small shrine, probably to one of the local sea-nymphs, a dozen yards from us, with a low wall around it.

'Fair enough,' I said. 'We'll sit down over there and you can tell me your version of things.'

'What d'you mean, my version?' He followed me over, and we sat. 'I told you, I don't know nothing about the old man's death. Nothing at all. Zero. Zilch.'

I shrugged. 'Your landlady and Atia's sister-in-law Gellia think you do. In fact, they have you pegged as the killer. Mind you, to be fair, they're both on your side.'

'Fulgentia's barking mad. And 'cording to Atia Gellia's a fucking drunk. They can believe what they like, the pair of them, but it don't make it true. I never touched Marcius, never even set eyes on him.' I said nothing, just waited patiently. 'All right. So what do you want to know?'

'You're having an affair with Atia, yes?'

He gave me a defiant look. 'If that's what you call it when some old bastard slimes in and marries your fiancée and you keep on seeing her, sure.'

'You were engaged?'

'Good as. Her father wouldn't have it, but she was working on him. Then Marcius turns up and flashes his money around and that was that.' He scowled. 'What'd you expect me to do?'

'Find another girl. Find another job. Maybe move towns. You have any ties here?'

'Nah. Me mam's long dead, dad skippered a cargo boat till it went down five years ago and took him with it. Couple of uncles and cousins, but they're in Tarentum.'

'So why not go there?'

He stared at me. 'And leave Atia behind? No fucking way!'

'That may not be a problem now that her husband's out of the picture.'

'Look.' He got to his feet. 'Are you trying to set me up for this? Because I've already told you–'

'That you had nothing to do with Marcius's murder. Yeah; I got that part. Even so, you won't come out of it too badly, will you? Girlfriend a rich widow, free to do as she likes, go where she likes. Remarry, even. Which, incidentally, your landlady tells me she's already planning to do, with you as the other partner to the arrangement. Oh, and by the way, the old man was killed just a few hundred yards from here, with what I'm reliably told was a belaying pin. Plenty of those in your boss's shop, I expect, and they make really good clubs, perfect for the job. So come on, pal. I need a bit more than just a bare denial here.'

He sat down again, slowly. 'All right,' he said. 'How can I make you believe me?'

'By being totally up front, for a start. First off: the affair – we'll keep calling it that, if you don't mind – has been going on ever since the marriage, yes?'

'Since the engagement. Marcius's engagement, that is, when Atia's father stopped us seeing each other. So for about a year now.'

'And you meet at your lodgings?'

'Twice a month. Every second Ninth Day. I get those off. When the old man was alive Atia'd make up some excuse to give him if he asked, say she was going out shopping or visiting a friend, something like that. When Gellia took up with her it was easy, because she was happy to cover for us.'

'Your landlady was okay with this? I mean–'

'I know what you mean. Sure she was. Fulgentia may have a few tiles loose, but she's okay. And she knew the history. Besides, she don't go out much nor have all that many visitors, so Atia's maid keeps her company while we're together.'

'Did Atia ever stay the night? When the old man was alive, that is.'

'Once or twice, yeah. When he was away on business.'

'She could do that?'

'She was safe enough. The family slaves all knew that if they peached she'd trump up an excuse and get them flogged. She'd've done it, too, no worries.' His lips twisted with pride. 'That's my girl, Corvinus. Tough as old boots, is Atia. Tougher than me, that's for sure.'

Yeah, I was beginning to appreciate that. Also, if I was reading things right, a whole heap less starry-eyed and more practical. It was easy to see who the brains was of the partnership. 'But she didn't sleep over the night Marcius was murdered?' I said.

'Nah. It was a Ninth Day night, sure, as I recall, but the old man was at home. Not that he paid her much attention in that way, but there was always the chance he'd come to her room, or tell her to come to his, so she couldn't risk it.'

'How about here, at the shop? Does she ever call in here, at all?'

'No way! Nor at her home. She ha'n't been near either of her parents since the wedding. Anyways, once she was engaged to Marcius her father wouldn't never've let the two of us meet, not even in the shop, not even if he was there himself.' He frowned. 'Hang on, though, I tell a lie. She did drop by, just the once.'

'Yeah?' My interest sharpened. 'When was that?'

Another scowl. 'Look,' he said, 'I don't carry a fucking calendar around in my head, okay? And there was nothing special about the visit; she was up this way with her maid in any case, she knew her father took an hour off for lunch at noon, she risked a quick visit and that was that. No big deal. The place was heaving, so we'd hardly time to speak, even, let alone anything else.'

'This was before her husband died or after?'

'Before. I remember that much. What does it matter?'

'It doesn't.' Yeah, right! Or possibly, right. 'I was just asking. So when did you find out about the murder?'

'From Atia, the next Ninth Day I was free.' So only half a month ago. 'But one of the customers'd mentioned it the day after the body was found, so I knew already.'

'Her father didn't tell you himself?'

'Nah. But then he wouldn't; he never so much as spoke Atia's name to me after the engagement. Far as I was concerned she din't exist no more.'

Fair enough. 'So what now? What are your plans, exactly? You and her?'

He shrugged. 'Ha'n't decided yet, not altogether. But like Fulgentia probably told you, soon as the time's ripe we'll get married, move somewhere else. Tarentum, maybe Puteoli or some other big port. Ostia, even. Use her money to open a chandler's shop, or buy one that's already there. I know where I am with chandlery.'

'What about her father?'

'That bastard? He can do what he likes, as far as we're concerned. Her mother, too. They sold her to begin with and we're finished with them.'

'And Atia's happy with all that? Running out on her family and being a chandler's wife?'

'Sure she is. We wouldn't be doing it that way if she wasn't, would we?'

'No, I don't suppose you would, at that.' I stood up. 'Okay, friend. That's your lot. Grilling over.'

He looked surprised. 'You're done with me?'

'I think so, sure. Certainly for the present. Unless there's anything else you want to say.'

'Nothing. There's nothing. I told you.'

'Right, then. Thanks, pal. I'll see you around.'

I left him sitting and walked back along the quay towards the Marcius building.

I was just coming in the door when I spotted Titus talking to one of the clerks.

Uh-oh.

He came over. 'Corvinus!' he said. 'I've just sent a message to your house.'

'Is that so?' I said cautiously. Then, to get in first: 'Any news of your daughter?'

'Yes. That was the reason for the message. One of the slaves from the local Isis temple came round with a letter from her while I was having breakfast. Seemingly that's where she is. She's decided to get herself initiated as a priestess.'

'Really?'

'Really.' He frowned. 'I can't say I'm altogether pleased, to put it mildly, but I'm not unduly surprised: she's always had a bent that way, and I knew she wasn't happy about the marriage. She's alive and safe, that's the main thing, but of course it throws this whole deal with the Pettii into the melting-pot. Quintus Cluvius is furious.'

'Yeah,' I said. 'He would be.'

'I'll try to persuade her to reconsider, naturally, as will Septimia, but I don't hold out much hope. If it had been something more straightforward, like an elopement, then no doubt something could have been done. As it is...' He shrugged. 'Well, it's no concern of yours.'

'She, uh, say anything in the letter about the missing ring?' I asked casually.

'No. Why should she?'

'No reason. I just wondered.'

'That's gone for good, I suspect. Not that it matters, except of course where the intrinsic value of the thing is concerned. Unless she changes her mind, which as I say is very unlikely, there'll be no wedding now, whatever else happens. So why are you here this morning, yourself?'

'Just a couple of things I wanted to check up on.' Considering the reason I had for making it, I wasn't going to mention the upcoming visit to the old offices to Titus; no way. 'You wouldn't know whether your brother's around, would you? I haven't managed to talk to him at all so far.'

'Aulus? No. He doesn't come in all that often. He tends to be out and about with his friend Marcus Cluvius most of the time.'

Said with a tone that was completely devoid of expression. Yeah, well; I wasn't particularly disappointed, quite the reverse: before I talked to Aulus Marcius I wanted to check out his love nest. If that's what it was.

'No problem,' I said. 'Uh...the other thing I had earmarked for this morning was a chat with your wife. You know whether she'll be at home later?'

'I really don't know. You'll have to go round and see.' He hesitated. Then he said, more quietly: 'It's... You mentioned both of them practically in the same breath. Septimia and my brother.'

'Did I? It wasn't intentional.'

'I'm not a complete fool, Corvinus, so don't take me for one. Nor am I blind.' I said nothing. 'I know perfectly well what's going on between them; I just don't particularly care, that's all. Perhaps now that Marcia has gone things will be different, but for the moment I'm content to leave well alone. Now' –

he raised his voice – 'I'll let you get on. I simply thought I'd better pass on the news as soon as I could.'

He gave me a parting nod and made his way between the desks towards the stair.

Uh-huh. Interesting. I carried on to Eudoxus's cubby and collected his spare key.

Sure enough, there was a wooden staircase on the blind side of the building, leading to a door at the top. I climbed it and put the key in the lock.

The key turned. What was more, unlike the one on the downstairs door, the lock had been oiled.

Bull's-eye!

The door opened onto a small lobby. Beyond it was the living-room of a self-contained flat, furnished – I could see in the shafts of light that came in through the slats in the shutters – with a low table, a couple of couches, a dresser with shelves, and two six-lamp candelabra. There was no trace of the musty, disused smell that I'd met with downstairs on my previous visit; if anything, all my nose picked up was a faint scent of perfume.

I left the front-facing shutters closed and went through to the neighbouring room.

The main bedroom, obviously, overlooking the harbour. This time I did open the shutters.

An unmade bed, with rumpled sheets and a blanket lying on the floor next to it. On the bedside table, a tray with a stoppered wine-flask and two cups, one still half full of wine. The room's single clothes chest had a man's clothes inside – just the basic stuff, underwear and a couple of clean tunics – while on top of the dressing-table next to the window was a bronze hand-mirror and a woman's make-up box. There was a small glass perfume bottle, empty, beside them. I picked it up, sniffed it, and put it back...

'Find what you were looking for?'

Shit! I turned round.

The guy was standing in the doorway leaning against the jamb, arms folded. Big, broad-faced, florid, with thick lips and a fleshy nose: a professional boxer gone to seed.

'Aulus Marcius, right?' I said.

'And you're Valerius Corvinus.' He uncrossed his arms and straightened, but stayed where he was, blocking the exit. 'Like to tell me what you're doing here?'

'Checking out the rest of the building. I was round a couple of days ago, taking a look at the offices downstairs. Turned out that was where your father was murdered.'

'Is that so, now?' Not a smidgeon of surprise, but then he'd've known that already. One way or another. 'So why come up here? As you can see, it's a completely separate property. And in use. Private use.'

I ignored the stress he'd put on the penultimate word. 'Yeah, well, I'd say that was rather obvious, wouldn't you?' I said. 'The key fits both doors, and separate or not they're both part of the same building.'

'Is that an accusation?' He said it quietly, with what, presumably, he meant as an undertone of humour but certainly didn't come across that way.

'Should it be?'

'You'd be a fool to make it if it was.' I tensed, but he still hadn't moved. 'You've talked to Marcus, I understand. Marcus Cluvius.'

'Yeah,' I said. 'We spoke.'

'So you'll know exactly where I – we – stand regarding the old man's death.'

'Uh-huh. According to him, the killer did you both a favour because he was getting in the way of your plans for the company. There was more, of course, but I think that about covers it.'

'Not quite. According to what he told me he also warned you to keep your fucking nose out of our private business. So I'd be very, very careful when it comes to tossing unsubstantiated accusations around.' He smiled. 'Or even substantiated ones, for that matter, if they're the wrong type.'

'You mean there's an overlap between your private business and my investigation into your father's murder? Now that *is* interesting.'

The smile disappeared. 'Don't be clever, Corvinus,' he said. 'Believe me, it isn't safe. You've had your warning, and that's that. You choose to ignore it, well, it's your funeral.'

'Fair enough.' I turned my back on him, and picked up the perfume bottle again. 'Nice little set-up you have here. Very comfortable. I hope Septimia approves.'

'She's not all that concerned about the decor.' No surprise in his voice this time, either. 'So you know about her and me?'

'Open secret, pal, according to your wife.' I replaced the bottle and turned back round. 'That worry you?'

'Not particularly.' He'd come a couple of paces into the room.

I moved further towards the window, trying not to make the move too obvious. 'How long has the affair been going on?' I said.

I needn't have bothered being careful; his eyes measured the change in the distance between us and he smiled again.

'About a year and a half,' he said. 'Maybe a bit longer.'

'But according to the janitor Eudoxus you only asked for the key to this place about two months ago. If it's so perfect then why not before?'

'Simple; because I hadn't thought of it. Then I did. And if you're being pruriently curious before that we used the spare room of one of the family's more venal freedmen. Pricey and fairly basic, but it served the purpose.'

'You come here a lot, the pair of you?'

'As often as we can. Which is maybe six, seven times a month.'

'Overnight?'

'About half of that. Neither of us has much difficulty with the partner side of things.'

'So would you and she have been here the night your father was killed?'
Silence. I tensed again, but he stepped aside, away from the door.
'Maybe you'd better leave now,' he said quietly.
I shrugged. 'Suits me, pal. I've seen all I wanted to see. A pleasure meeting you at last. Oh, and I'd have a word with whoever cleans the room. Or doesn't, rather. The place is a pit.'
And on that cheap note I left.

Okay, so now for the other member of the partnership, if she was around. I'd just, of course – unexpectedly, although never mind that – talked to Aulus, but I'd no other plans for this morning, and Septimia might be more forthcoming. Plus there was the Sextus Pettius side of things to look into.

According to the door-slave, the lady was in but being dressed and having her hair done, so I kicked my heels on a stool in the atrium for half an hour or so before she finally turned up.

'Valerius Corvinus,' she said. 'What a pleasure.' Not according to her tone of voice, mind, and the look I got would've curdled milk. She sat down on the chair next to the ornamental pool and straightened the folds of her impressive and seriously-pricey mantle. 'I'm afraid I have to go out very shortly, so your visit will be brief. Given that, how can I help you?'

'I've just been round to the company offices,' I said. Her blue-tinted eyelids flickered. 'The new ones, that is. According to your husband you've had news of Marcia.'

'Yes indeed.' She frowned. 'Silly girl. She always was obsessed with that sort of thing, even as a small child, but to actually decide to give up a perfectly good prospective marriage and make it her life simply beggars belief. I'll talk to her, of course, and to the High Priestess, in the hope that one of them will see sense, but I'm not optimistic.'

'Yeah,' I said. 'That was more or less your husband's view. So you're disappointed that the marriage won't happen after all?'

'Of course I am. It was all arranged months ago, and naturally now all the arrangements have to be cancelled. Not to mention this agreement with the Pettii, although that is Titus's concern far more than mine.'

'You'll be sorry to lose Sextus Pettius as your son-in-law too, I expect.'

She shot me a suspicious look, but I was keeping my expression neutral. 'Not particularly,' she said. 'Not in himself, although Marcia could have done much worse. Why do you ask that?'

'No particular reason.'

'Well, then.' She made a move to get up. 'If that's all you came for I really must be–'

'Aulus Marcius,' I said.

She sat down again. 'What about him?'

'I was just wondering. You and he spend a lot of time together in the flat above the old company offices overlooking the Neck, yes?'

She was staring at me. *'How dare you?'*

'Where, if you didn't know already, your father-in-law was murdered. At least, it was done in the offices themselves, on the ground floor, but it comes to the same thing.'

'You will leave! Now! Or I'll have the slaves throw you out!'

I didn't move. 'You want me to draw my own conclusions and take things from there, lady?' I said. 'Or do we talk this through sensibly?'

She was quiet for a long time. I waited. Finally, she said: 'Aulus didn't kill his father. And neither, before you ask, did I.'

'So who did?'

'I have absolutely no idea.'

I sighed. 'Okay. Perhaps you should tell me what happened from the beginning. You were both there that night, weren't you?'

'As it happens, we were, yes.' She gave me a defiant look. 'My hearing is much more acute than Aulus's. It must have been about midnight, perhaps a little before, when I heard noises downstairs.'

'What kind of noises?'

'Voices. Raised voices. Two men, I think, although I can't be totally sure. The floor is thick planking, and the sounds were very muffled.'

'Uh-huh. They were arguing?'

'It sounded that way, certainly.'

'You didn't hear anything of what was said?'

'No; as I say it's a very thick floor. Finally, there was a series of thumps, and then silence.' She hesitated. 'We were...rather busy at the time, so it was several minutes before I told Aulus about it, and he took the key and went down to see what was going on. There was no one about, but the downstairs front door was open. My...according to Aulus, my father-in-law was lying on his front just inside, with the back of his head beaten in.' She paused, took a small handkerchief from her mantle-fold, and dabbed at her lips. 'Quite dead, of course, that much was obvious. Aulus dragged the body over to the window, opened the shutters and tipped it over the sill into the Neck. Then he closed the shutters, locked the door behind him and came up and told me.'

'You didn't think, either of you, that it might've been a good idea to have left things as they were, I suppose?' I said. 'Reported what had happened in the morning?'

She just looked at me. 'Certainly not. We had our reputations to consider, and the old man was dead, after all. Added to which the current would carry the body down towards the sea, so there would be nothing to link the office building – and us – with the murder. Everything considered it was all rather fortuitous, really. We went back to bed, and that was that.'

Gods! Talk about callous! Still, looked at from their point of view – and given the type of people they were – it was fair enough. 'He – Aulus – didn't see the murder weapon?' I said.

'He didn't look for it. Why should he? All he was concerned about was getting rid of the body itself. Besides, it was pitch dark, of course, until the shutters were open, and he had only taken down the one lamp.' She smoothed down her mantle again. 'Now, if that really is everything you need from me I must be–'

'Not quite, lady,' I said. 'You're also having an affair with Sextus Pettius, yes?'

Her hand paused. 'Who told you that?' she snapped. I waited. 'So what if I am? What business is it of yours?'

'Does your brother-in-law know?'

'Absolutely not! And he mustn't; Aulus would kill him if he ever found out. He's very...possessive.'

'How long has that been going on?'

'Not very long. For just under a year.'

Since the marriage and the deal with the Pettii were arranged, in other words. Which made complete sense. 'Did you start it, or did he?' I said.

'He did. If you must know.' She was pouting slightly, like a spoilt child. 'Corvinus, this has nothing whatsoever to do with my father-in-law's death. The business at the old offices, yes, I grant you, you were within your rights to question me about those, but my relationship with Sextus is–'

'He's been using you to get inside information on what's happening on the Marcius side of the fence, hasn't he?'

'On occasion, yes. Although I know very little about the business aspect of things, and neither Titus nor Aulus discuss them with me.' She allowed herself a small smile. 'For differing reasons, naturally.'

'You told him about the terms of the new will?'

'Yes again, as it happens. What was wrong with that?'

'So what were your intentions after the marriage? Where the affair was concerned?'

She smiled again. 'Oh, I doubt if that would have changed things much,' she said. 'You've met my daughter, so you'll agree that she would hardly have been the sort of wife to keep Sextus's interest alive past the wedding night, if that. As long as Aulus remained in ignorance I would have been quite happy to have let things go on as they were.'

'What about your husband?'

'Finding out, you mean?' Now she actually laughed. 'Oh, dear, I really couldn't care less about that eventuality. Besides, Titus is the most incurious man I know. I could commit adultery with either Aulus or Sextus under his very nose and I doubt if he would even notice.' Yeah, right; I already knew how valid a judgment *that* was, as far as Aulus was concerned, at least. It would be interesting to know just how far the second part held good. 'Still, I suppose now that Marcia has decided to devote herself to a life of chaste piety there will have to be a certain amount of adaptation.'

'Assuming that Sextus is still interested in you,' I said.

The smile disappeared. 'I beg your pardon?'

I shrugged. 'I've met your daughter's fiancé as well, remember, and he didn't exactly strike me as the burning-with-passion type either. Now that the business part of the deal has fallen through – as, presumably, it has – I'm wondering what's in it for him any longer. Apart from your physical charms, that is. Just a thought.'

She coloured to her plucked eyebrows and got to her feet. I thought she was going to slap me, but she simply said, very coldly: 'You will leave now. *Go!*'

I rose. Yeah, well, possibly not the most tactful observation to come out with at the end of an interview, but I hadn't been able to resist it. And it was certainly true enough: as far as her role as provider of inside information went, sweet Septimia had served her purpose. 'A pushy bitch who believes she's the gods' gift to men', wasn't that the way Sextus had described her to me when I'd talked to him? He could've been covering, of course, but taken all in all with how the guy had come across in general I'd say it had been the closest you'd get to an honest opinion.

I almost felt sorry for the lady. Almost, but not quite.

Anyway. Home, to check up on what was happening there.

12.

Bathyllus was waiting for me in the lobby when I opened the door. I swapped my damp cloak for the cup of wine he was holding.

'The mistress back yet?' I said.

'Yes, sir.' He hung the cloak up on one of the pegs. 'She's in the study. And you had two messages come for you this morning shortly after you left.'

'Two?' I carried the wine-cup through to the atrium. 'One was from Titus Marcius, I know. About his daughter. Who was the other from?'

'Lucius Pettius, sir. He said it was urgent, and would you come round to his offices as soon as possible.'

'No details?'

'None. I did ask, but the messenger refused to say.'

Odd; the last time – the *only* time, two days before – that I'd seen Pettius Senior he'd made it clear that as far as he was concerned if our paths never crossed again it'd still be too soon. Also, that the investigation into old Marcius's death had nothing to do with him and he'd prefer if it stayed that way until hell froze. So why the change of mind? Not to mention the urgency?

Yeah, well; whatever it was it could wait until tomorrow. The rain had started in earnest, I really didn't fancy a return trip to the harbour district involving a two-way crossing of the Neck this late in the day, and whatever had got the old man's knickers in a twist he could just possess himself with patience. I collected the wine-jug from Bathyllus and took it and the cup through with me to the study.

Perilla was stretched out on the reading-couch with a book roll.

'Oh, hello, Marcus,' she said. 'Successful day?'

'Eventful, certainly.' I kissed her, set the cup and jug down on the table, and pulled up one of the wickerwork chairs. 'You?'

'Not particularly. Sentia took me to visit some friends, but the weather was absolutely foul and when we left I decided to come straight home and finish Eumenes off before Sentia took him back. Which I've almost done.' She laid the roll aside. 'So. Did you talk to Atia's boyfriend?'

'Yeah.' I gave her the details. 'He may still turn out to be the killer, but I doubt it: he hasn't got the mileage, and he struck me as genuine. Simple, but genuine. Atia herself, mind, she's another matter entirely; I reckon given the necessity she could have done it without batting an eyelash. Planned it out, too, right to the extent of filching a suitable weapon from her father's chandlery.'

'Surely that's an argument against her being responsible? After all, if she's as clever as you say then she'd know that to use something from the shop to murder her husband would attract attention. To her or at least to your Frontius.'

'Yeah. True. Plus from what Septimia said – I'll come to her later – the murderer was probably a man. Although to be fair she couldn't swear to it.' I drank some of the wine. 'It was only an idea. But having seen the boyfriend I can understand why she would be desperate to make the switch. Simple the guy may be, but he is pure maiden's-prayer beefcake.'

'Really?' Perilla said drily.

I grinned. 'Believe it. No wonder Landlady Fulgentia was so taken. If Atia waits one minute longer than the minimum-prescribed mourning period to hitch up with him I'll eat my sandals.'

'So. What else did you do today besides drooling over Adonis lookalikes?'

'Checked out the flat over the old Marcius offices,' I said. 'And it *was* a flat. Oh, and got caught by Aulus Marcius while I did it.'

'*What?*'

'No sweat. Strangely enough, barring a smidgeon of natural indignation he didn't take it too amiss as such that I was furkling around up there. Not that there was anything incriminating to find, mark you, given that he was pretty well up-front about the Septimia side of things.' I gave her an outline. 'The really interesting thing was the conversation I had with Septimia afterwards. Seemingly she and Aulus were in residence the night of the murder and were responsible for getting rid of the body.'

I told her the whole story.

'You believe her?' Perilla said when I'd finished.

'Yeah, I think so,' I said. 'Certainly what she said fits the facts as far as we know them. Plus pitching the corpse into the Neck and going back to bed as if nothing had happened is just the sort of thing that pair of lovelies would do. And with the two properties – upstairs and downstairs – being completely separate, given that there were no lights showing in the flat the killer wouldn't know there was anyone else in the building at all.'

'Unless he or she already knew and didn't care. Quite the reverse, in fact.'

I frowned. 'Ah... just run that last bit past me again, would you?' I said.

'It's just a thought. What if the killer knew that Aulus and Septimia were using the flat upstairs for their meetings? And that he'd chosen the venue for the murder deliberately because of it? If the old man were found dead in an unused set of offices to which his younger son was known to have the key, and that furthermore he was using the flat upstairs as a place to conduct his affair with Septimia, then... You see?'

Oh, shit. I leaned back. 'You're saying the plan was to frame Aulus for the murder?'

'It's certainly one possibility, isn't it? Given you accept that Septimia is telling the truth and Aulus was genuinely innocent.'

'Yeah. Yeah, it is.' Gods! It would've worked, too: if Septimia hadn't heard the noises and sent Aulus down to investigate, the body would've stayed where it was until someone thought to check the offices themselves. Which, no doubt following an unobtrusive prompt on the part of the killer, whoever he or she might be, would've happened pretty damn soon. And assuming said killer had made the running initially as far as setting up the rendezvous was concerned it would certainly explain the choice of venue. 'So. If you're right then where does it leave us in the way of possible perps?'

'Obviously with anyone who for any reason wanted Aulus gone.'

'Fair enough.' I reached for the wine-cup and took a decent swallow. 'Let's start with Brother Titus.'

'Very well.' Perilla shifted on the couch and straightened a fold in her overmantle. 'Motive?'

'Two of them. Aulus is screwing his wife and he's also his main rival in the succession stakes. I'd say that makes him pretty well a front runner.'

'Hold on, dear. You're forgetting that the murder happened before the new will was read. As far as Titus was concerned at that point he was his father's named heir, home and clear. And do you actually *know* that Titus was aware at the time of his wife's adultery? Not to mention where she and Aulus were meeting.'

Bugger, I hated it when she nit-picked! 'Look, lady,' I said. 'This is your theory, not mine, okay? You want to take over, you go ahead. Otherwise just keep it shut. Bargain?'

She smiled and ducked her head. 'All right. But they are valid points, both of them.'

True, unfortunately. 'As far as the second goes the answer's no to both halves,' I said. 'I don't know; not for sure. Still, let's indulge ourselves for now subject to later correction and assume that he sodding well was aware, both of the existence of the affair itself and the location. Agreed?'

'Very well.'

'Thank you. First point. The succession. Even if, technically, Brother Titus was down to succeed the old man we know that things weren't that simple. Aulus and Marcus Cluvius had been carving out a separate niche for themselves in the company and gathering a lot of support, which meant chances were that by the time Marcius Senior finally keeled over Titus would have a real fight on his hands, to say the least of it. Plus, of course, there was the upcoming problem of Sextus Pettius. By killing his father and implicating his brother he'd be killing two birds with one stone. Three, in fact, because with the old man out of the picture and him left in charge the agreement with the Pettii needn't be a done deal any longer. Particularly since it'd be his own daughter providing the link.' I swallowed some more of the wine and refilled the cup. 'So. Happy with all that?'

'Mostly, yes.' She was twisting her lock of hair. 'Even so, he would still have to have come up with a decent excuse for bringing his father to the offices, wouldn't he?'

Jupiter give me patience or strike me dead! 'Gods, Perilla, what do you want, jam on it? Of course he fucking would! *Anyone* would, down to and including the family cat! Just forget about means for the present, will you? We're only looking at possible motive here, nothing else, okay?'

'All right, dear, there's no need to swear. And yes, as far as motive goes all that qualifies Titus quite well, I think.'

'Good.'

'Who's your next candidate?'

'Yeah, well, that'd be Sextus Pettius.'

'Hmm.' She looked doubtful. 'Go on. Reasons?'

'Not the jealousy aspect. Oh, sure, given he's having an affair with Septimia himself that might've figured, technically at least, but that horse won't run. First, he's known all about her relationship with Aulus from the start, and it doesn't bother him; quite the opposite, because I reckon it was his main reason for getting involved with her in the first place. The business side of things, now, that's another matter entirely. He's a cold fish, Sextus, and unlike Aulus and Marcus Cluvius, who are just thugs pure and simple, he's very, very smart. This way he'd be getting rid of his main potential rival without any risk to himself.'

'Yes, but surely killing the old man would be completely counter-productive.' She pulled on the strand of hair. 'After all, it's totally in his best interests to keep him alive, at least until after the wedding.'

'Unless he knows about the contents of the new will. Which, if you remember, he does.'

'But he got that information through Septimia, who presumably had it either *propria persona* if she was present when it was opened or afterwards from Titus or Aulus. In either case, obviously, the murder had already happened. Besides, why should knowing the terms affect anything at all?'

I shook my head. 'Uh-uh. First, we can't be absolutely certain about the timing here. Oh, sure, the likelihood is that he only got the information after the fact, but like I said when we discussed the will in the first place, leaks happen. Second, if he *did* know beforehand that, with the old man gone, the probability was that he'd be facing not walkover-Titus but his pushy brother as his de facto rival then coming up with a scheme to anticipate things by getting rid of Aulus would make perfect sense.'

'Not perfect, dear; far from it. You're fudging again and you know it.'

'Yeah? How so?'

'I said: killing Marcius would put his own position in serious jeopardy, particularly if the death took place before the wedding. It was Marcius who brokered both the marriage and the agreement, and who, if your theory holds good, would be instrumental in manoeuvring Sextus into a position from which he could eventually take control of the company. Surely the game would simply not be worth the candle; it would be far, far too risky. Now please do be sensible.'

'Okay. Fair enough. So just answer me two questions, will you?'

She sniffed. 'Very well.'

'One. Where was the body found?'

She gave me a blank look. 'I beg your pardon?'

'It's a simple question, lady. No tricks.'

'Floating next to the quay further down the Neck, of course. What has that got to do with anything?'

'Not where the killer left it, in the old offices underneath the flat where, at the time of the murder, Aulus was having it off with Septimia, then?'

'Marcus...'

I held up a hand. 'Look, all I'm saying is that if the plan was to nail Aulus as the killer, it didn't work, okay? So as far as motive goes we're dealing in might-have-beens. Agreed?'

'I suppose so, yes. Go on. Second question.'

'So Aulus is still around. Second question: who's running things at present, on a day-to-day basis?'

'Marcus, I really think–'

'Just answer the question.'

She sighed. 'From everything you've told me so far I would assume Quintus Cluvius.'

'And is he for or against the deal with the Pettii?'

'That's a third question, dear. And this is getting very silly.'

'You're obfuscating, lady. Or possibly just trying to bugger me about. Let's just have an answer, please.'

'Very well. He's in favour of it. As far as we know.'

'Right. And that's with the lad still alive and kicking, with his honour unsullied. So back to the might-have-been. If Aulus had been chopped for parricide according to plan – and you can bet Cluvius would've stood back and applauded while it happened, because there's no love lost there – the smart money would've been on the marriage and the deal going ahead regardless. Only this time with just Titus in the opposite corner.'

'What about Aulus's partner? Cluvius's son? He would be even more dangerous, surely.'

'Not without Aulus himself to give him legitimacy. Marcus Cluvius could be the power behind the throne, sure, no question, but never the actual boss. Anyway, I reckon Sextus could take him, easy.' I emptied the wine-cup and poured myself a refill. 'So. That's the theory, as far as he's concerned, anyway. What do you think?'

'It's still very thin, dear, to put it mildly. But I have to say you made a better case than I thought you would.'

'Gee, thanks.'

'Anyone else?' She frowned. 'No, there isn't, really, is there? Not if you're taking removing Aulus as your primary factor.'

'Actually, yeah, there is. Quintus Cluvius.'

She sat up straight. '*What?* Marcus, you can *not* be serious!'

'Why not? I just said, he's no fan of Aulus Marcius, far from it. That much was obvious when I talked to him. Nor of Aulus's and his son's plans for the company, either. On the other hand, reading between the lines, he's got more time for Titus and his picture of a better, cleaner world than most. Yeah, I'd take a side bet on Cluvius being our perp any day.'

'For goodness' sake! He was Marcius's deputy and friend for over twenty years!'

'Admitted. The deputy part, anyway; the friend bit we're only taking on trust.'

'That is pure supposition, and not even credible supposition, at that! Besides, apart from his dislike of Aulus what motive could he possibly have had?'

'The up and coming wedding and the deal with the Pettii, for a start.'

'*What?*' She sat up on the couch. 'Now you wait one small second, Marcus! You've just said yourself – and used as part of an argument, what's more – that Cluvius was in favour of both. So how the *hell* can you suddenly–'

'Don't swear.'

'–decide to do a complete *volte-face* and cite opposition to them as his reason for killing a friend and colleague of twenty years' standing? That is pure unadulterated sophistry, it makes no conceivable sense, and I will swear if I like, when and whenever I choose to do so!'

I grinned; it wasn't often that Perilla lost the rag. 'Yeah, well, I was making a case for Sextus being the perp then, wasn't I?' I said. 'This is a different scenario altogether. Oh, sure, the guy claims to be in favour of the deal, no question, but that's all it is, a claim; when push comes to shove his word is all we have to go on.'

'Why on earth *shouldn't* he be in favour? After all–'

'Look, Perilla. While Marcius was alive he wouldn't have had much of an option but to agree, okay? Oh, he may have privately disapproved, maybe even argued the toss with the old man before things were settled, but don't forget that Marcius had the final word. Even so, the companies had been at loggerheads for practically a generation. The fact that old Marcius had decided unilaterally to bury the hatchet doesn't mean to say that everyone else was happy to do it. Far from it; in fact the chances were that given the option they'd rather see hell freeze first. And forget the move towards shifting the company's activities into more legitimate channels; if Marcius's plan were to go through to its logical conclusion it'd be business as usual, only with a Pettius in charge. How do you think Cluvius would feel about that?'

'None too happy, I admit. But unhappy enough to commit a murder?'

'The guy's no shrinking violet, lady. If he thought it was necessary, and the only way forward, yeah, I can see that he might. And with both Marcius and Aulus disposed of as the de iure and de facto head of the company Titus would be off and running.'

'There would still be the question of the marriage.'

'Maybe Cluvius had plans to stop that too. We don't know; it's another of the might-have-beens. In any event the chances are that now Marcia's done a runner the deal is off the board altogether, so that's something he doesn't need to worry about. Even so–'

'Excuse me, sir. Madam.'

I turned round. Bathyllus had just buttled in through the door.

'Yeah? What is it, Bathyllus?' I said. 'Not dinner time yet, surely?'

'No, sir. It's Alexis. If you're free he would like a word.'

Hey! The wanderer returned! 'Yeah, fine,' I said. 'Send him in.' Bathyllus exited and the lad himself shuffled round the jamb. 'So, Alexis, how's it going? Anything to report?'

'Not really, sir.' He cleared his throat. 'Or at least nothing much, and it's probably not important. In fact, it's not even current, as it were, far from it. Still, I thought–'

'Come on, pal,' I said. 'We're hoping to be home before the Winter Festival. Spit it out.'

'I'm sorry.' He reddened. 'It was only a rumour, even at the time, and the man I was talking to could provide no corroborating details whatsoever, but–'

'Alexis...'

'The dead man's first wife, sir. Faustina, her name was. According to my informant the rumour at the time she died was that Marcius had killed her.'

'*What?*' I goggled at him. 'How? *Why?*'

'I've no idea, sir. I'm afraid that's all there is, because as I said, the man couldn't supply any details. And it was over twenty years ago, after all. All the same, I thought you would want to know.'

'Yeah. Yes, I would. Do. Whatever.' Gods! 'That's really all he could tell you?'

'Yes, sir. Mind you, he was pretty pi-' – he glanced at Perilla – 'drunk at the time. We were in a wineshop.'

'Yeah, I'd sort of gathered that.' Well, like the guy said it probably wasn't important, and as news went it wasn't so much old as fossilised. Even so, that figure of twenty-odd years was cropping up with monotonous regularity, which was far too close to a coincidence for comfort. Certainly it was something worth checking up on further. 'Well done, Alexis,' I said. 'Keep up the good work. You still all right for cash? No, never mind.' I opened my belt-pouch, took out two or three silver pieces and a few coppers, and handed them over. 'That should keep you going, just in case.'

'Thank you, sir.' He hesitated. 'There was one strange thing happened, though.'

'Yeah? What was that?'

'We were talking, the other customer and I, I'd steered the conversation round to the Marcius family, and he'd just told me what I told you when a man who'd been drinking at the other end of the bar came over and deliberately jogged my elbow so that I spilled my drink.'

'Deliberately? You're sure?'

'Absolutely. It was a full cup, too. We had words, and he drew a knife.'

Oh, shit. I goggled, and Perilla was staring at him as well. Alexis is no puny weakling, sure – all that double-digging and mulching has put on serious muscle where it counts, and he's a big enough lad to start with – but he's no bar-room brawler, either. I should've thought of that aspect of things before I sent him out, at least as a possibility, however many warnings to be careful I laid on him.

'But you're...ah...okay, are you?' I said cautiously. Which, if you like, was a pretty stupid question under the circumstances, but there you went.

'Yes, sir, completely, thanks to Titus Satrius.'

I blinked. 'Come again?'

'That was the strange thing, sir. He–'

Gods! 'Hold on right there, pal,' I said. 'Explanation first. Where does Satrius fit into all this? He was with you?'

'No, sir. I didn't know he was there at all until that point. He must have come in behind me and been sitting at one of the corner tables.'

Jupiter, the slimy, conniving..! 'So what exactly happened?' I said.

'Well, as I say, the man drew a knife and then suddenly Satrius was there and broke his wrist.'

'Just like that?'

'Exactly like that, sir. I heard the bones snap. Five seconds max, from start to finish.' He grinned. 'Very neat, really.'

'What happened then?'

'Nothing. He told me to fu-' – he glanced at Perilla again – 'to go, sir, and it seemed a pretty good idea, so I did. I came straight back here.'

'Fair enough, Alexis,' I said. 'Congratulations again. Uh...maybe on second thoughts you should let things settle for a while.'

'You don't want me to go out again?'

'Not for a couple of days, no. We'll chase this one up first.' Plus the question of Titus sodding Satrius. Oh, sure, I was grateful to him for playing what must essentially have been guardian angel – if the term wasn't laughably inappropriate – to Alexis, really, really grateful, but the bastard could at least have told me what he was up to. One set of mysteries in any given case was quite enough to handle. Whatever joys tomorrow brought – and finding out what was biting Lucius Pettius topped the list – I'd definitely be paying a visit to Satrius's girlfriend in that lingerie shop of hers. If said girlfriend and said shop had any physical existence, that was, which on current showing was a moot point. And now, of course, we had this other business to look into...

Still, we'd see what tomorrow brought.

13.

I was round at the Pettius offices the following morning by midway through the second hour, and I knew it was serious as soon as I set foot inside the building. On the last occasion the clerks' room hadn't exactly been bright with merry carefree banter, but now there was a sort of hushed stillness like you'd get in a house where someone has just died. Which, as it was to transpire, was smack on the button.

The guy on the desk showed me in to Pettius's office without a word and closed the door behind me. Pettius was sitting at his desk. From the looks of him, the guy had slept in his clothes, or more probably hadn't slept at all. Washed or shaved, either.

'You sent a message saying you wanted to see me,' I said. There was a stool to one side of the desk. I pulled it up and sat.

'That's right, I did.' His hands were resting on the desk-top. I noticed they were trembling. 'Sextus was killed two nights ago.'

'*What?*' I stared at him.

'Stabbed in the back on his way home from his local wineshop. The body was found yesterday at first light.'

Shit. 'Uh...I'm sorry,' I said.

'Are you? Are you, indeed? Well, that's nice to know.' His hands balled into fists. 'I just wanted you to take a message back for me. Since you seem to be that fucking family's intermediary at present. You tell Aulus Marcius he's a dead man walking.'

Something cold touched the back of my neck. 'Aulus?' I said. 'Why Aulus?'

'Look, Corvinus, let's not mess about, okay? You know that as well as I do.' He was speaking quietly enough, but he fists were still clenched, so tight that the skin was stretched and white over the knuckles. 'Sextus and Aulus were both screwing that bitch Septimia, Aulus found out he wasn't the only one getting inside her pants, and he decided to sort things out. End of story. The guy's a walking corpse. Tell him.'

'You knew about your son and Septimia?'

'Of course I fucking knew! Gods help me, the affair was my idea in the first place. If she hadn't been of use to us Sextus would've had nothing to do with that conniving whore.'

Yeah, well, I was glad to have that part of it confirmed, at least. 'And that's it?' I said.

'That's what?'

'The only proof you've got that Aulus Marcius was responsible.'

'It's enough. There isn't a mugger in the city would've dared touch Sextus. Besides, his purse was still on his belt.'

'I'm not talking about muggers.'

He frowned. 'If you're saying this had anything to do with Titus Marcius's murder that's garbage.'

'Is it? You're absolutely certain?' The frown didn't shift. 'Look, I'm levelling with you here. You may be right, it could well have been Aulus, absolutely no argument. But there's also a possibility that someone else – someone who has a vested interest in getting rid of him – is trying to set him up.'

'Like who, for example?'

'I don't know yet. Not for sure.' Mind you, with one of our three frame-Aulus-scenario suspects suddenly out of the picture in no uncertain terms the field was shrinking fast. 'Even so, it's a distinct possibility. Kill Aulus now and you might be doing whoever-it-is's job for him. Leave it with me for the moment. See what I can come up with.'

He was quiet for a long time. Then he shrugged.

'Fair enough,' he said. 'You've got five days.'

'Come on, pal! I can't possibly promise to–'

'Five days, Corvinus. On the sixth the bastard's cat's-meat, you have my word on that. It's the best deal you'll get, so take it or leave it.'

Jupiter! 'Okay,' I said. 'I'll take it. Five days. Deal.'

'Deal, then. And if you do find out that it wasn't Aulus Marcius after all then you give me a name. No faffing about, no clever-clever sleuthing stuff, that part's not negotiable. Understood?'

'Yeah. Understood.' He spat on his hand and stretched it out. We shook. 'So. I need to know where it happened. Particularly where this wineshop is.'

'I'll get someone to take you there now. Plus clear it with the owner that it's okay for him to talk to you.' He stood up. 'You're wasting your time, though. I know Aulus fucking Marcius, and he's guilty as hell. Five days.'

I'd imagined, for no good reason, that Sextus's place, and so his local wineshop, would be closer to the town centre than it actually was, but in fact the distance was no more than a few hundred yards. The alleyway where the body had been found was just that: a narrow, barely shoulders-width, passage between two main streets that would've acted as a short-cut between the two, so long as you knew where you were going in the darkness and didn't worry too much about nocturnal entrepreneurs with designs on your purse.

The wineshop itself was on the main drag, and seriously upmarket. Which, I supposed from my brief encounter with Sextus Pettius, wasn't surprising: I couldn't see a guy like that frequenting the sort of spit-and-sawdust places that you got down by the docks themselves, where two or three copper coins would get you not only your jug of wine but the serving girl as a chaser. It was busy, too, despite the early hour.

I went up to the bar.

'Yes, sir, and what can I–?' The barman clocked Pettius's gofer over my shoulder. 'Ah.'

I'd been eyeing the wines chalked up on the board. Greek again, mostly – for some unfathomable reason, these chic bars in the big eastern ports seem to go for Greek – but there was an Alban among them, and since thanks to Sempronius bloody Eutacticus I'd missed out on my usual wineshop binge in Castrimoenium I might as well have it by proxy.

'Make it a cup of the Velletrian,' I said. 'Plus the answers to some questions re Sextus Pettius.'

The guy darted a look at my minder.

'That's perfectly in order, Paullus,' the man said. I'd been expecting, when Pettius had told me he was detailing a facilitator, that it'd be a bare-fisted walnut cracker like Satrius or his local pal Carpus, but in this instance all that was needed, seemingly, was one of the squad of weedy-looking pen-pushers from the clerks' room. Evidently organised crime in Brundisium was a lot more into the soft side of the corporate management ethos than you'd expect. 'Tell the gentleman what he wants to know.' Then, to me: 'I'll be getting back now, sir.'

'Come on, pal.' I took some coins out of my belt-pouch. 'Have a cup of wine before you go, at least.'

But he was already on his way out. Conscientious as well as nerdy: the world of crime certainly wasn't what it used to be. I turned back to the barman and waited until he had filled the cup and returned the flask to its cradle.

'So,' I said. 'Talk to me. What exactly happened? Regarding the killing, I mean?' I took a sip of the wine. Not bad, not bad at all.

'Can't help you much there, sir, I'm afraid.' The barman picked up a cloth and began drying cups. 'Master Sextus left just before closing – that's midnight, when there's a crowd in, which there was – and that was the last I saw of him.'

'He come in here regular?'

'Regular enough. He had his cronies, and I' – he dropped his voice – 'well, between you and me, sir, I know gambling's not allowed as a rule, strictly speaking, but I turn a blind eye so long as it's kept friendly. I've a back room there, just behind the bar, that they use when they've a game on.'

'They used it two nights ago?' I said.

'That they did, yes.'

'And was it? Kept friendly, I mean?'

'It always was. There's nothing in that direction to give you pause, sir, I'd take my oath on that. Money changed hands, 'course it did, but it were never a lot, no more than would pay for the evening's drinks.' Yeah, well, judging by what the one cup of Velletrian had cost me that wouldn't exactly be peanuts. Still, I doubted that it'd amount to anything like a motive for murder. 'And before you ask it were the same five, half dozen gentlemen every time, or some of them, depending who had business elsewhere. No strangers, ever.'

'You see many strangers in here as a rule?'

He laughed. 'Just look around you, sir.' I did; as I said, the place was heaving. 'And compared with the evening shift it's quiet at present. I couldn't put a name to more than two or three of them faces you can see, and I'd wager most of the others'll be up and gone elsewhere before the month's out. We're a port. The place is always full of strangers.'

'So you wouldn't have noticed anyone following him out, then? Sextus? When he left?'

'No chance. Like I said, I'm rushed off my feet evenings as it is, and I've better things to do near closing time than watch who goes out the door, saving your presence. Truth is the emperor Claudius bloody Caesar himself togged out in his purple mantle and olive wreath could've followed the poor gentleman outside and I still wouldn't've noticed. I'm sorry, sir, but that's just how things are.'

Bugger. Well, it had been worth a try. I thanked him, downed the rest of my wine, and left.

So. Next, because we were within striking distance of the market square here, Titus Satrius, via his bit of squeeze, if she existed, the lingerie lady; what was her name? Porcia. Near the temple of Rome and Augustus, Satrius had said, and opposite a wineshop. If he wasn't putting me on it should be easy to find, which was just as well because I didn't particularly relish imagining the looks I'd get if I had to ask for further directions.

It was; another seriously upmarket establishment with three or four expensively-dressed ladies doing a browse and eyeing me keenly and suspiciously in the process while I shifted from foot to foot and waited to be professionally taken notice of. Which I was, ten or so minutes later, after the proprietrix finished serving an obviously pernickety customer and came over.

'Yes, sir. How can I help you?' she said. Guarded as hell, but then who knows what place cross-dressing had in the best Brundisium society? And if this was Porcia then her name was bang on: I didn't know, or particularly want to, if the lady wore any of her own stock in her private moments, but if she did there would be enough material to make a small tent. Clearly Satrius liked them big.

'Yes and no,' I said. 'I've a message for your friend Satrius. Could you tell him–?'

'I beg your pardon?'

'Satrius?' Blank incomprehension. '*Titus* Satrius? Your boyfriend from Rome?' Still nothing, but her colour mounted visibly. 'You, uh, you are Porcia, right?'

Her lips formed a tight line. 'My name is Tullia, I am a respectable married woman, and I have never even heard of a Titus Satrius, from Rome or anywhere else. Or, for that matter, anyone by the name of Porcia. You have obviously been misinformed, or you have the wrong establishment, or you are drunk. Most probably, from the smell of wine on your breath, the last. You will please leave forthwith.'

Shit. I would *kill* bloody Satrius! 'Ah...right. Right.' I backed away towards the door. 'My mistake, lady. Really, *really* sorry to have disturbed you.'

I exited, hurriedly. Yeah, well, at least I'd given the wealthy female browsers something to gossip about at their next cake-and-honey-wine klatsch: most of the interested glances had been directed at me, sure, but there were a couple of speculative ones in Tullia's direction, too.

The lad himself was waiting on the pavement outside the wineshop opposite, and grinning like a drain.

I crossed the road.

'You bastard!' I said. 'You complete and utter total *bastard!*'

'Come on, Corvinus!' Satrius said. 'No hard feelings, okay? Come inside and I'll buy you a drink.' He was still grinning as he led the way into the wineshop and up to the counter. 'You have to admit that was a pretty good joke, though. Peeved, was she?'

'Bastard! Hundred-per-cent, cast-iron, twenty-four fucking carat–!'

'Answer's yes, then. Two cups of Tarentine, Lucius,' he said to the barman. Then, while the guy was pouring, he turned back to me. 'I thought you'd enjoy the Porcia bit, too. I've seen the lady a few times in the past outside the shop, sure, but she could've been called Valeria Messalina for all I knew.' He sniggered. 'She'd have to shed twenty years, lose a few pounds, and do something about that face of hers first, of course. What was her name, as a matter of interest? She tell you that?'

'Tullia. You've been tailing me all along, haven't you? Right from the word go! *Bastard!*'

'Tullia, eh? Put it on my tab, Lucius. Some relation of the chickpea guy's, do you think?' I didn't answer, just glared. 'Of course I've been fucking tailing you, some of the time, anyway. What'd you expect? The boss told you right at the start that that's my job, watching your back. And, as it sodding turned out, the back of that gormless slave of yours that you have nosing around the wineshops into the bargain. As a result of which I've been rushing around between the two of you like a fucking blue-arse fly, making sure no one puts a knife between your ribs. So less of the grousing, because you owe me, pal.'

He picked up his cup and carried it over to one of the tables. I followed him with mine.

'You could've told me,' I said.

'No I couldn't. Not my shout; boss's orders.' He pulled up a stool and sat. I squeezed myself onto the bench by the wall. 'He's a smart one, the boss, he knows you work better when you're not being crowded, so he tells me to keep a low profile.' He grinned again. 'Besides, being stuck with you for half a month was more than plenty. You've been safe enough so far, and I've got Carpus keeping an ear out on the inside and ready to blow the whistle if it seems the bad boys are thinking of turning nasty. Which they well might after Alexis's little run-in yesterday, so you just watch your step from now on, okay?'

'I should thank you for that, at least,' I said. I took a sip of the wine. Tarentine, eh? Nowhere near as good as the Velletrian I'd had earlier, but pretty decent for all that, and half the price. Plus I recognised a peace offering when I saw one, so I wasn't inclined to be picky.

Satrius shrugged. 'I told you. It's my job. By the way, did Alexis tell you the punter with the knife was your friend Brinnius?'

'Was he, indeed?' I grinned; the broken wrist couldn't have happened to a nicer guy. 'No, he didn't, but then he wouldn't have known, would he?'

'True. I said at the time you could've taken him yourself, Corvinus, and I meant it. That bugger's a rank fucking incompetent. No kidding, talk about walkovers, I felt embarrassed for him, I really did. Some people have no professional pride.'

'You think he touched a nerve somewhere? Alexis? Asking about Marcius's first wife?' I said.

'Search me. That's your department. But these guys – just to be clear, we're talking Marcus Cluvius and Aulus Marcius, right? – they don't like too many questions being asked on principle. Makes them jumpy, and that pair don't do jumpy.'

'You don't know anything yourself? About what's-her-name Faustina's death?'

'Nah. Never heard word of her at all, not even her name, until Alexis's wineshop pal brought it up.'

'You don't know anyone who would know? From the company side?'

He shook his head. 'Uh-uh. Remember, Corvinus, you're talking more than twenty years back. Most of the guys I know in the business were either still at the apple-scrumping stage, were still sucking their mother's tit, or hadn't even been born yet. I'll ask around, though.'

'You do that. Thanks.'

'You're welcome. Meanwhile, I'll let you get on with things. You got any plans? Just so's I know, plan ahead myself, like.'

'Yeah,' I said. 'I thought I'd go over to the Isis temple, have a word with young Marcia's maid.'

His eyebrows lifted. 'Capra? Why her?'

'Titus Marcius mentioned she'd been his mother's while she was alive. If anyone knows anything about the death then she's the most likely candidate.' I hesitated. 'You, uh, do know what happened to the ring, don't you?'

He looked guarded. 'No, why should I? I said, Corvinus: the sleuthing part of the business is your province; me, I just–' He stopped, the guarded look vanished, and he lowered his voice. 'Fuck! You clever bugger! You've found out who took it, haven't you?'

'Better than that, pal, *way* better than that.' I gave him the story. 'Mind you, if Eutacticus reckons he has a vested interest in it things might get a bit tricky.'

'Nah, the boss won't care. It was never his in the first place, and to tell you the truth he wasn't all that easy in his own mind about where it came from. Plus if the wedding's off there's not much point to it now, and technically it belonged to Marcia anyway.'

'The wedding's permanently cancelled in any case,' I said. 'As of two nights ago.'

'Yeah?' He gave me a sharp look. 'And why would that be?'

'Something else you're missing,' I said. 'I've just been talking to Lucius Pettius.' I told him about Sextus.

He downed his wine in a oner and set the cup down. 'Fuck!'

'Yeah,' I said. 'That more or less sums it up.'

'You any idea who killed him?' He frowned, and shook his head. 'No, scrub that. I don't want to know.'

'Fair enough.' I finished off my own wine and stood up. 'In that case I'll be getting along. Oh.' I stopped. 'In the highly unlikely event that I really need to get in touch with you without risking having my lights punched out by offended Brundisian matrons how would I go about it?'

'Simple. Just tell Lucius here. I've got a room above the shop.'

'Really?'

'Really.' He grinned. 'No kidding this time. It couldn't be better. You'd be amazed how many of Porcia's – sorry, Tullia's – customers want a man's opinion on how they look in the lingerie they've just bought before they try it out on their hubby. The direct approach doesn't work every time, sure, but I haven't been short of company these last few days.'

The mind boggled. Still, there was no accounting for female taste. Or the lack of it. 'Fine,' I said. 'Then I'll see you around. Or possibly not, depending.'

I left.

I was lucky: the first person I saw when I came through the temple doors was Marcia herself, re-stocking the incense-burner in front of the goddess's statue. I waited just inside the threshold until she'd finished, seen me, and come out from the *abaton* into the public area.

'Valerius Corvinus,' she said. 'I didn't expect another visit. Is there a problem?'

'No, no problem.' She was looking much more relaxed and at home now; priestessing – or at least what in her case was presumably its preliminary stages – must be doing her good. 'And before you ask it's got nothing to do with the ring.'

'What, then? You haven't come to persuade me to go back, I hope? Father and mother have tried already, both with me and the High Priestess.' She smiled. 'Not that they got any change out of her. She's a Cornelia Lentula, with all that implies, and people like my parents are less than dust beneath her chariot wheels. I never thought I'd see my mother come off second best, but the Mistress had her on the defensive in two minutes flat and running for cover after five. Which, it has to be said, was a better show than my father put up. Lentula wiped the floor with him practically at the start.'

'There wouldn't be a wedding anyway,' I said. 'Sextus Pettius is dead.'

Marcia's smile disappeared. '*What?*' she said. 'How can Sextus possibly be–?'

'He was killed two nights ago. Stabbed in the back on his way home.' I'd been watching her closely, but there was nothing in her face but shock and surprise. 'So you're off the hook as far as that side of things is concerned. If it makes a difference.'

'It doesn't. I'd've gone eventually anyway.' She was still looking pole-axed. 'Who would want to murder Sextus? I mean, granted, I didn't like the man, in fact I loathed him, but I wouldn't wish him ill. Not to that extent, anyway.'

'That I don't know,' I said. I wasn't going to bring up the subject of Aulus and her mother, not unless she did first. 'Actually, though, that's not the reason I'm here.'

'No? What is, then?'

'I was hoping to have a word with your maid.'

'Capra?' She frowned. 'Why on earth would you want to talk to her?'

'Is she around at present?'

'Yes, she is, as it happens, but–'

'Maybe somewhere private.'

That got me a long, slow, considering look. Then she shrugged. 'Very well. There's a room we use for private talks, if you insist that that's what it is. I'll take you there now. Follow me.'

We went through the doorway to the left of the entrance that she'd come through on the previous occasion and along the short corridor beyond. There were several closed doors. She opened the first one and stood aside.

'Wait here,' she said. 'I'll send Capra to you.'

I went in and she closed the door behind me. The room was more or less what I'd expected: bare except for three wickerwork chairs and a portable shrine against the back wall, with a statuette of the goddess on top of it. No incense pan this time, but there was an oil lamp burning at the goddess's feet and two small bowls, one of fruit, the other of dried flowers, to either side.

I sat down in one of the wicker chairs and waited. Five minutes later the door opened and Capra came in. I'd expected that, like Marcia, she'd be wearing the usual uniform white linen shift, but she had on her ordinary slave's tunic.

'The mistress said you wanted to talk to me, sir,' she said. Neutral voice, blank expression, but the eyes were wary.

'Yeah, that's right, Capra.' I indicated the other chairs. 'Have a seat. Make yourself comfortable.'

She didn't move, or smile. 'I'd rather stand, if you don't mind,' she said.

Bugger; it was going to be like that, was it? 'Look,' I said. 'No hassle, none at all. I just need some information, that's all. And I thought you might be the best person to give me it.'

Her eyes shifted. 'Information about what?'

'You used to be old Titus Marcius's first wife's maid when she was alive, didn't you?' I said. 'Faustina, wasn't it?'

'Yes, sir, I did.' Guarded as hell; interesting. 'But that was a long time ago. Twenty years and more.'

'Yeah, I know,' I said. 'That's the point. Thing is, I've heard there was a rumour at the time that her death wasn't a natural one. Would you know anything about that?'

Long silence. Finally:

'No, sir.' Lips set straight as an architect's rule.

'In fact, that Marcius himself was responsible for it.' Silence again; her eyes were fixed beyond me, on the side wall. 'Come on, lady! I told you, no hassle, and that's a promise. This is just between me and you, no one else involved, and I'm telling no one. So what was it made him kill her?'

Her face shut. I could see the muscles of her jaw clench, as if she was forcing her teeth together even harder to make sure that not a sound, let alone a word, could escape. The eyes, focused on a point in the wall above and behind my left shoulder, didn't move. I waited, giving her time to change her mind. Nothing; as far as Capra was concerned I might as well not have existed.

Finally, I sighed and stood up.

'Fair enough,' I said. 'If you won't talk then you won't. But my guess is that the answer's important. If I'm to find out who killed the old man–'

'Master Titus was a monster. I hope he's burning in hell.'

I blinked. That had come out completely flat. And neither her eyes nor her face had moved.

'Is that right?' I said carefully. 'And why would that be, then?' Nothing. 'Come on, Capra! If you hated him that much then you must've had a reason.' I was talking to myself, or for all the reaction I got I might as well have been. I shrugged. 'Okay. Have it how you like. But you know where I am, and like I say it's important. Or could well be. Think about it, and if you change your mind let me know.'

I left her sitting there and went back to the exit.

Once outside, I glanced up at the sun. Not bad; I made it just shy of the eighth hour, which meant that I still had a fair slice of the afternoon to play with. So. Possibly a good time to chase up the prostitute that Julius Montanus had mentioned and given me the address for. Messia Postuma, right? Working from, to use Bathyllus's phrase, a brothel by the name of Calypso's Purse, in the alley behind the Temple of Vulcan. At least I was on the right side of town, in fact I was practically sure I'd passed Vulcan's temple on the way over, or at least spotted the frontage at the end of one of the streets I'd come along.

I wasn't wrong; the temple turned out to be only a five minute walk away back towards the centre of town. I skirted the raised podium and took a left down the alleyway between its rear side and the line of buildings – the featureless backs of two-storey houses, mostly – that lay behind it.

The alleyway neither looked nor smelled salubrious. For a start, the back end of the temple had provided a very convenient – and private – vertical surface for the local male population to empty their bladders against, while householders and passers-by in general had obviously viewed it as an adjunct to the quarter's rubbish tip. The entrance to the brothel itself was about half way along: a grilled metal door with an inspection hatch at eye level and the place's name written on the stone jamb next to it, under which – in case you were in any doubt as to what was on offer – some obliging punter had scrawled an erect phallus.

I knocked and waited. Silence. I knocked again, louder this time. There was the sound of footsteps inside, and the hatch snapped open.

'We're not open till sunset,' a man's voice said. 'Bugger off.'

I sighed, took a couple of silver pieces from my belt-pouch, and held them up level with the grille.

'Look, pal,' I said. 'I just want a word with Messia Postuma, if she's around. Or if not whoever happens to be handy.'

There was the rattle of a key being turned in the lock and two solid clunks, top and bottom, as bolts were shot. The door opened. Behind it was a little guy in a slave's tunic holding a mop and bucket. He set the latter down, took the coins from my hand, and shut the door behind me.

'Messia, you say?' he said.

'Yeah, that's right. She works here, doesn't she?'

'Worked.' He picked up the bucket again. 'You'd best talk to Madam Hermione. Follow me.'

Shit; I was getting a bad feeling about this. I followed him along a short corridor to what was obviously a sort of clients' common-room.

'Wait here,' he said, and left me to it.

I sat down on one of the stools and looked around me. The place wasn't quite the dive that I'd expected from the outside; not top rate, by any means, but probably getting there by Brundisium standards. Decent – if that wasn't an inappropriate word, considering their subject matter – frescos, comfortable, well-upholstered couches with inlaid tables beside them, half a dozen ornate bronze candelabra, and even a few marble copies of what I recognised as original Greek statues. Not bad; not bad at all.

'Philip tells me you want to speak to Messia.'

I turned round. The woman was a looker, and it wasn't down to make-up, either: I contrasted her mentally with Frontius's landlady Fulgentia, who must've been about the same age, mid- to late fifties, and who'd fitted the brothel-madame stereotype far more neatly.

'Uh...yeah,' I said. 'Yes, if she's around. I know she was pretty badly injured, but–'

'She's dead. She drowned herself a month ago.'

Gods! 'I'm sorry,' I said.

'I'm sure you are.' She didn't sound it; quite the reverse. 'In any case whatever your reasons were for wanting her, specifically, you're out of luck. Now as Philip no doubt explained we don't open for business until sunset. If you come back then I'm sure we can cater for any other requirement you may have.' She stepped aside, leaving the doorway clear. 'Meanwhile if you don't mind, I'm very busy.'

'Marcus Cluvius,' I said. 'That name ring any bells?' Obviously from the look I got and the way her jaw had tightened it did, and not the friendly, tinkly sort, either. 'Look, lady, just give me ten minutes of your time, okay?'

'If that's who sent you,' she said, 'you can just–'

'*No!*' I held up a hand. 'Ten minutes. Please?'

She folded her arms. 'Very well. But we'll make it five. Maybe. After that I have Philip throw you out.'

Yeah, well, having seen the guy already I'd take that particular threat with a large pinch of salt. Even so, I wasn't going to argue. 'Fair enough,' I said. 'You want to sit down?'

'I'm quite comfortable standing, thank you. Get on with it.'

'All right.' I hesitated. 'It's pretty complicated and there're lots of other factors involved that have nothing to do with Messia. But basically I want to nail the bastard's hide to the wall.' She blinked but said nothing. 'I was hoping that Messia would help me do it, that's all.'

'Does that purple stripe mean you're official?'

Time, clearly, for a bit of fudging with the best possible motives. 'I was sent down from Rome,' I said. 'And I've got the support of the garrison prefect Julius Montanus. That enough for you?'

'It'll do for a start.' She moved over to the nearest couch and sat. 'But no promises. Not yet. What exactly did you want from Messia?'

I shrugged. 'To tell you the truth I wasn't sure. To get the facts clear in my mind, certainly. You know what those were, yourself, by the way?'

'Yes.'

Nothing more, just the one word. I sighed. 'Look, Hermione...it is Hermione, right?'

'Lucretia Hermione, yes.'

So; a freedwoman. She'd done pretty well for herself if the decor was anything to go by. Which made sense: unless I missed my guess, Lucretia Hermione was a smart, tough cookie. Not altogether, under the circumstances, a good thing because if we were to get anywhere here I had to break through that hard shell. Which was not going to be easy.

'Fine,' I said. 'Okay, I'll tell you what I already know. Or assume, rather. Cluvius and his partner Aulus Marcius are running a protection racket, yes?' She hesitated, lips pursed. 'Hermione, I can't know for sure unless you tell me. And if I don't know I can't help. There'll be no comeback, I guarantee it.' Silence. Bugger. 'The way these things usually work, the bastards cream off a bit from the top every month in exchange for not wrecking the place or hassling the punters. Not a fortune, but then it doesn't have to be, because they've a lot of other businesses on their books to collect from besides yours. So you pay up just to avoid the hassle. Correct so far?' A nod; barely perceptible, sure, but it was a lot better than nothing. 'Thing is, if you cause any trouble – even look like you might be thinking of causing any trouble – they hit you quick and hard. Straight in, no second chances, because it sends a clear message to their other customers. That what happened to Messia?'

She was quiet for a long time, but this time I waited.

'Not quite,' she said finally.

'Tell me, then.'

'Cluvius took his...call it his monthly contribution in kind, and in person. From Messia, specifically; he always insisted on her. I won't go into details; suffice it to say that eventually things got too extreme and she refused to do as he wanted. He said nothing at the time, but the next day on her way to the vegetable market two men grabbed her and hustled her into an alley where one of them slashed her face open with a razor.' All spoken in a voice completely devoid of expression. 'She didn't know the men herself, and they weren't recognisable from her description later, so there was nothing more to be done.' She shrugged. 'That's all there was. And that's all I can tell you.'

'She drowned herself, you said?'

'Yes. A few days later. Not that I blamed her. After all, who would pay to lie with a whore with one eye and half her face missing? Cluvius hasn't visited us since. I think he thinks that if he did I'd put a knife between his ribs while he slept.' She gave me a straight look. 'He wouldn't be wrong, either.'

Said with a matter-of-fact coldness. I winced. 'That may not be necessary,' I said. 'If you help me, though, the end result'll be the same. I promise you that.'

'Help you how?'

'Tell Montanus what you've just told me.'

'Officially?'

Bugger; from her change of tone I knew what was coming. Still, there was no way round this.

'You'd have to talk to him personally, yeah,' I said. 'Or give him a signed deposition that I could pass on. But–'

'And when Cluvius gets to know about it? Not if, when, because believe me he will. And pretty damn soon, at that.' I didn't answer; I was remembering how fast news of my own visit to Montanus had been relayed back. 'Is your friend the cohort commander going to lend me some of his men on a permanent basis to stop the bastard sending someone round in the night with an oil jar and a torch? Because that will be exactly what will happen.'

She was right; it would, and even to try to argue otherwise wouldn't've been fair. So that was that. I sighed mentally and turned to go.

'Fair enough, lady,' I said. 'Thanks for your time.'

I'd already crossed the room and I had my hand on the door-knob when she said, 'Wait!' I turned back. 'Corvinus, isn't it?'

'Yeah. Marcus Valerius Corvinus.'

'Very well, Marcus Valerius Corvinus,' she said. 'I'll make a bargain with you. If you can find proof from elsewhere reasonably sufficient to send that man to the public strangler then you let me know and I'll go to Montanus gladly. And not only me. Messia was a popular girl, in the non-professional sense. She had a lot of friends, many of whom had dealings of their own with Cluvius and would be delighted to dance on the bastard's grave. I think I can speak for them too. Will that serve? Are we agreed?'

Hey! 'Sure,' I said. 'Absolutely.'

'Then it's a deal.' She held out her hand like a man, and I shook it.

Yeah, well, hardly a clear win for the home side; if actual convincing proof existed then, short of it coming from people like Lucretia Hermione in the first instance, I'd no idea where to get it from. Still, a part-win was better than nothing. Far better.

Enough for the day. Home.

14.

Perilla wasn't around when I got there – out gallivanting, according to Bathyllus, with her new pal Sentia on some historical jag beyond the city walls, visiting what was left of the siege fortifications from old Julius's blockade of the Pompeians ninety-odd years back – so I settled down on the atrium couch with a half jug of wine and put my thoughts in order. Such as they were.

She finally rolled in just short of the dinner gong, by which time I was most of the way down the jug. Nonetheless, things had started to crystallise, and I was feeling a lot happier. Never underestimate the beneficial effects of red wine on the brain cells.

'So how was your day, Marcus?' She held out her cloak for Bathyllus to take and hang up. 'What did Lucius Pettius want you for?'

'His son was killed two nights ago,' I said.

She stared. '*No!*'

'Believe it.'

'What happened, exactly? Do you know?'

'Uh-uh. Or not all that much as far as the details are concerned. All I've got is that he was on his way home around midnight from an evening with his gambling pals in one of the local wineshops when he was stabbed in an alleyway not far from the Pettius offices.'

'That's fairly near the main harbour area, isn't it?' She settled down on the couch opposite me. 'Not a very nice part of town away from the main streets, so it could always have been a simple robbery. After all, if he'd been gambling and left the place with a heavy purse then he'd have been a natural target for anyone who'd noticed. Particularly if he was walking home by himself.'

'According to his father the purse was still on his belt. Besides, again according to his father he was well-enough known for your ordinary jobbing knifeman to have left him alone.'

'So if there is a connection with the case then who killed him, and why? Do you have any idea?'

'Pettius blames Aulus Marcius. Understandably enough, and who's to say he's not right? He has a clear motive, and it's the most likely explanation by a long chalk.'

She was frowning. 'Pettius knew that both of them – his son and Aulus – were involved with Septimia?'

'Yeah.' I topped up my wine cup. 'Not only that, but it turns out that he suggested that Sextus start an affair with her in the first place, to keep the Pettii up to speed where the Marcius family's private affairs were concerned. Anyway, the bottom line is that he's breathing fire and planning to cut Aulus Marcius's throat.' I took a sip of the wine. 'Which, to tell you the truth, would solve a lot of problems in the long run.'

'And you're simply going to let him?' She sat up straight. 'Marcus, you can't!'

'Frankly, there isn't a whole lot I can do to stop him. I managed to get him to agree to a five-day moratorium, which will give me a bit of space to nose around, see if I can pick up any proof one way or the other, but that's about it.'

'Surely if you tell Julius Montanus, or if I have Sentia pass the message on to him–'

I shook my head. 'Uh-uh. That wouldn't do any good. Believe me Montanus just wouldn't want to know.'

'Whyever not? After all, if you say you have clear evidence that Lucius Pettius is planning a murder then–'

'No. It should work like that, sure, only it doesn't. Not this time. We're moving in a different world here, Perilla. If Montanus can nail Aulus and his sidekick Marcus Cluvius for crimes against honest citizens then he will, and gladly; I've his word on it. But if crooks like the Pettii and the Marcii go on killing each other until the cows come home with no collateral damage then that is absolutely fine with him because Brundisium would be a whole lot better off without them.'

'That is completely unfair!'

'Fair or not, it's the way of the world. Besides, by rights Aulus would have it coming even if he didn't kill Sextus.' I told her about my talk with Hermione, and what had happened to young Messia. 'They're a pair, those two. Me, I'm with Montanus; as it is, they've been getting away with murder, literally. With them dead the town would be a far cleaner place.'

'You could at least look into Sextus's death a bit more closely. If only for the sake of your own conscience. After all, if your original theory is correct and someone *is* trying to get rid of Aulus by proxy then–'

'Look, lady,' I said. 'I've already been doing my best in that direction, okay? Like I say, Pettius has given me five days' grace to come up with a viable alternative, which may not be much but at least it's something. Assuming, of course, that Aulus isn't the fucking perp to begin with, which six gets you ten he will turn out to be. In which case if Pettius goes and sticks a knife in him considering the circumstances I'll be happy to stand aside and whistle while he does it.'

'Calmly, dear. I'm not criticising. Not as such.' She paused. 'So. What else can you actually do?'

I shrugged. 'I've been thinking about that. Nothing from the actual killing side of things, that's for sure. Whoever did it must've known where Sextus would be that evening, gone to the wineshop and hung around until he left, then followed him out. All that's obvious, no argument. Trouble is, I've talked to the guy who was behind the bar at the time and there isn't a hope in hell of matching the perp with a face. And, of course, there were no witnesses to the murder itself. So from that direction it's a dead end.'

'But? There must be a "but", surely?'

'In a way. Not that it's any kind of a biggie, mind, and it may not exist at all. It has to do with where and when the murder happened. Aulus lives near the centre, so if he's our perp it would be easy for him to get from his house to where Sextus was killed. Which like I said, was on the same side of the Neck, further on in the direction of the harbour. Say a twenty-minute walk, sure, but with no complications.'

'All right. So?'

'So if Aulus did do the job then that's that, we've no chance of tracing his movements, certainly not at that time of night when there was probably no one else around in the first place. But if it wasn't him, and the actual killer was from this side of town, then to get to where the murder happened he'd've had to get across the Neck.'

'Or make his way around it.'

'No. That's the point, lady. He could've done that, yes, no argument, but the chances are that he wouldn't bother, because it'd mean walking into the centre then all the way back the way he'd come, only along the opposite bank. And the same for the return trip. That's quite a hike; we're talking the best part of an hour each way, at the very least, in pretty filthy weather. Certainly, unless he was being super-cautious, and why should he be, something not worth the effort if he could avoid it.'

'So?' She frowned. 'I'm not with you. Oh, I know there are ferryboats that cross from one bank to the other and would cut the time to a fraction, but they wouldn't operate at night, certainly not that late.'

'Actually, they do. Or at any rate according to my informant one of them does. The ferryman's a guy by the name of Milvius, works out of a berth about half way along this side of the Neck. I'll try to catch him tomorrow, see if he remembers taking a passenger over to the other side and back two nights ago.' I shrugged. 'It's an outside chance, sure, and frankly like I say my money would be on Aulus to begin with, but it's certainly something worth checking up on. If only just to show willing.' I up-ended the wine jug over my cup and a dribble came out before the thing dried. Damn. 'Oh, and apropos checking there was something else of interest came up today. Or rather in the event there wasn't.'

'Pardon?'

I grinned. 'Yeah, well, I'm afraid that pretty well sums it up, as it happens. You remember Alexis's rumour that Marcius had murdered his first wife twenty-odd years back?'

'Yes, of course I do.'

'After I left Pettius I called in at the temple of Isis to have a talk with Marcia's maid Capra.' Following a short detour to the centre of town, true, but I'd be keeping the pseudo-Porcian business under close wraps as far as Perilla was concerned. It had nothing to do with the case, and honesty between husband and wife need only go so far. 'You know she was the dead wife's, Faustina's, at the time she died?'

'Yes. So you told me. And?'

'And nothing. Zilch. Zero. Nothing whatsoever. She wouldn't talk about it. Shut up tighter than an oyster right from the word go.'

'Really?'

139

Spoken with an evidence-of-interest rating, on a scale of one to ten, of hardly a blip. 'You don't find that odd?' I said.

'Not particularly, dear. Besides, why on earth should it matter in the first place? You said it yourself: the woman's been dead for over twenty years.'

'Come on, Perilla!'

'You come on. There are such things as loyalty to one's mistress – ex-mistress, in this case, but nevertheless – and prurient nosiness. All Capra's silence shows is that she possesses the former herself and suspects you of the latter. Quite justifiably so, in my view.'

Ouch. 'Okay. So why the loyalty?'

'I beg your pardon?'

'Loyalty, if it involves silence, implies that, ipso facto, there's a reason for it, right? After all, why keep schtum about something if it isn't important? Particularly something that far back?'

'I told you. She probably considered it to be none of your business.'

Gods give me strength! 'Fine,' I said patiently. 'So if the rumour's true, and Capra knows it, then by not talking to me who would she be protecting?'

Perilla frowned. 'What?'

'It's a simple question, lady. Marcius kills his first wife, Capra's mistress. More than twenty years on, I ask her if she knows anything about the death and she gives me the straight finger. No messing, not even a token attempt at a denial or a lie or prevarication, just the door slammed in my face. So why should she do that? The thing's ancient history, Marcius himself is dead and buried, where she is now she can virtually tell the rest of her world to go and fuck itself–'

'*Marcus!*'

'–so where would be the harm? Quite the reverse, in fact, because if the bastard did kill his wife and she's kept the knowledge to herself all these years she'd be desperate to pass the details on, particularly to a complete outsider. Unless.'

'Unless what?'

'Unless her mistress was the guilty party. To some extent, anyway.'

Silence; Perilla was twisting a stray lock of hair. Finally:

'Adultery,' she said.

'Yeah. That was my thought.' I picked up my wine cup and drank the last half inch or so. 'Which, as far as the case is concerned, opens up some interesting avenues. Now doesn't it?'

She sighed. 'Marcus, we're still talking, as you said, ancient history. Even if whatever happened involving this Faustina does turn out to have some relevance it can't possibly have a direct bearing on Marcius's murder. Certainly not if you're thinking in terms of a motive, of personal involvement or even interest. Twenty-odd years ago most of the people concerned in the case who might be suspects either hadn't been born or were scarcely more than children.'

'Okay. Fine. So we're left with the other two oldsters, Marcius's contemporaries. Quintus Cluvius and Lucius Pettius.'

'And all this fits in with Marcius's own murder how, exactly?'

'Yeah, well, I'd've thought that was–'

'Let me guess. You're going to say that twenty-odd years ago one of them, Cluvius or Pettius, had an affair with Titus Marcius's wife, that he found out and killed her. Correct?'

'More or less.' I was guarded. Shit; I hated it when she did this. It usually meant that a bit further down the line I would find myself well and truly screwed. Still, I had to make the effort, if only out of sheer bloody masochism. 'Why not? It's a reasonable theory. And if it was Pettius then it'd explain the antagonism between the two firms. That seems to have started at about the same time, doesn't it?'

'So if Marcius knew that Pettius was the other half of the affair, which ipso facto he must have done for the rift to have happened in the first place, then why not kill him straight away as well?'

'I don't know. Maybe he thought it was too risky. After all, treating the guy as an enemy as far as business is concerned would be one thing; starting up a blood feud with the Pettii and probably ending up dead himself as a result would be something else.'

'And twenty-plus years later everything was forgiven and forgotten to the extent that Marcius was willing to marry his only granddaughter to Pettius's son and lay the groundwork for a virtual joining of the two firms, yes? In fact, to the extent that he made the suggestion himself with that aim in mind.'

'Ah.' Bugger; I didn't deserve this. 'Maybe. For all we know–'

'There's another thing. Does any of this sound in the least like typical behaviour on Marcius's part? According to what you already know about him as far as his character goes, I mean?'

Hell and damnation. I was beginning to sweat. 'Okay,' I said. 'Granted. Perhaps it doesn't, at that. Or not as such. On the other hand, he might not have known that Pettius was guilty at the time and only found out recently. That'd explain–'

'How?'

I blinked. 'How do you mean, "how"?'

'How, after all this time not knowing, did he suddenly find out who the responsible party was? Not from Capra; her loyalty lay with her mistress. And if she had any to spare, under the circumstances, then it would go towards protecting her mistress's lover rather than revealing his identity to her killer. And if from someone else then who? And in *that* case the original objection applies: why did whoever it was not tell Marcius right at the start, or at least at some other point between then and now?'

'Shit, lady, I don't know!' Jupiter! 'It's just a theory, okay?'

'Not to mention that it was Marcius himself who ended up dead, not Pettius.'

At least I was on firmer ground there. 'Yeah, well, there's an easy explanation for that, isn't there?' I said.

'Is there, indeed? Namely?'

'That in the event the attempt went wrong. Instead of Marcius stiffing Pettius according to the original plan things happened the other way round, with the old man ending up as the corpse and Pettius walking away free.'

'Hmm.'

I grinned. In situations like this the lack of an immediate sassy comeback on the lady's part was always a good sign, because it meant that she hadn't got one. I pressed my advantage. 'Actually, that'd fit the facts pretty well, wouldn't it? After all, the murder happened at the old family offices, that Marcius knew would be empty and that he had a key to. It would've been easy for him to arrange a clandestine meeting there, kill Pettius, tip his body into the Neck, and slope off home with no one the wiser. Only he botched it. Maybe Pettius had got suspicious and come prepared, or the surprise attack just didn't come off and he managed to turn the tables. That side of things doesn't really matter, because however you like to play it at the end of the day we have a name for our perp. Case closed.' I leaned back against the headboard of the couch. 'What do you think? Possible, yes?'

'I suppose so, dear.' She was twisting her lock of hair. 'So. Let's be clear about this. What you're saying is that Lucius Pettius killed Marcius, but only, as it were, in self-defence; that in actual fact Marcius himself was planning to murder Pettius and the attempt went wrong?'

'Uh...yeah. More or less.'

'And that the whole thing, the olive branch to the Pettii, the negotiated engagement, the suggestion of a future merger, was simply bait to lull Pettius into a false sense of security in order for Marcius to arrange his murder, yes? In eventual reprisal for Pettius's seduction of his wife a generation previously?'

Bugger; I was getting a bad, bad feeling about this. 'Well,' I said, 'put like that maybe there are a few points that need–'

'You don't think that, as an explanation, it's just a tad overcomplicated? After all – and we've been through this already – if Marcius knew that Pettius was responsible from the start then he could have engineered his death, openly or clandestinely, at any time during the previous twenty-odd years. And if he didn't, and the knowledge came after the *entente* with the Pettii was already up and running, then how did he come by it at this late date? Not forgetting, of course, that we don't actually know for a fact that there was an adulterous affair in the first place.'

Hell's bloody teeth! She was right, though, I had to give her that. As a theory it had its merits, sure, but it also had holes you could drive a horse and cart through. Time for a bit of retrenching.

'Okay,' I said. 'But sticking with the seduction angle. Leave Pettius aside for the moment. If not him then how about Quintus Cluvius?'

She sniffed. 'Marcus, admit it. You're floundering.'

'True. Admitted. Even so, if the whole Faustina business does happen to be relevant–'

'Which it most probably isn't.'

'–which I think it is, then assuming the reason for her death was an adulterous affair he's someone we have to look more closely at.'

'Very well. Go ahead, if you absolutely must.'

'Pluses: he's the right age – in fact, he's the only other candidate, as far as we know – and as Marcius's deputy he's practically part of the family already, so access to the lady on a regular basis wouldn't be a problem. And as far as the old man's murder goes where he scores over Pettius as a candidate for perp is that the love affair angle – revenge for Faustina's death – need only be an additional motive to his main one. Which, if you recall, we've already covered.'

'And that was? Remind me.'

Tone hardly redolent of wholehearted encouragement. Gods! She was really being difficult here, wasn't she? I took a deep breath. 'Cluvius is Old School, right? He's deputised for Marcius practically all his life, and all that time the Pettii have been, if not the enemy, then the next thing to it. Now it suddenly turns out that not only is his friend and boss thinking of making peace but he's very likely also manoeuvring for a Pettius to be either de iure or de facto head of the company when he retires. Solution: put the guy in an urn before any of this happens, keep control of the company yourself while systematically, in one way or another, getting rid of the potential opposition and the problem's solved, in both the short and the long term. Motive in spades, right?'

'I suppose so. Yes.'

Grudging as hell, but at least – again – there had been no snappy comeback. 'Look, lady,' I said patiently. 'I'm open to other suggestions, okay? You have any of these at present?'

She smiled and ducked her head. 'Not as such. No.'

'Then keep it zipped. Whether you like it or not, the Faustina side of things is crucial; that I'd bet a year's income on.'

'Very well, dear, have it your own way. For all I know you may be right.' *And pigs might fly*, her tone said. However, at least she wasn't rejecting the theory out of hand any longer. Good sign. 'You think there's a chance of Capra changing her mind and talking to you?'

'Uh-uh.' I shook my head. 'Not before hell freezes.'

'Then you're stuck. Obviously you can't approach either Quintus Cluvius or Pettius themselves for information, and no one else is of the right generation. It has to be Capra.'

'Not necessarily.' I picked up the wine cup, remembered it was empty and set it down again. 'I was thinking about that before you came in. You remember me mentioning a guy called Carpus?'

'Satrius's friend. Of course.'

'When we were talking in the wineshop, that first day, he mentioned that his father had worked for Marcius and the two were pretty close. He'd be no Capra, sure, with an in to the family's private affairs, but at least he would've been around at the time. I could talk to him, see what he's got. If anything.'

'He's still alive?'

'I think so, from what I can recall of the conversation, anyway. Certainly worth a stab.'

'You have his address?'

'Not at present, but I'm sure I can get it. Anyway, I'll–' There was a polite cough behind me. I turned. Bathyllus. 'Yeah, Bathyllus. What is it?'

'Only dinner, sir. If you and the mistress are ready.'

About time; it'd been a busy day, I hadn't eaten since breakfast, and I was starving. 'Sure.' I stood up and collected the empty wine jug and cup. 'We'll go straight in.'

Perilla had got up too. 'There is one thing, Marcus,' she said. 'Not connected with the adultery theory, or even directly with Marcius's death.'

'Yeah?' I said. 'And what's that?'

'Just a thought I had when we were discussing Sextus Pettius's murder. You think that Aulus actually was responsible, don't you?'

'Like I said, it seems the likeliest explanation. And?'

'Septimia told you that she'd been very careful to keep her affair with Sextus a secret from him, yes?'

'Uh-huh. Or so she claimed.'

'And you believed her. But in that case, if Aulus was the killer, when and how did he find out?'

Ah.

15.

I was up and around betimes the next morning.

If I wanted to find Carpus's father, the most obvious way of going about things was to ask someone at the Marcius offices, but that I didn't want to do, no way and nohow: if I was right about the Faustina connection being important, and Quintus Cluvius did turn out to be our perp, then I'd no intention of risking him getting wind of possible developments. Besides, I had a viable alternative. I headed across town towards the centre and the wineshop Satrius was using as his base.

The wineshop was open. So, unfortunately, was the lingerie shop across from it, or at least it was in the process of opening, because I arrived just as Tullia-aka-Porcia was taking the padlock off the shutters. When she saw me she stopped what she was doing, straightened, and gave me a glare. I gave her my best smile in return and slipped in through the wineshop door.

Open for business the place was indeed, but clearly only just; Lucius the barman was stacking wine jars in the rack behind the counter.

'Hi,' I said. 'Remember me?'

'Sure.' He settled the jar he was carrying into its cradle. 'Corvinus, right? You looking for Satrius?'

'Is he around?'

'Nah, and won't be for a few hours yet. He got lucky yesterday, one of the regulars from across the street, not-so-little brunette married to an inspector of aqueducts.' He winked. 'Out of town at present checking for leaks. Was it important? Because if so I can–'

'No, that's okay, pal. Actually I wanted a word with his mate Carpus to ask him for his father's address. You know where I can find him?'

'Carver? No idea, not at present, anyway.' He hefted another full jar into position. 'But his father, sure, that's easy, I can tell you that myself. He's practically a neighbour, one of our regulars. End of the road, Market Square side, turn left, go down fifty or sixty yards and you'll see a cobbler's shop on your right. He lives in the flat above, on the first floor. If you've any trouble finding it ask for Gaius Vestius.'

Great! 'Thanks, friend.' I turned to go.

'Cup of wine first? On the house.'

'No, I'd best get on. Things to do.'

'As you like.' He reached for another jar. 'I'll tell the lad you called.'

I found the cobbler's shop and the staircase next to it that gave access to the first floor. There were two doors at the top. I knocked on one, but there was no answer. I thought the other was going to be a dud as well, but after the third knock I was on the point of leaving when I heard shuffling footsteps on the other side and the door opened the barest of cracks.

'Yeah? What is it?' An old man's voice, thick with suspicion.

'Gaius Vestius?' I said.

'Maybe. Depends who wants him and why.' The door opened fully. Well, the age was certainly right for Carpus's father. The build, too: old the guy might be, but he was almost as tall as me even allowing for the stoop, he had the breadth to match, and there were still serious muscles beneath his tunic. Carpus again, thirty years on. Only he was blind. The white-clouded eyes stared past my shoulder.

'You don't know me,' I said. 'The name's Marcus Corvinus. I'm–'

'The purple-striper from Rome. Sure. My son Gaius mentioned you. So?' Tone still suspicious as hell, and he hadn't moved.

'I was hoping you might be able to help me out with something,' I said. 'The answers to a few questions. Can I come in?'

'Suit yourself.' He stood aside for me to pass. 'I'm not busy. Questions, is it?'

The room was small but surprisingly neat. From what I could see of it, anyway, once he'd closed the door behind me.

'Yeah, that's right,' I said. 'If you can spare the time.'

He chuckled. 'Time I've got in spades, that's not a problem. Answers, though, well, they're another matter. You'll want some light. Open the shutters. This time of year I keep them closed to keep the wet out.' I did; not that it made much difference, because the flat was north-facing, but at least what we had now was gloom rather than actual darkness. 'There's a stool by the wall. Use it.' He was feeling his way across to the wickerwork chair by the window. While he got settled I carried the stool over and sat down opposite him. 'Now what's this about? Gaius tells me you're some sort of investigator looking into the old master's death. That be right, would it?'

'Yeah,' I said. 'That about covers it.'

'Then you're wasting your time with me, boy. I'm long gone, fifteen years or more. I don't know nothing about nothing since then.'

'Uh-uh,' I said. 'It's not about the murder. Or not directly. You were with the firm twenty-odd years back, yes?'

'I was, and just as long before that an' all. Started when I was hardly more than a nipper. So?'

'The old master – Titus Marcius – he was married then, right? To a woman by the name of Faustina?'

'That he was. And?'

'She died. Under suspicious circumstances.'

Silence; *long* silence. Finally: 'Is that so, now?' he said.

'The rumour is that Marcius killed her. Or had her killed. You know anything about that?'

'Not a thing.'

'You're certain? It can't be a big deal, surely, not after all this time. If you do remember something, anything at all, then–'

He held up a hand. 'Look,' he said. 'Me, I was just a gofer, know what I mean? Maybe a bit of muscle, when I had to be, like what my son is now. That sort of stuff I don't know nothing about, not now, not never, because it was none of my fucking business. You understand?'

'So you wouldn't know if she was having an affair? With Lucius Pettius or Quintus Cluvius, for example?'

'If that's what you think then you're dreaming. The mistress wouldn't have looked twice at either of them.'

'But she was having an affair with somebody, right?' I persisted. Silence again. 'Come on, pal! You may only have been the hired muscle but according to your son you and old Marcius went back a long time together. Maybe you weren't friends exactly but my guess is that as far as the family were concerned you were a lot more of an insider than you claim to be. Now I may be wrong, but I think that if we want to find out who killed Titus Marcius then finding out what happened with his first wife is important. You with me there or not?'

He frowned. I waited. Finally: 'Fair enough,' he said. 'Like you say it's water under the bridge now, and if it'll help nail the bastard then what does it matter? If Faustina did have an affair, an' I'm not saying for a fact she did, mind, chances was it was with Sextus Pettius.'

Bull's-eye! Eat your heart out, lady! 'You mean Lucius Pettius?' I said. 'But you just said that–'

'I may be blind, boy, but I'm not senile. I know who I mean. You asked and I'm telling you.'

Yeah, well, as far as senility went I reckoned that the jury must still be out after all. 'I'm sorry,' I said, 'but it's Lucius right enough. The father. Sextus is his son.'

'Fuck that.'

I blinked. 'How do you mean?'

'Lucius Pettius is the lad's uncle.'

Shit. Evidently one of us was mad here, and I was pretty sure it wasn't me. 'Look, Gramps,' I said patiently, 'I may only have been in this town for five minutes but I can't've missed something like that. Trust me, if they'd been uncle and nephew someone would've mentioned it somewhere along the line. As it is the consensus is pretty clear, and just for the record I'm including the pair of them in the mix. We're talking father and son, that is definite. Finish, end of story.'

'Never mind your end of story, boy, I'm telling you like it is. You don't want to listen, that's your look out.'

'Tell me, then.'

'Sextus – that's Lucius's brother Sextus – died three days before the kid was born, he was their first, and his mother died having him. Lucius and his wife couldn't have kids of their own so they took him on and named him for his father.'

Gods!

'"Took him on"?' I said; my brain had gone numb. 'Adopted him, you mean? Even so, they'd have had to–'

'Nah. Where was the need? An' we're not dealing with one of your fancy upper-class Roman families here. It happens that way all the time. Fact is, he was Lucius's son right from the day he was born, an' far as anyone knows or cares nowadays that's who he's always been. Barring Lucius and the boy himself – and maybe not even him, for all I know, if he was never told – it's just oldsters like me remember anything different.'

I leaned back. Jupiter! We'd still have to work out how everything fitted together, sure, but I reckoned Tithonus here had just blown the case wide open. 'So how exactly did Sextus – your Sextus – die?' I said carefully. 'Was Marcius involved in that too?'

'Nah. The master hadn't nothing to do with it. And before you start thinking otherwise I'm telling you that's straight fact.'

'Yeah? So how *did* it happen?'

'You know Master Titus and Lucius Pettius started out as partners?'

'No. No, I didn't.'

'True. I'm talking fifty years back, mind. There were four of them all told, grew up together further down the coast in Valetium, like I did myself. Master Titus, the two Pettii brothers, Lucius and Sextus, an' Quintus Cluvius. They was all pretty much of an age, late teens when they started out proper, but Sextus, he was the baby of the set, ten years younger than his brother, from a second marriage, so he came into the business a tad later on. You with me?'

'Uh-huh. "Business" doing what, exactly?' I said.

He scowled. 'Look, boy, you know what I mean well enough. If you're going to play coy and sneer you can just fuck off now, okay? Oh, sure, none of it was legal, far from it, but they was no worse than some and better than most. Understand?

'Fair enough,' I said. 'I'm sorry. Carry on.'

'Anyway, by their mid twenties the three of them – four now, I should say, with young Sextus added – they'd built up a pretty smart operation. Master Titus, he was the brains, Cluvius was the muscle. The Pettii had family connections in the area from way back, they made the contacts, kept their fingers in the different pies, spotted the openings and the one-off chances. Only thing was, Valetium was a small place, opportunities was limited. By that time they had the town pretty well stitched up and was looking to move up the ladder.'

'So they came here?' I said.

'The three of them did, Master Titus, Lucius an' Cluvius; young Sextus, he stayed behind to keep the Valetium side of things going, look after their interests there, see no other firm slipped in behind their backs. Me, I came too, along with most of the other grunts. It wasn't no stroll, mind; those days, Brundisium was Victorini territory, had been for fifty years and more, so we had to go careful, keep our heads down, build things up gradual. Master Titus, he was good at that, and luckily for him the Victorini had got slack, come to take things for granted. So by the time they woke up to thinking maybe they should take our boys more serious, five or six years down the road, the lads'd already cut themselves a big slice of the cake while they wasn't looking and they found they'd a real fight on their hands.' He paused. 'Hold up, boy. I'm not much for talking as a rule, and my throat's drying out. There's wine and a couple of cups in the cupboard behind you. You want to pour me some, have some yourself?'

'Sure.' I stood up and did like he'd asked. I expected the wine to be thin, second-rate stuff, but it turned out to be the same Tarentine that Satrius had ordered in Lucius's wineshop. 'So. Don't think I'm hassling you, pal, and all this is fascinating, but where does Faustina come in? Not to mention Sextus Senior?'

'Hold your horses. I'm getting there, son. You ask for the story, you get the whole boiling, okay?' I waited while he took a long swallow of the wine and cleared his throat. 'Faustina, she was a real catch. Father was in the shipping business, the dodgy side of it if you know what I mean, so that was a plus to begin with, added to which he'd had dealings regular with Master Titus from the start, and he knew we was on the up and up. So a joining made good sense. The other two, Lucius and Quintus Cluvius, they was married already when she came onto the market, and Sextus, he was still back in Valetium. So it was Master Titus that put in for her. We're talking forty years ago now, you understand? A tad back on ourselves, two years after the lads made the move from Valetium.'

'Fair enough,' I said.

'She was a looker, too, the mistress, he'd no cause for complaint on that score, either.' Vestius drank some more of the wine and set the cup down on the table beside him. 'Anyways, to cut the story short, they was wed just shy of her sixteenth birthday, she'd two babes before she was twenty, and that was that for the next ten years. You with me?'

'Uh-huh.' I took another sip of my wine.

'Well, by this time we was pretty much level-pegging with the Victorini. We'd the whole side of town west of the Neck in our pockets, they was the same for the east, with the harbour area and everything beyond Market Square up for grabs. Meaning it was pretty much a constant battleground with neither of us getting the upper hand or being willing to back off. Finally Master Titus, he reckons the time's come to go all out. So he tells young Sextus to wind things up in Valetium and move everything over here. Money, manpower, the lot. The whole shebang.'

'So Sextus moved too.'

'Sure he did. Like I say, it was a total up-stakes job, nothing and no one left behind. Sextus, he was wed himself by this time, to a Valetian girl. I forget her name, not that it matters. It weren't a love match by no means, not on either side because the girl was no picture and Sextus' – he grinned – 'well, to put it politely he hadn't the makings of a family man to begin with, nor planned on being one after he was hitched. Still, her father had useful contacts along the Greek coast the other side of the water, which was something the lads'd been looking for for years, so he was happy with the arrangement.'

'So he comes to Brundisium and starts up an affair with Titus Marcius's wife?'

'Just you wait, boy.' Vestius frowned. 'Don't you jump to no conclusions. I told you, I don't know that for a fact. Maybe he did, maybe he didn't; I can't say one way or 'tother. What I do know is the way young Sextus was made he couldn't see a good-looking woman, married or single, without trying to put her on her back. He'd manage it, too, a lot oftener than you'd think because he was a good looking bastard and he had the patter in spades. Plus like I said the fact he was married himself didn't slow him down any.'

'It takes two to commit adultery, pal,' I said. 'What about Faustina?'

'The perfect little wife and mother, she was. On the surface, at least.' His hand felt for the cup and closed on it. He drank and held the cup out. 'Pour me some more, would you, boy?'

I did, and sat down again. 'But?' I said.

He set the cup down. 'You know yourself the way these things go without me telling you. Faustina was still the right side of thirty, still pretty much the stunner even after having the two kids. Sextus, he was her age, more or less, like I say good looking and good with women, and he didn't make no secret about not being a model hubby. Reverse of the coin, like Sextus's her marriage'd always been more a business arrangement than a love match, Master Titus was ten years her senior, and he hadn't been no sculptor's dream to begin with. Plus – and this isn't just me talking, ask anyone you like that knew him – he was a hard, cross-grained bastard with the charm of a wolverine. So if she and Sextus did start an affair – and I'm not saying they did, because like I told you I don't know the truth of it one way or 'tother, and if they did then they was pretty careful about it – it was an accident waiting to happen. Particularly since Sextus's wife was in the family way an' he was at a loose end, as it were.'

Gods! He sounded a real charmer, this bastard, and no mistake. Still...

'Marcius himself didn't know?' I said. 'Or even suspect?'

'That I don't know either. He could of done, sure; he knew the sort of man Sextus was, no doubts on that score, an' he was no fool, the master, quite the contrary. Far as opportunity went, mind, the two of them would've had plenty of that. Faustina was no prisoner, and Master Titus, he was too busy most of the time with his own concerns to bother with hers. If her and Sextus was carrying on together an' he'd got wind of it somehow then it didn't show in how he behaved to them, and at least to my knowledge he never let on to no one, not even to Lucius or Cluvius. But then that in itself don't signify; he always played things close to the chest, did the master, kept his own counsel till he was ready. An' more often than not not even then.'

'So what exactly happened in the end? How did Sextus die?'

He picked up the wine cup and swallowed another mouthful. 'We're talking, what, maybe four or five months after the move from Valetium, yes?' he said. 'So twenty five years back.'

'Okay.'

'We'd got a shipment coming in, courtesy of Faustina's father. Luxury goods that he'd–' He stopped and grinned. 'Yeah, well, never mind that part, it's not important. All that is is that the boss – Master Titus – he didn't want to risk the port authorities asking too many questions when we landed it. There's a cove a mile or two along the coast, pretty much isolated, perfect for that sort of thing. And I told you we was having this ongoing war with the Victorini boys at the time, right?'

I nodded, then remembered. 'Yeah,' I said. 'You told me that.'

'So. The boss had arranged the rendezvous at the cove as usual. Cluvius an' Sextus, they was to take a couple of mule-carts and half a dozen of the lads, me included, across at first light, load up the goods that the ship's captain had dropped off above the shoreline the night before and bring them back to town. Meanwhile the captain himself would've carried on up the coast, put into the harbour in the normal way, unloaded the rest of his cargo and paid the port taxes on it in full like the upright tradesman he was, with a fat bonus in his belt-pouch and no one, including the ship's owners, any the wiser. Easy-peasy, we'd done it a score of times over the years with no hassle.'

'Only this time there was?'

'Right. We was loading the goods onto the carts when the bastards jumped us, a dozen of them at least. They must of been there all the time hid among the bushes just a few yards away, because we didn't have no warning. It weren't much of a fight; our lads had weapons, sure, but they had their hands full at the time an' they wasn't expecting to have to use them. We lost four men straight off. Cluvius, he was all for making a stand, but one of the bastards cut him in the face an' that was him out of things. The rest of us too, because three minutes in we was four to their twelve, so we ran.'

'And Sextus?'

'He was one of the four that went down right at the start; how, I din't see at the time, but when we came back for the bodies later on he was lying there with his head stove in.'

'And you're certain it was the other gang? The Victorini?'

'Sure I am. Who else could it have been?'

Good question. 'You tell me, pal,' I said. 'It just strikes me as a bit too coincidental to be coincidence, if you see what I mean. Certainly convenient from Marcius's point of view if the guy was screwing his wife.'

'Yeah, well, there again you don't know that for a fact, do you, boy, no more'n I do. Anyway, the upshot was that as far as the master was concerned now – Lucius Pettius, too, of course – it was war to the knife, with no quarter asked or given.' He grinned. 'The Victorini caved in inside of three months, and before the year's end we'd rolled the bastards up like a rug.'

'Okay,' I said. 'So that was Sextus gone. What about Faustina?'

'Long gone herself by this time, hardly more'n a month after Sextus.' I must have made a movement that he picked up, because he shook his head. 'Nah, it was an accident, pure and simple. One of the house slaves spilled oil on the floor while he was filling the atrium lamps, the mistress comes in while he's off getting a cloth, she slips, goes backwards, catches her head on the marble wall round the pool an' breaks her neck.'

'Uh-huh.' I kept my voice neutral. 'Anyone see it happen, by any chance?'

'Must of done, since that's the story.'

Jupiter! So much for logic! 'Yeah. Right,' I said. 'What about the slave, the guy who spilled the oil? What happened to him?'

Vestius grunted. 'What you'd expect, with the mistress dead. Master Titus chopped the bugger himself, straight off.'

'He was in the house at the time?'

'Maybe. Maybe not. How the fuck should I know?' He shifted irritably. 'Look, boy, you wanted the story, you've got it, all of it, far as I'm concerned. What you make of it's up to you, okay? But don't go trying to pin nothing on the master from what I've told you and using me for proof. Even if you're right – an' I'm not saying one way or the other, because I don't know and it's none of my business – it was years since, Master Titus is dead, and if the mistress was carrying on behind his back she deserved all she got. Catching the bastard who killed him's one thing, that I'm all for. But that's as far as I go. Understand?'

'Yeah,' I said. 'I understand.'

'So fuck off, leave me alone, an' get on with it, okay?'

'Fair enough.' I stood up. 'Thanks, pal. Believe me, it's been more than helpful.'

Gods! That was putting it mildly. And what I really needed to do now was to talk to Lucius Pettius.

16.

Okay, there were significant bits of the puzzle still missing, sure, but all things considered I reckoned we'd got our perp; certainly as far as making out a decent case was concerned. The problem now – and it was going to be a real bugger – would be proving it.

First stop in any event was the Neck, and a chat with the night-time ferryman, Gaius Milvius.

He wasn't at his berth when I reached it, but I could see what was obviously a ferry-boat that'd just landed a passenger on the other bank, so I gave the guy a wave and he started back across.

'Gaius Milvius?' I said as he pulled in to the mooring.

'That's me, sir.' Fifties, ageing wide-boy type. He looked and sounded wary. 'What can I do for you?'

'No hassle, pal.' I opened my belt-pouch and took out three silver pieces. 'And I don't want to cross, at least not yet. You want to come ashore?'

He shrugged. 'Fair enough.'

I waited while he tied the boat to the stanchion and climbed the steps onto the quay.

'Now, sir,' he said; the wary look hadn't shifted, in fact it'd gone up a notch since he'd clocked the stripe on my tunic. 'What's this about?'

'Just a couple of questions I need the answer to.'

'That purple stripe mean you're some sort of official?'

'In a way. No hassle, though. I said.' I held up the coins. 'None whatsoever.'

Another shrug, more relaxed this time as his eyes did the arithmetic. 'Fine,' he said. 'You're paying. Ask away.'

'You were working three nights ago? Around midnight?'

'Sure. Sunset to midnight, at any rate. This time of year I pack in about then, 'less I've a pickup arranged. Specially when the weather's dodgy like it is at present.'

'And did you, three nights ago? Have a pickup?'

He shook his head. 'Uh-uh. Didn't have no customers at all that evening, going or coming.'

'You're sure about that?'

'Certain.'

Yeah, well, it'd been worth a try. And to tell you the truth I wasn't all that surprised; quite the reverse. If anything, it was a relief because there went one bit of the puzzle that probably wouldn't need solving after all. 'Okay,' I said. 'Second question, a bit more difficult this time. We're talking, what, a month and a half ago. Middle of September, just after the Ides. There was a murder near here, an old guy by the name of Titus Marcius. You hear about that?'

'Marcius?' His interest had sharpened. 'Sure I heard. Who didn't? That's what you're about?'

'Uh-huh. You happen to recall whether you were working that night as well?'

'Not as such. But I probably would've been. So?'

I crossed my fingers. 'So I was hoping that, if you were, you might remember if you had a passenger. It'd be late, well after sunset, starting out from the other bank. And he'd've arranged a return trip an hour or so later. Probably a tall, well-built man in his sixties, spry for his age.'

'If you mean Lucius Pettius, then sure.'

Jupiter! *'You know him?'*

'By sight, yeah. I couldn't swear to the actual day, mind, but it must've been then or thenabouts.'

Sweet immortal gods! I'd got him cold! 'You're absolutely certain of that?' I said.

''Course I am.'

'You happen to recall where you dropped him off, exactly?'

'Sure. A bit further up, at the quay just past the old Marcius offices. Collected him from there as well an hour later. Funnily enough–' He stopped, and frowned as the penny dropped. 'Here, hang on a minute, squire. You're not saying he's the one that done it, are you? That I had Old Man Marcius's murderer in my boat?'

I handed over the coins. 'Let's have that crossing now, pal,' I said. 'Pettius company offices, or as close as you can manage. You know where they are?'

''Course I do. No problem.' He hesitated. 'You'd be wanting to talk to the gentleman himself, though, would you, sir? In person, like?'

'That was the general idea, yeah.' I was heading for the steps. 'So?'

'It's just that...well, maybe I can save you the journey.'

I stopped. 'How do you mean?'

'Happens I brought him over this side myself this morning.'

I stared at him. 'You did *what?*'

'Sure. Hardly an hour since. Dropped him at the same place, in fact. 'S why I thought it was odd, you asking, but there again–'

I didn't stop to listen. I was already heading for the Marcius offices at a run.

The door was open, which, if I'd stopped to think, should've seemed odd, but I didn't. I went inside.

Cluvius – Quintus Cluvius – was sitting hunched over on a stool beside one of the desks. He looked up, saw me, and gave the faintest of nods and a half-smile. Pettius was lying face-down on the floor between us; dead, obviously, and – judging by the pool of blood spreading out from beneath his chest – stabbed to the heart.

Yeah, right. So much for that part of it. I came further in. Cautiously.

'So it's yourself, Corvinus,' Cluvius said. He still hadn't moved. 'I wasn't really expecting you, but you're welcome all the same. Pull up a stool.'

I did – well out of reach; both his hands were hidden by his cloak, there was still at least one knife to account for, and I didn't trust the bastard an inch – and sat.

'And you've worked out that Lucius was the killer,' he said. Conversationally: we might've been chatting about the weather, for all his tone suggested.

'Yeah.' I risked a quick glance down at the body. The blood looked pretty fresh, and a runnel of it was still making its slow way towards a crack in the flagstone floor. Shit; he couldn't have been lying there for any more than a few minutes, tops.

'Impressive.' Another half-smile, or maybe it was just a twist of the lips. 'When did you manage it?'

I shrugged. 'Only this morning, more or less. As a certainty, at least, although to be fair by then I was working with a fairly short list. You?'

'Five days ago, when we talked last and you told me that Titus had been killed here, and with a belaying pin. It had to be Lucius; no one else fitted.' He grunted, and his right hand moved inside his cloak. I stiffened, but he made no other movement. 'The rest, the whys and wherefores, they were just details. And I had help with them.'

I let that part of it go for the present. 'You, uh, didn't think to let me in on things at all in the meantime?' I said.

I'd spoken quietly, but he scowled, and I tensed. 'Look, boy,' he said. 'I told you how things stood right at the start. Despite what Sempronius Eutacticus may think you were never either wanted nor needed. Any problems we've got, they're no one else's business but ours, and we deal with them in our own way. Which I've now done. You got a problem of your own with that, or Eutacticus does, then the pair of you can just go fuck yourselves.'

I winced. Mind you, if I was being honest with myself, Pettius's death was pretty convenient: I doubted if, for all his protestations, Julius Montanus would've been too happy to take a hand at this late stage in the game, and otherwise all I could've done would have been to report back to Eutacticus in person. Which, if we were being realistic, would probably have had the same result, and left me responsible for fingering the guy in the first place. Also, like I'd told Perilla, we were moving in a different world here; normal rules didn't apply. 'Fair enough,' I said. 'You want to tell me the whole story, though? Like you say, the whys and wherefores of it? Maybe answer a few questions as well. Just for my own satisfaction, you understand.'

'If you like. But that depends on what you know already.' He shifted slightly on his stool and drew in a sharp breath. Again, his hand moved under the cloak. 'No point in wasting time for both of us if I don't need to, is there?'

'You all right?' I said.

'I'm fine.' He wasn't, not by a long chalk: I'd seen dishrags a better colour. Still, like he'd said, that was his business and I wasn't going to press the matter. 'So how much do you know?'

'First of all: I'm assuming that Sextus Pettius's death – the brother's, not the son's, if we can still call him that – was Pettius's reason for killing

Marcius, yes? And that Marcius engineered that in revenge for Sextus having seduced his first wife?'

That got me a wry chuckle. 'You've been a busy little beaver those last few days, haven't you? I didn't find that out myself until a day or so back. But you're right, all the same. Who told you?'

'I got the bare background facts – them and nothing else – from Carpus's father. Me, I just strung them together and made a few guesses where the links went. You know Carpus?'

'Carver? Sure. Good man. His father, now...that'd be old Gaius Vestius, wouldn't it? He still above ground? Well, well!' Another chuckle. 'And yes, he'd remember what happened, all right. The bit about Sextus Pettius – the young version – not being Lucius's son, too. There's not many know that nowadays, nor ever did for that matter. I'd almost forgotten it myself.'

'Uh...incidentally, while we're on the subject,' I said diffidently, 'you weren't responsible yourself for that killing, were you? Young Sextus's?'

'No. Why should I be? I'd nothing against the boy, whatever his father – uncle – had done. That was Aulus.'

'You're sure?'

'Sure I'm sure. Absolutely. But don't concern yourself with him, Corvinus, he's already been dealt with.' He must've noticed my look, because he smiled. 'I told you, we handle our own problems, and it was a family matter. That stupid bastard could've started another blood feud, and all because of a bitch of a woman who couldn't keep her pants on for five minutes straight. I asked Aulus round here this morning to have a private word before Lucius arrived. He's upstairs now.'

'Dead?'

'He was when I left him. You can check that out later, if you like, but I'm fairly sure he's stayed that way.'

Gods! 'Speaking of blood feuds,' I said, 'you don't think maybe a little thing like killing the head of the Pettii family would have a few repercussions of its own?'

The smile disappeared. 'Suppose you let me worry about that, boy,' he said carefully, 'because again it's no fucking business of yours. Now. We were talking about what happened twenty-five years back. How much did old Vestius tell you?'

'Nothing about the adultery side of things, or nothing definite, at least. But he said Sextus had been killed in an ambush along the coast. A smuggling pick-up that went wrong.'

Cluvius was nodding. 'The Victorini boys. Just an unfortunate balls-up, someone getting pissed and shooting his mouth off in the wrong company. Or so we thought at the time; so I'd always thought, until a couple of days ago. It happened, now and again, on both sides.' He pointed to his eye-patch. 'That was when I lost this.'

'But it wasn't the Victorini, was it?' I said. 'And it was no balls-up, either, not the way you mean it, quite the contrary: Marcius had arranged the attack himself, as background cover for stiffing Sextus. Pretty clever, really; he gets his revenge on the man who seduced his wife without risking setting the guy's brother at his throat, and at the same time he puts a bit of ginger into the feud with the opposition that's enough to finish them off. Two birds with one stone. Not bad going.'

'Yeah, Titus always was a smart bugger. Brains of the team, and no mistake.' Cluvius frowned. 'The lads who attacked us were from out of town, where exactly I don't know, Tarentum maybe. I should've spotted they were all strangers rather than the boys Victorinus usually used as muscle, but everything happened so fast it didn't register. Then afterwards it didn't matter, and I hadn't thought of it since.'

'Until...what did you say? Two days ago?'

'Yeah. Right.'

'So where did the information come from? That, and the Aulus side of things.'

He told me. Uh-huh. Well, that made sense. And it answered one or two very pertinent questions that'd been buzzing round my brain for the last few days.

'And Pettius?' I said. 'How did he know? About his brother having been set up, I mean? Same place?'

Cluvius shrugged, and winced. 'Search me, boy,' he said. 'That he didn't say, and I didn't ask, because it wasn't important. All I wanted from him when I sent the message telling him to meet me here was the admission that he'd killed Titus and confirmation of his reason for doing it. Both of which I got.'

'And then you stabbed him.'

Another scowl. 'Look, let's get this straight, okay?' he said. 'I'm no murderer. Nor was Lucius, for that matter, not the way I see it. He knew why he was here, just like the last time when he was the one to arrange things with Titus, and he'd come prepared. Like I knew he would, like Titus would've known he would. It was a fair fight both times, on both sides, and if it was Titus got stiffed first time round and him second, well, that's just how things go. If you don't believe me look at his right hand.'

I did. Pettius's arm was stretched out away from his body, partly under one of the desks. The hand still held a knife.

'Okay, pal,' I said. 'Apologies. I'm sorry. Even so–'

'Fuck that, Corvinus!' He was really angry now. 'There's no even so about it, not by my reckoning, not by his. You might have your law, but we've got ours. And by the gods I've done nothing against it, no more than Lucius did when he killed Titus.'

'*Even so*' – this time I stressed the words – 'the killing's got to go on now, hasn't it? That much I do know. The guy's son, nephew, whatever you like to call him, he's already dead himself, sure, but when word gets out – as it will – that you've killed Pettius there'll be someone else who'll be out for your blood. And so on and on, back and forth until there's no one left on either side. According to what you say is your law that's the way it works, right?'

'Right. Only under the circumstances it won't be necessary.' He moved his cloak aside. The whole right side of his tunic, shoulder to hem, was a single, sodden red mass. 'I reckon I've got another, what, ten minutes before I pass out, maybe fifteen, if I'm lucky, and that'll be that. With me gone there's an end to the matter, far as the Pettii are concerned. All done and dusted.'

Shit. I didn't say anything, just stared. Cluvius replaced the cloak.

'Off you go, Corvinus,' he said quietly. 'Back to Rome. You can tell Sempronius Eutacticus that's job done.' He grinned, or tried to. 'And next time tell him to keep his fucking nose out to begin with, okay?'

There wasn't anything I could do, and besides from the looks of him ten minutes, let alone fifteen, was optimistic.

I left him to get on with it.

Where now?

Well, that much was obvious. There was still a fair chunk of the morning left. Plenty of time to pick up Titus Satrius if he wasn't still out tomcatting and pay a call on our real murderer.

When I walked into Lucius's wineshop he was sitting at one of the tables with a half jug in front of him, working his way through what was either an early lunch or, given the circumstances, a late breakfast.

'Hey, Corvinus!' he said. 'How's the lad?' Well, someone was in a good mood. Whoever she was, the lady must've been worth the trouble. 'You want some of this?'

'No, it's okay.' I pulled up another stool and sat down facing him. 'Some wine would be welcome, though.'

'Lucius!' He turned to the barman behind the counter. 'Another cup over here, quick as you like.' He turned back to me. 'Well? How's it going? You solved the case yet?'

'Yeah, as a matter of fact I have.'

He stared at me. 'You're kidding, right?'

'Uh-uh.' Lucius had brought the cup over. I filled it from the jug and sank the result in a oner. 'All done. At least, as far as laying the finger on the actual guy who did it is concerned.'

'Great!' He was beaming. 'Who was it?'

'Lucius Pettius.'

He set down a half-chewed chicken leg. '*What?*'

'Fact. No doubt about it. Only he's already dead. Aulus and Quintus Cluvius too.' I refilled my cup and gave him the whole story. Barring Cluvius's final message to Eutacticus, of course; heartily though I concurred with the sentiment expressed that was a detail I would not be passing on.

'So we can fuck off back to Rome?' Satrius said when I'd finished. 'The boss'll be delighted.'

'Yeah, well, not quite.' I emptied the last of the wine into my cup. 'There's one small loose end I have to tie up first. At least, one that I can tie up.'

'And what's that?'

'I have to talk to the bastard who was really responsible. For all of the deaths, bar none, from Marcius's onward. Or rather, *we* have to talk to him, because you're Eutacticus's rep and he has to be given the whole boiling. Which is why I'm here. So if you've finished your lunch, pal–'

'Breakfast.'

'–or whatever it might be we can go and get this over with. Okay?'

We set out for the Marcius offices and a final word with Brother Titus.

He was in his office working his way through a pile of flimsies with an abacus at his elbow. Par for the course: that was the guy all over, the quintessential businessman-cum-administrator-cum-glorified clerk. I nearly threw up on his cedarwood-boarded floor. Give me straightforward bastards like Quintus Cluvius or Marcius Senior any day; at least you know where you are with them, and even when they kill they do it face to face.

I hadn't knocked. He looked up in annoyance.

'Corvinus,' he said. 'This is a surprise. What–?' Which was when he saw Satrius coming in behind me and stopped, frowning. One thing you can say about Titus Satrius, he fits in with your everyday commercial office environment as neatly as a two-ton rhino would in a ladies' cake-and-honey-wine klatsch. He closed the door behind him and set his very considerable back against it.

'Quintus Cluvius is dead,' I said. 'If you hadn't heard already.'

'I beg your pardon?' Titus was staring at me.

'Same goes for Lucius Pettius.' I pulled up a stool and sat down. 'And your brother Aulus. You'll be glad to know that Cluvius killed them both. Only he got himself fatally stabbed in the process; I'm assuming by Pettius, because he was the second victim, but I can't say for certain. Anyway, the result's the same. You can tick another three boxes. Congratulations, pal. Job done.'

'Corvinus, really, I haven't the slightest idea what you're–'

'Don't talk. That comes later. For now you just listen, okay?' I shifted on the stool. 'You want the who's, the how's and the why's? Fair enough; easy ones first. Aulus died because you told him your wife was double-timing him with Sextus Pettius. As a result, he flies off the handle, as you knew he would, and the next thing is Sextus finds himself down an alley with your brother's knife in his back. Now, I don't know whether you fingered Aulus as the perp to Cluvius or the old man knew about the affair and put two and two together himself, but it doesn't matter either way. In any event, to avoid the truth getting out and the resultant start of a new inter-family feud, Cluvius zeroes the guy himself. So while we're about it we can add Sextus to the tally, can't we?'

Titus was staring at me like I had two heads. He was almost purple with rage, although he was holding it in well.

'Look,' he said, 'you've obviously been drinking. I can smell the wine from here. I'll take that into consideration as an extenuating circumstance. But unless you leave my office this minute – both of you – I'll have you thrown out.'

I glanced round at Satrius, still standing with his shoulders against the door.

'Will you, now?' Satrius said. 'Fair enough, pal, you go right ahead and try to do that small thing.' He folded his arms and grinned. 'Or, there again, you can just keep your fucking trap shut like you've been told and let the man finish. Your decision.' I turned back; Titus's lips had set in a tight line. 'Wise choice.'

'What I do know for definite, though,' I went on, 'because he told me himself before he died, is that you told Quintus Cluvius that your father had arranged the death of the other Sextus Pettius – Lucius's brother, and Sextus's real father – twenty-five years back. And, extrapolating from this, that you'd been the one to slip the info to Lucius Pettius himself, probably anonymously through a note or a letter, although that's just me guessing. Thus providing him with a reason for killing your father in revenge, which, of course, as you well know, he did. Tick another of the boxes. Your father's, this time.'

'Corvinus, how the *hell* was I supposed to know about that?' Titus snapped. 'For the gods' sakes, I was only just into my teens, and I knew nothing whatsoever about my father's business! And as far as Sextus Pettius Senior is concerned I can't remember even seeing the man!'

I could sense Satrius shifting his bulk behind me. I held up a hand, and he subsided.

'Yeah, well, that was one of the questions I wanted to ask you, pal,' I said. 'Me, I think your daughter's maid told you. Capra. Along with the details of your mother's affair with the guy. Probably – although again I'm guessing here – about the time of the betrothal. Am I right?'

'Why the *fuck* would she do that?' Good sign; he was obviously beginning to get rattled.

'To put a stop to the marriage. She knew your daughter didn't want it, and Capra would do anything for young Marcia. Again I'm guessing, but I reckon I'm on fairly safe ground here. Capra's a slave, sure, but that doesn't mean she's thick, it only means she's powerless. My guess is that she came to you, as Marcia's father, knowing that you weren't in favour of the match either, and spilled the secret she'd been holding for the past twenty-five years in the hope that you'd use it in some way, maybe blackmail your father into cancelling the wedding by threatening to pass it on to Pettius. Plus, as an added incentive, blowing the whistle on young Sextus's affair with your wife just to show you, if you didn't know already, what an out-and-out bastard the man was. So. I'll ask you again: am I right?'

Silence; *long* silence. Finally:

'Very well,' he said. 'Yes, you are. Completely, on all counts, even the guesses. But as you'll admit yourself what's important, or should be, here, legally speaking, is that I haven't actually killed anyone *propria persona*. I'm not like my father and old Quintus, let alone my brother. I never have been. Violence appals me, and I certainly wouldn't...*couldn't*...do murder, either in hot blood or cold. Ever.'

I said nothing; I didn't trust myself. Behind me, Satrius grunted.

Titus laid his hands flat on the desk in front of him. 'You have to believe me in this, Corvinus,' he said. 'If I did manipulate things I did it for the best and most unselfish of reasons. I told you when we first talked, I want to make a complete break with my family's past. Turn the company into a legitimate business.'

'Okay. Fine,' I said. 'And the way to do this is to get rid of everyone who might have other plans, right? Sorry. Engineer things so they get rid of each other.'

'Yes. Why not, if their plans were criminal and allowed for the maiming and murder of innocent people? How else could I have done it?' Yeah, well, to be fair I could see where he was coming from. Even so... 'The only death I regret is Quintus's. That was never meant to happen, never! He was the only one who was fighting my corner, and he had the authority to hold everything together while we made the change. As for the rest, including my father's, maybe I should feel some guilt, but I don't, not a shred. They were vicious crooks and killers, pure and simple, and the world is a better place without them.'

I winced; I'd said pretty much the same to Perilla, about Aulus and Marcus Cluvius, when we were talking about Sextus's murder. Yeah, well, maybe I didn't have much of a right to claim the high moral ground after all. Which reminded me. 'There's still one left, isn't there?' I said. 'One box still to be ticked. Cluvius's son Marcus. Were you planning to get rid of him as well?'

'If I could, yes, of course I was. I still am, actually.' He spoke completely calmly. 'The man's no more than a thug, and without my brother to provide him with a legitimate link to the family it shouldn't be too difficult, one way or another.' He must've seen the look on my face because he frowned. 'Come on, Corvinus! Be honest! Marcus Cluvius is a vicious, psychopathic brute, and if you had the chance you'd put him in an urn yourself. Or am I wrong?'

'No, you're not wrong,' I said slowly. 'Difference is, I'd do it legally.'

'So would I. Will, if possible. But if it isn't? Exactly how far would your scruples extend?' I didn't answer, which, I suppose, was an answer in itself. 'Right. So.' He took a deep breath. 'What happens now?'

Good question, and one I'd been asking myself all the way over. Not that I had the answer to that one, either. The guy was right; four people might have died, but technically – legally speaking, like he'd said – his hands were clean. And if the end result was that the Messia Postumas of this world, let alone – what was the kid's name, the one who'd burned to death in her parents' bakery? – the Turia Gemellas, ditto, went unscathed in future then who was I to pontificate, never mind pass judgement?

Mind you, fortunately this time round I didn't have to: the guy hadn't actually committed a crime in any form, and even if he had I knew in my bones that trying to involve Julius Montanus would've been a complete non-starter. What Sempronius Eutacticus's reaction, if any, might be when Satrius reported back to him was up to that bastard himself, but I'd be willing to lay a pretty substantial bet that once he knew the ins and outs of it he'd be happy to leave things alone.

Life could get pretty messy sometimes, and when it did all you could do was shrug and say, 'What the hell?'

Which was more or less what I did.

17.

And that, by rights, should've been it for the case. Not that it was a perfect ending by any means, all nicely tied up with a pretty ribbon round it, but like I said life's never neat and sometimes you just have to settle for what you can get, grit your teeth, and carry on regardless.

Only it wasn't the end, not quite.

We'd been twiddling our thumbs for three days while Satrius organised the trip back – snail-pace transport again, whoopee, which meant we had another fifteen days of the bugger's dubious company to look forward to – and were just on our way out to the promised dinner with Montanus and Perilla's pal Sentia when the lad himself rolled up, looking like the cat that'd not only swallowed the canary but had the rest of the aviary into the bargain, with fruit and nuts and possibly a cabaret to follow.

'Hey, Corvinus,' he said. 'I'm glad I've caught you.' Yeah, well, there was more than one opinion on that score. Still... 'Out on the town, are we?'

'Uh-huh.' I opened the carriage door and helped Perilla in. 'Life for us purple-stripers is just one long party. We're having dinner at Julius Montanus's place.'

The grin spread even wider. 'Now that, boy, is what you might term a fortunate concatenation of circumstances.'

'Yeah? Is that so, now?' I followed Perilla in and settled down into the cushions. 'How many syllables does that make altogether?'

'Fuck that.' He reached under his cloak, produced a roll of flimsies held together with a leather lace, and handed it over. 'Here. Don't say I'm not good to you. Read and marvel.'

I frowned, undid the lace, opened out the roll and scanned the first flimsy...

Shit!

I leafed rapidly through the remaining sheets. They were all the same format.

'Good, aren't they?' Satrius said. 'And the handwriting's Marcus Cluvius's. That's for certain. I checked with Carpus.'

My brain had gone numb. 'Where the *hell* did you get these?' I said.

Satrius scratched his head. 'Yeah, well, it's a bit of a mystery, that,' he said. 'Lucius the barkeeper, he got them from one of his customers last night. Complete stranger, like, never been in before. Handed them over without so much as a word when he was paying for his drink and told Lucius to give them to me next time he saw me. Which as things turned out was half way through this morning. Me, I'd say they came from that slimy bugger Titus, but that's just a guess.'

Yeah, I'd go for that explanation myself: they weren't the sort of thing Cluvius would've left lying around – definitely not! – and the covert method of delivery was Titus Marcius's style to a T.

List of punters being soaked. Names, addresses, amounts, dates, the lot. And ongoing; the fact that the date given at the top of the last column to be filled in on the bottom flimsy was only five days previously, plus the existence of the empty columns to the right extending as far as the flimsy's edge, confirmed it. And as a clincher the entries against two names on the top sheet – Gaius Vecilius and Gaius Turius – stopped half way along the line, and the names themselves had been scored through. Vecilius, I remembered, had been the guy that Montanus had told me had been found badly beaten up in an alley; while Turius must've been the dead toddler Turia Gemella's father. The man who owned the bakery that'd caught fire, probably not long after the date when the payments stopped...

Got the bastard! Got him cold, five ways from nothing, and legally, into the bargain!

'Marcus?' Perilla was staring at me. 'What on *earth* is the matter with you?'

I must've been grinning at least as broadly as Satrius. Yeah, well, slimy bugger or not I owed Titus for this, in spades. And that he was the one responsible I didn't have the slightest doubt: with Marcus Cluvius gone – and gone he would definitely be when Montanus saw these flimsies, permanently, courtesy of Brundisium's public executioner – he'd've made a complete sweep of both the competition and the opposition. I'd bet good money that Septimia was living on borrowed time to boot, although I doubted if she had anything worse than divorce coming to her: Titus might be a slimy toad in many ways, but he was honest and law-abiding enough according to his own lights. And I had to admit, although I hated doing it, Brundisium would be a whole lot healthier a place with him heading the company than it would've been with one of the bastards he'd shafted in charge. Certainly I couldn't see Sempronius Eutacticus minding overmuch.

So maybe the case hadn't finished on as much of a downer as I'd thought it had.

'Marcus?' Perilla said again. 'If it's some sort of a joke, then–'

'No joke, lady. Certainly not one that Marcus Cluvius is going to find funny. See for yourself.' I handed her the flimsies and closed the carriage door.

We set off for Montanus's.

Printed by Amazon Italia Logistica S.r.l.
Torrazza Piemonte (TO), Italy